P9-BYS-940

The First Move

"Hugo," said Miss Gorringe.

"Yes?"

Miss Gorringe sat behind the smaller desk, halfway down the long cool room. Her own desk was less cluttered with bric-a-brac than Bishop's: instead of green-jade ornaments she had a stock of neat black files, perfectly tabulated; instead of tobacco-jars, pipes, motor-magazines and ivories, she had an array of notebooks and reference tables that would have delighted a chief-editor whose business was curious crime.

Miss Vera Gorringe, M.A., was a good lieutenant, a well-groomed, middle-aged, elegantly dressed electric brain with a sense of humor and a flair for unearthing the unearthly.

She was doing it, even now.

She said: "Professor Scobie won't be dining with us tonight."

Bishop swung his lean head to face her.

"Oh. What's his excuse?"

"The best in the world," she said. "He's dead."

————

ALSO BY ADAM HALL

Knight Sinister
Queen in Danger
Bishop in Check
*Rook's Gambit

Published by
HarperPaperbacks

*coming soon

ADAM HALL

Pawn In Jeopardy

HarperPaperbacks
A Division of HarperCollins*Publishers*

This is a work of fiction. The characters, incidents, and
dialogues are products of the author's imagination and are
not to be construed as real. Any resemblance to actual
events or persons, living or dead, is entirely coincidental.

HarperPaperbacks   *A Division of* HarperCollins*Publishers*
10 East 53rd Street, New York, N.Y. 10022

Copyright © 1954 by Elleston Trevor
All rights reserved. No part of this book may be used
or reproduced in any manner whatsoever without
written permission of the publisher, except in the case
of brief quotations embodied in critical articles and
reviews. For information address HarperCollins*Publishers*,
10 East 53rd Street, New York, N.Y. 10022.

This book is published by arrangement with the author.

Cover photography by Herman Estevez

First HarperPaperbacks printing: February 1991

Printed in the United States of America

HarperPaperbacks and colophon are trademarks of
HarperCollins*Publishers*

10 9 8 7 6 5 4 3 2 1

For Irene and Michael

1st

MOVE

FOR A moment the silence was absolute. A pause had come between the soft cool gusts of the little wind, leaving this aching silence in the faint light of stars. The mouth of the tunnel lay to the south; it was a black hole in the grey of the gloom. Northwards, there stood the signal-box, with a yellow gleam making a blotch of light that picked out the thin threads of the rails and drew them towards the tunnel.

A mass of leaves lay silent, sprawled across the land from here to the roadway; in them, no bird sang, as late as this.

The train's sound came as softly as if the wind had blown up again to touch the leaves; but in moments the sound grew too great for the wind, and the thin-drawn metals between the tunnel and the signal-box carried it here, trembling to the coming of vast weight at speed.

The sound reached the stones of the tunnel and began to echo, clamoring in and calling down through the heart of the hill, long before the train became a point of light between the shadows of the landscape.

It was the Midnight, from London to the coast. From the signal-box, a man watched it, his shirt-sleeved arm crooked at the window. The long linked blaze of it came by, thrusting into the hill; and its whistle screamed, as if in sudden terror of the dark.

One by one the bright links were lost, and there was gloom again. Slowly the tumult died, leaving a long-drawn sigh in the tunnel's throat; then, after minutes, the silence was back, numbed and absolute.

The gleam of yellow that was shed downwards from the signal-box picked out the threads of the rails, and the heap of stones below the steps, and the gradient-post on the far side of the track, and the white face of the man who lay on his back.

He lay a dozen yards from the tunnel, his limbs flung out awkwardly, in the untidiness of death. His eyes stared at the stars. His mouth said nothing. His hands held only stones, and the dark of his own quick blood.

He had come to be here when the train had screamed, as if in sudden terror of the dark.

The cat sat with statuesque quiet, at the end of the limed-oak desk. It stared at Bishop. Only once, in the past few minutes, had it moved its head, to follow a curl of smoke that had gone drifting up from Bishop's pipe. Smoke fascinated the Princess Chu Yi-Hsin; she was a Siamese, and perhaps her Oriental mind composed fantasies of smoke as she watched it moving in the quiet air, but much more likely she was thinking of edible fish and the cream off the top of the milk.

"Scat," said Bishop.

She sprang off the desk, and be damned to him.

"Hugo."

"Yes?"

Miss Gorringe sat behind the smaller desk, halfway down the long cool room. Her own was less cluttered with *bric-à-brac:* instead of green-jade ornaments she had a stock of neat black files, perfectly tabulated: instead of tobacco-jars, pipes, motor-magazines and ivories, she had an array of note-books and reference-tables that would have delighted a chief-editor whose business was curious crime.

Miss Vera Gorringe, M.A., was a good lieutenant, a well-groomed, middle-aged, elegantly dressed electric brain with a sense of humour and a flair for unearthing the unearthly.

She was doing it, even now.

She said: "Professor Scobie won't be dining with us tonight."

Bishop swung his lean head to face her.

"Oh. What's his excuse?"

"The best in the world," she said. "He's dead."

His mouth tightened, instinctively. Slowly he said:

"Professor Scobie is dead?"

"Yes. Listen."

She folded the newspaper exactly down the middle, and began reading.

" 'The body of Professor Gordon Scobie was found shortly after midnight last night near Henford Tunnel, on the London-Brinton line. One of the younger members of the jet-development team at Farley Research Centre, he was believed to have been on board the last train to the coast, on his way to Brinton. It is thought that he fell from his compartment soon after the train passed through Henford. The police do not at the moment suspect foul play, but fuller inquiries are being made. Professor Scobie was forty-three.' "

Bishop got up from his enormous chair, and reflectively laid his *meerschaum* in a bowl.

"Is that all, Gorry?"

"Enough, I think."

"M'm . . . " He stared out of the window for a moment and then said: "Quite absurd, isn't it?"

"Absurd?"

"I mean that bit that goes: 'Fell from his compartment.' Only a small irresponsible child or a doddering nonagenarian can *fall* from a train, accidentally. This poor devil was neither."

"Yes, quite. But news-reports . . . Should we telephone his wife?"

Bishop shook his head.

"I don't think so. All we can say is how sorry we are, and there'll be enough people doing that. Not the sort of message that's really appreciated—too much pain attached. I'll drop her a line, instead."

He came over to her desk, and leaned on a corner.

"This is a bit sad, Gorry. I've never met his wife but I believe they got on pretty well—and two boys doing fine at school—"

"Poor little beggars."

"Yes . . . "

She got up, meticulously placing her pen-rack an inch lower on her desk, so that he shouldn't send it spinning when he stood up. This corner was a favourite spot of his, for idle perching when he had something to think hard about, and she'd tried to wean him away from it for years.

She said quietly, "I suppose I'd better go and rearrange the dinner-table, as Scobie won't be along."

He emerged from reverie.

"M'm?"

"Never mind."

The telephone rang as she turned towards the door. She stopped, and crossed the long room to Bishop's desk, picking up the receiver.

"Yes?"

Bishop was gazing moodily at his shoes. Watching him, she doubted if he had even heard the phone ring, or knew what room he was in. There was an absurdity in Scobie's death. Only children and nonagenarians fell from trains, by accident. It had him thoughtful.

A voice on the phone said just a moment please.

She waited.

"Hugo?" a man's voice said.

"No, this is Gorry. Good afternoon, Freddie."

Inspector Frisnay said good afternoon. "Is your impossible boss available?"

She glanced across the room again. Bishop still stared at his shoes. She said: "Available, but not fully conscious. Shall I try to break through the fog for you?"

"If you will. It's a little important."

"All right Freddie."

She cupped the phone.

"Hugo, Freddie's on the line."

"M'm?"

Patiently she said: "Detective-Inspector Frederick Frisnay has telephoned us. Are we alive or dead?"

"Oh." He slid off her desk and took the receiver. "What's he want?"

"Try asking him."

She went over and stood by the windows, looking down at the buses in King's Road. Chelsea looked hot, and a little jaded, at the end of a summer afternoon.

She listened carefully. It was her job. She was, among a hundred other things, a mental memorandum-sheet.

"'Lo, Freddie."

Frisnay said hello and then said: "I understand you're a guest short, for dinner tonight."

"Yes, but you can't fill the bill. We dine only the more enlightened set." He said it without humour in his voice, automatically. He and Frisnay had talked like this since they'd kicked each other round the Junior Common Room after Prep, twenty years before.

"Hugo, I don't dine in a dead man's shoes, on principle. But I'm interested in Professor Scobie's, and so are you."

"Oh, why?"

"Because you can't keep away from sudden death. You even lay a place for it, at your table. I want to talk to you, about Scobie. Not over a phone."

"Come round for a drink."

"I can't leave the office—"

"So you ring up Mahomet. All right, make it ten minutes."

He cocked a glance at Miss Gorringe, who nodded. He had no appointments.

He rang off. She asked:

"So Freddie's working on the Scobie case?"

"If it's a 'case'."

"You don't think it's an accident. You said so."

"Nor does Freddie, I agree."

"Then if it's a case for the Yard, it could be one for us."

He picked up his *meerschaum* and gently tapped out the ash.

"A police-inquiry might not necessarily unearth material for a book like ours, Gorry. But we live in hopes, as ever."

He put the pipe into his pocket, and went down the room to the main door. From the davenport, the Princess Chu Yi-Hsin watched him, with amethyst eyes.

"I'll let you know, Gorry."

He opened the door.

"And I suggest we dine out tonight."

"Might feel a bit morbid, here, even with the table rearranged."

"Yes."

He went out. She moved back to her desk, and methodically cut out the news-report, and filed it. For the new book by Hugo Ripton Bishop there were so far only three stories set down. Scobie's might make a fourth. It would have to fit a certain pattern, and the title: *Personality Under Stress*. It would have to feature the almost documentary story of a man who was driven to stark extremes, by pressure on his mind.

For a moment she stared at the file, thinking how odd her job would seem to others, wondering how many others would care to take it over. Not many, probably: and she'd fight those few, because she prized it. Working for a man like Bishop was a rare experience that she'd never easily give up.

She closed the file, left her desk, and went into the dining-room. Scobie had been moved from his place at the table here, and was now in the neat black file.

Frisnay lit a cigarette and looked hard at Bishop and said: "This is very confidential, I must warn you."

"All right."

"We don't know what we're coming to, yet. Perhaps you can help. Professor Scobie was going to have dinner with you, this evening. That right?"

Bishop tilted back in the visitors' chair and said: "Yes, that's right. How did you know? Mrs. Scobie tell you?"

Frisnay's round wooden face gave an almost human smile.

"Yes, Hugo. We have—as you suspect—interviewed Mrs. Scobie. One of the things we learned was he had an appointment with you, for tonight." He watched his cigarette in silence and then added: "For the night after he died."

"You don't merely suggest he fixed his appointments in an impracticable order, Freddie . . . I suppose most people have appointments when they die, unexpectedly, and can't keep them."

"My dear Hugo, I'm not suggesting you know anything more about Scobie's death than we do—"

"But you hope to heaven I might . . . "

"Not even that. I just want to build up a picture of Scobie's affairs, during the last few weeks of his life. So you come into it. And as you're forever raking about for morbid material for that damned book of yours, I wondered if we might help each other."

Bishop watched him, and when Frisnay didn't add anything, said:

"You don't think this is just an accident, then?"

"Do you?"

"I hate to seem pernickety . . . but I asked you first."

Frisnay shrugged, heeling over in his chair and leaning one elbow on the window-sill, gazing out. His voice was deflected by the glass.

"No, we don't really think it was an accident."

"What," asked Bishop carefully, "do you think it is?"

"Except for one little point, suicide. Scobie had money-worries, and he'd been working at very tough pressure for a very long time. In addition—"

"The—er—'one little point' seems more interesting, Freddie. Has it a name?"

Frisnay turned back to face the office. He nodded.

"Yes. Scobie was seen talking to a man in the corridor of his train, not long before it reached Henford."

"Ah," said Bishop gently.

"A man nobody can describe, unfortunately. There's always a lot of confusion and confliction, you know, when you start digging up evidence after sudden death. People are caught on the wrong foot by the shock, and you can't get much out of them. Won't commit themselves." He waved a vague hand.

Bishop said quietly: "Freddie, you said something about our helping each other. You got me here, so you begin. I'm not really expected to sit here while you throw small-calibre bombs about at half-cock. You've made the whole thing stink of murder without anything solid to help me."

He crossed his legs, propped his pipe in his cupped hand and said: "I'm listening, sweetheart."

Frisnay sighed. He said:

"Well, there are three lines we can work on. Take the accident first. I don't really see a man in full possession of his wits falling out of a train that's travelling at full-blast. People do it when they're drunk, or when the train's pulling into a station and they open the doors in too much of a hurry, or when the corridors are jammed to the gunwales and a door gets pushed open in the general chaos. But Scobie wasn't drunk: the midnight London-Brinton was less than a quarter full; and it wasn't pulling up at Henford station. Along that stretch of line, it was travelling up in the sixties."

Bishop said: "All right. On the face of it, we rule out accident. Apart from the one little point about the man Scobie was seen talking to, what other ideas have you got, on the angle of murder?"

"None, Hugo. Not one. There's not a scrap of evidence or suspicion. Certainly, Scobie was working on top secret research with jet-aeroplanes, and a jet-aeroplane is a war-weapon, and men like Scobie have a peculiar importance when the international situation gets on the simmer. But that's not evidence of murder; it's no more than ground-work for theories about motive."

"Very well, what about suicide?"

Frisnay spread his hands flat on the desk and looked at them. "There *are* one or two pointers, Hugo, and we're checking up very carefully. It's not easy, because people don't chuck in the sponge for any clear single reason. It usually happens after a long period of strain, mental agony, frustration ... I don't need to tell you—you've written enough technical works on the subject yourself."

Bishop said half-aloud and slowly: "Once you've got beyond the unimaginative stage of dismissing all suicides as cowards or lunatics, their minds are worth looking ino. I'd like to see into Scobie's ... he wasn't a coward, and no lunatic. If he took his own life, it was because his mind was under some enormous pressure ... "

Frisnay grunted. "His personality was under stress ... I hear from Gorry that it's your new title."

"M'm? Yes." He frowned suddenly and said at a complete tangent, "Freddie, have you heard of Gregg, Taplow, Moss and Parish?"

Frisnay looked at him across his desk.

"They sound like estate-agents."

"But they're not. Three of them are scientists."

"Indeed?"

Frisnay looked interested. He waited. In a moment Bishop told him:

"The three scientists are Sir Bernard Gregg, Dr. Taplow, and Professor Parish. Moss—the fourth name I mentioned—is an explorer, by his own choosing. Those four men went on an expedition, two years ago, to the Antarctic."

Frisnay listened carefully. This was why he had asked Bishop here. Bishop had lost a dinner-guest, suddenly; and Bishop wasn't a man who would merely think of someone else to invite instead. He had known the dead man slightly, and he would have known him better—paradoxically—now it was too late.

He was saying: "The expedition was Sir Bernard Gregg's idea. It was Charles Moss who financed it, and planned the technical details. They were reported as having gone to the Antarctic to study *flora* and *fauna*, and anything else they might chance upon."

He looked directly at Frisnay and said: "They came back, a month or two later, and reported nothing definite. The voyage was dismissed, in the newspapers and in the scientific journals, as just another survey."

The silence lasted a few seconds, then Frisnay said:

"Well?"

"There was a fifth member. Another scientist. Scobie."

"I see."

Lightly Bishop said: "I just wondered if the expedition might have had some bearing on this death; but it's pure speculation."

Frisnay got up and walked about. The telephone rang and he snapped a switch, blocking calls. His short body, propped on its energetic legs, went up and down the room inquisitively.

"Sir Bernard Gregg . . . is he the researcher-chemist?"

"That's the one."

"What do the others do?"

"Dr. Taplow's a biologist, retired. He keeps a sort of private zoo, in the grounds of his house. Charles Moss, as I've said, is an adventurer, in the more sporting sense. The other one—Professor Parish—I don't know anything about. And of course there's Scobie."

Frisnay stopped pacing, and made a note on his pad.

"I'll check on them. You never know."

Bishop looked at the clock on the wall.

"I'm going, now. Any questions?"

"No, old son. You may have helped—shan't know, yet. Keep in touch. If we pick up anything we can release, you'll have it."

As Bishop opened the door he said: "What's the scene like, down at Henford?"

"Nothing much there. Scobie died on the lines, but whatever killed him was on board the train—whether it was an impulse of his own, or a living person. It was the train we combed more thoroughly, and the people on it."

"Yes of course. All the same, I'll run down there. So-long, Freddie."

The sun was down behind a silhouette of Surrey pines; their shadows were gangling, sprawled across the fields. The road ran curving between bracken hills, and the dust of a long summer day fanned out behind the car. It slipped with quiet elegance toward Henford, the engine almost silent, as it had been for over thirty years of motoring. There was only one make of machine that men had designed to go on forever, with quiet perfection and disregard of age; and Bishop had bought it; he had no choice.

Gorry, sitting beside him, said: "Hugo, why exactly are we going to Henford?"

There was a little silence. He was driving by instinct, consciously occupied with the problem of Scobie. Vaguely he murmured:

"M'm?"

"To Henford," asked Miss Gorringe, "why exactly are we proceeding? Don't give me a snap answer; I've all the time in the world."

In a few moments he said: "To look at the tunnel."

"The police must have been over the spot very thoroughly."

"Yes. But they might have missed something. Even the police miss things, sometimes. I believe they go so far as to run a Missing Persons Bureau."

Patiently she said: "When we get there, what d'you want me to do?"

"If I miss anything, too, just put it under my nose."

The ancient grey Rolls-Royce whispered past a huddle of barns, and turned between high banks, nearing a wood.

"Five hundred yards," Miss Gorringe said. She had spent some time with a large-scale local map, and knew the place where the road passed the railway.

"Your precision is perfection," he murmured absently.

"If it weren't, you'd give me the sack. Not that I'd mind, I could spend the twilight of my days in blessed peace—"

"And die of boredom. It's only the sweet mystery of what comes next that keeps you alive."

"But when it comes, it so often looks like death. Pull up here." The car stopped, soundlessly. "Through that gate and across the cart-track. You'll find the mouth of the tunnel right in front of you."

He got out, closing the door. She said: "You don't want me to come with you?"

"Not this time, Gorry."

He climbed over the green-slimed gate and crossed the ruts of the cart-track. Above the spinney, birds were darting in the bright evening light; the air was still. When he came to the lines he stopped, leaning on the wire fence that bordered the mass of leaves. He stood there for ten minutes, listening; and then the sound came, faintly from a long way off, the sound of a train.

He didn't move, but turned his head, watching the train as it grew from the green landscape, rocking towards the tunnel-mouth, passing him with a racketing rush whose sound was almost lost in the sudden scream of the whistle that went piercing ahead of it, into the dark mouth of the hill.

He saw the painted numbers on the doors, the lamps of dining-cars, small white faces at windows, a steward walking with a tray, then the glint of bicycle handlebars in the luggage-coach, then nothing more but the lines, the tunnel, the fields opposite. All the small pounding world of a few hundred strangers had come and gone, with a whistle, into the hill.

Leaves turned over, on the sleepers, and the air was still. A blackbird called, somewhere in the wood.

He climbed over the wire fence, and crossed the track, looking at the ground and stopping for a moment near the tunnel-face, turning the stones with his foot. Then he walked off, south-wards, to the signal-box.

There were ten timber steps, leading up to the door. He climbed them. The door was wide open, letting in the air. The signalman had his jacket off; his bare arms were brown and leathery. He looked at Bishop in surprise.

"Good evening," Bishop said.

"Evening, sir."

"You don't get many callers, here."

"It's not allowed."

"Of course not."

The man hesitated, then said: "What can I do for you?"

"I wondered if you'd help me. That poor devil who fell out of the Brinton train last night ... you didn't see him, from here?"

The man shook his head, resting his arm on a tool-shelf near the row of levers.

"Not from this box, no. He fell the other side, see."

"Ah. And when the train was going by . . . you didn't see anything unusual?"

"What like?"

Bishop leaned against the door-post, looking down the lines, following them with his eyes to the black hole in the hill.

"Well," he said, "I don't know anything about trains, but you must have seen an awful lot of 'em go by, and you'd pick out any little detail that might not seem . . . right, you know what I mean?"

The man didn't know what he meant. He shook his head.

"They go by pretty fast, you know, along this stretch—them as don't stop at Henford, up the line. If he'd come out *this* side, we—ell, I might've spotted him, yes, though there'd have been precious little I could've done about it, I reckon."

"Yes, quite." He looked away from the tunnel, and waved a vague hand. "That train that went by just now—it blew its whistle, before the tunnel. They all do that?"

"Oh yes." The man looked slightly shocked. "Where there's tunnels, there's whistles. Never can take no chances, see."

"Yes, I see."

"You the police?"

Bishop said: "No, I'm not the police."

He leaned away from the door-post, and stood down on to the top step.

"Who are you, then?"

Bishop turned idly and started down. "Oh, nobody you'd know," he said over his shoulder.

He heard the man crossing the wooden floor, above him now.

"Well p'r'aps I'll just have your name—"

A bell sounded. The man's feet stopped, and Bishop reached the gravel below the signal-box. Faintly he heard the man's voice, talking into a telephone. He crossed the lines and went over the wire fence, moving quietly into the trees.

Sitting on the running-board of the car, Gorry looked up and said: "Had a nice time?"

"Yes, thank you."

"Find anything?" She got into the car.

"Not really. Just took a sniff round." He filled his *meerschaum*, narrowing his eyes against a spread of late sunlight that seeped through a rift in the clouds. On the hill, the stems of the pines stood black and gold. "I had a chat with the man in the signal-box, but he didn't see anything last night."

He lit his pipe and got into the car. "While I was down there, Gorry, a train came through. You must have heard it. The thing blew its whistle."

"Yes. For the tunnel, obviously." She looked at him.

"Ah, so you know about trains." His voice had gone vague again. He murmured: "That's right ... where there's tunnels, there's whistles ... that's what the man said."

Miss Gorringe wound her window down, to let the pipe smoke out.

She asked mildly: "Is that significant of anything?"

Dreamily he said: "*Everything* is significant of *something*, you know. Otherwise the whole dipsy-doodle wouldn't work."

"You're rambling."

"Yes."

"No, I didn't mean that. You're on to something, aren't you, in your strange twisted mind ... "

He started the engine, and slipped into gear.

He murmured: "We'll be getting back now. I'd like to find out a bit more of Scobie's background, now that we know his world ended ... not with a bang, but a whistle ... "

2nd

MOVE

SUNLIGHT, EVEN daylight, had gone. A green-shaded lamp stood on the desk, casting a flat white light across the opened books. Beyond the lamp the study was shadowed. Reflected light picked out the gold tooling on books ranged along the walls, winked in the eye of a bronze dragon that crouched on a shelf near the deep-set window, gleamed on the gilt of a French clock whose tick matched the only other sound in the room: the scratch of the pen.

Sir Bernard stopped writing, and stared for a little time at the blotter on his desk, not seeing it. Scobie had been his friend, a fellow-scientist. He looked at the blotter, as he had looked at the wall, a chair, a picture, a window, to see Scobie's face. A face still young, still set in determination; a clever face.

Gregg's face, now seen pallidly against the shadows beyond the lamp, was not young. More than merely clever, it was wise. More than determination was set in the mould of it: the eyes were philosophical, the mouth adamant, the fine brow square and hard.

He had been fond of young Scobie, and for a time they had worked together, just for amusement, on a theory that had lain in neither of their specialised fields. Now, as he stared at Scobie through the blotter, there seemed a struggle in his expression. He tried to philosophise over the death of a good friend, and at the same time to bring adamancy to bear: he had work to do. Scobie had made aeroplanes; his death must not get in the way of his work, here. Cancer was still an evil in the world, and when at last men had success, Gregg would be one of those who had helped to stamp it out.

He looked down, at his graphs. His pen began moving again. The hand that moved it was tired, but it was strong. It formed the figures surely, and without haste.

Half an hour passed, and a knock came at the door.

He frowned.

"Yes?"

The door was opened.

"I'm sorry to disturb you, sir."

Without looking up he said:

"I rather wish you hadn't, Mrs. Cobb."

She was used to rebukes, when he was working. She had forgiven them all, for years.

"I know, sir, but it's the doctor."

"Dr. Taplow?"

"Yes, sir."

He put down the pen, shifting himself in the chair. His back was cramped.

"All right, if it's Dr. Taplow."

He pressed the bridge of his nose, closing his eyes for a moment.

"In here, Sir Bernard?"

After a few seconds he opened his eyes and said:

"No, I'll come to the drawing-room."

"Yes, sir."

She went quietly out, a round small woman with responsibilities.

Dr. Taplow was waiting, in the larger, cooler room.

"My dear Clive," said Gregg.

Taplow was standing by the hearth, hands behind him, a thin dry-faced man with soft-grey tangled hair. There was a faint trace of Welsh in his accent.

"I knew you'd be working, Bernard, but—"

"And I knew you'd be coming . . . I can do with a break—sit down. Something to drink?"

"Thank you." He did not sit down. He was a restive man. "You keep up a lot of pressure."

Sir Bernard went to the rosewood cabinet, and opened the doors.

"There's a lot to do. You'd like a whisky."

"I would." Taplow was watching him, the droop of the great shoulders, the tilt of the fine head. He said: "I shall have to talk to Joanna."

Gregg poured two whiskies.

"She's not home yet, it's her late night."

"I mean I shall have to talk to her about you. Keep up this pace and you won't live to see the results of your work."

"As long as the others live as a result of it, I'll be more than satisfied. You can't kill cancer by sitting and looking at it, and that'll be enough about me and my work. I don't kindly play the martyr."

He gave Taplow his drink.

Gregg said: "Well . . . here's to Gordon Scobie. Hope he's found peace."

"Gordon," Taplow said.

"There's not much more we can say, I suppose."

"He's dead, and there's an end. And there was nothing his friends could have done."

"They tried, Clive, they tried."

Taplow looked at him steadily.

"Then it wasn't an accident . . . "

Gregg stood his glass on the mantelpiece, and shrugged.

"As far as I'm concerned, it was. The world doesn't care much, one way or the other, but we owe it to him to let them think what they choose."

"You—weren't surprised, then?"

Sir Bernard looked away and said: "I was bewildered, Clive." He made a sudden decisive gesture—"Sit down, you look restive, man. I'm going to tell you about Gordon Scobie."

Taplow found the nearest chair.

Gregg sat down too and said with his head in his hands:

"He was in trouble. He was here, last night— came here before he caught his train, as I was obliged to tell the police."

"They've been to see you?"

"Yes. An inquiry—routine. They came here because there was a cheque in Gordon's pocket, signed by me."

"Ah," said Taplow. He waited.

Gregg lifted his head, and leaned back in his chair.

"I'd been on the telephone to him, earlier in the day. He sounded worried. I asked him to come along, if he felt like it, and he accepted the invitation—oh, late in the evening. We had a drink, bit of a talk—Joanna was out so we weren't disturbed—and in the end I said I'd be glad to help him."

Taplow watched his face. He had not imagined anything like this.

"I suppose," Sir Bernard said, "I would have told the police about this, even if they hadn't found my cheque. There had been a death, and I knew more than most people about the circumstances—I couldn't very well have said nothing at all, when—"

"Of course not. I'd have done the same thing."

"Thank you. It's pleasant to try glossing over a thing like this, for the sake of the dead, but . . . " At a sudden tangent he said quickly: "Of course the odd thing is, with my cheque in his pocket, the worst of his troubles were over!"

"I'd been thinking that, Bernard. Queer."

"I couldn't have given it to him, you see, without also giving him the chance of returning it over quite a long period—a period of years. That was agreed. He needed time, to pull out—everyone does, when they're in a jam, and things have got on top of them—"

"Then what made him . . . ?"

"Clive, I don't know. His troubles were over, for a long time. I don't know what made him."

Taplow crossed his legs, the nervous energy

of his frame keeping it on the move, even seated.
He said:

"He must have made up his mind, before seeing you."

"It could have been like that, yes. He was in that mood."

"And it would have taken more than a slip of paper to pull him out of it—"

"Yes, I should have seen that—known him better—"

"You can't be expected to get inside a man's mind."

"I know, but I blame myself, just the same."

"Man, what more could you have done?"

Gregg shrugged his hands out. "Seen him safely home, all the way if necessary. I might have, if I'd realised that when a man is in the black pit he'll do things he'd never think of doing otherwise."

Taplow leaned forward, nodding quickly.

"Rushing along in a train, alone in the dark . . . the way out must look so easy—must *be* so easy."

"Yes," Gregg said wearily, "yes, Clive. But I didn't think. I wanted to get back to my laboratory, finish off a bit of work—and of course I thought I'd done all that was necessary."

With quiet conviction Taplow said: "I'd say you had, Bernard, against any argument."

"Well . . . we're both proved wrong. Joanna

drove him to Victoria—she was just coming in as he was leaving, and offered to take him there. She told the police, today, that Gordon had appeared normal when she'd seen him off. But it's odd how we only notice afterwards the little signs that there's something badly wrong. Then it's too late."

Taplow got up, and moved about. He said:

"Well we can't blame Joanna—she's a young girl, and—"

"Oh, I don't, Clive—"

"And you can't blame yourself. Either Gordon was so deep in his depression that he couldn't believe his worries were over, or he came face to face, suddenly on that train, that he'd gone from debt to borrowing . . . and got out of the train and the world, in one move, on a blind impulse."

He touched an ornament on the shelf, turning it in the light of the standard-lamp. "He didn't leave a note, I suppose?"

"If he'd been reasonable enough to write a note, he'd have had time to think of his wife, and the boys, and his work. And he wouldn't have done it at all."

He finished his drink and put down the glass.

"You must be right, you know, Clive. It can only have been sheer impulse—a thing few of us can control."

Slowly Taplow said, watching the ornament: "Yes . . . the big bang comes, after the fuse has been creeping so long that you've not got the strength or even the sense to stamp it out . . . "

Sir Bernard turned his head, looking at him.

"You sound as if you'd been faced with the same situation."

Taplow jerked round and gave a short laugh.

"I? Not on your life, man. I'm not the one for chucking things when they get on top of me. When death comes for this old chicken, it'll have to come out of the dark."

Gregg got up, stiffly.

"Well it's a morbid enough thought, at a time like this."

He took his glass over to the cabinet. "I think that's Joanna, coming in. Stay for a while, Clive —she won't let me do any more work for to-night."

"More power to her." He turned as the door opened.

"Hello, Daddy . . . Clive—I didn't know you were here—"

"My dear Joanna, you're as bad as your father, working as late as this."

She brushed her hair back quickly with her crooked fingers and looked at her father.

"Greggy . . . you haven't been working again tonight?"

"Oh, a few notes that couldn't wait—and I'm not in the mood for brow-beating. Will you have a drink?"

She stood on the hearth-rug, with her hands thrust into the pockets of her skirt. She watched him, and saw that he was tired.

"No, thank you—"

"Clive, another whisky—"

"No more, Bernard, no—"

"Daddy, you promised me you'd take at least two nights off, this week. You gave me your word." She spoke steadily, controlling impatience. Her dark eyes were serious. "You're killing yourself with work, and that's not noble or heroic or even very intelligent. It's obsessive."

He gave himself another short Scotch and said:

"Nonsense, Joanna."

She glanced at Taplow. He shrugged, he liked her spirit, but no spirit in the world would stop Bernard working. She was right: he was obsessional about it.

She said: "It was this kind of thing that killed Gordon Scobie, or helped to."

Gregg turned to face her. He drank some whisky and in a moment said:

"Scobie . . . what made you say that?"

She looked down. "It was overwork that partly made him do it."

32

Taplow said gently: "You think it wasn't an accident."

She flashed him a swift look.

"Only a fool would believe that. When the police came to question me at Farley Research, I couldn't clearly remember how Gordon seemed, when I left him at the station; but afterwards I realised, slowly. Yes, he seemed quiet. Yes, he was preoccupied. He had something bad on his mind—"

"Oh, we're all of us worried about something or other."

She didn't glance at her father. His remark wasn't worth it. She said:

"Happily, only a very few of us worry ourselves to death, and work ourselves to death. One of them's going to be you, Daddy. It's not too much to ask—just that you relax now and then, for your own sake and for the sake of the people you're trying to help. That's all."

Taplow's voice came from near the windows, where he was wandering restively.

"That's reasonable, Bernard. You can't say it isn't."

Irritably Gregg said to both of them: "I'll do my best, but I've a great deal of work to get through." He raised his tumbler.

Joanna glanced at him.

"You sound as if time were short."

"No, there's time enough, but the job is long. Now if you'll forgive me, I'd prefer to talk of something else."

In the long Regency room, the notes of the piano came with a brittle clarity, as melodious as breaking icicles. Bishop's hands fanned across the keyboard, here and there touching a variation of his own.

When Miss Gorringe came in, he went on playing. She waited for perhaps ten minutes, sitting on the davenport with the Siamese on her lap, stroking the smoky ears. Lamplight fell across her quiet face, its pink glow suiting her make-up.

He stopped playing and looked around, remembering that the door had opened.

He said sincerely: "You make a nice picture, Miss Gorringe."

"Thank you, sir."

He closed the piano and said: "You have also got news on your mind."

"Yes. The coroner's verdict has come in. Professor Gordon Scobie took his life while the balance of him mind was disturbed. Unquote."

"I see."

"You don't seem impressed."

"One isn't often impressed by the totally expected."

"You don't agree with the verdict, Hugo."

"I expected it to be one of suicide, and if I hadn't agreed with it, I should have given the coroner my reasons—it would have been my duty. The thing is, I've no reasons, but only odd instinctive ideas on the subject that I can't possibly trust. But they nag. Obviously Scotland Yard hasn't any good reasons, either, or the verdict would have been stood over while they made fuller inquiries."

He filled a pipe. For a minute there was silence in the room. Gorry said at last:

"Instinctively, what would you say the true verdict is?"

He struck a match. From where she sat, the Siamese watched the smoke as it clouded up.

He said: "Murder by a person or persons unknown."

"What evidence?"

"Except for this vague man who was seen talking to Scobie in the train, no evidence. Not a damned shred. Just these Jack O'Lanterns, flitting through my head. The plain fact that Scobie had a nice wife and two kids; the fact that his work meant life to him, and his work wasn't finished; and the fact that they always whistle . . . just there by the tunnel. The trains."

She watched him steadily. She said: "That sounds pretty irrelevant."

He turned and faced her, speaking rapidly and trying to pin down his own ideas.

"Gorry, a couple of thousand trains have blown their whistles at that point on the London-Brinton line—a couple of million, it doesn't matter how many. But that one . . . just that one of them, a week ago, was different. That one screamed for Scobie."

Quietly: "Strip-cartoon stuff."

"All right, I'm a clown full of dreams. I don't blame you—it's not evidence. But by God, if there's any to dig up, I'll get it."

He turned towards his desk.

"Now these people," he said, "Gregg, Taplow, Parish and Moss. All on the expedition with Scobie. Who else?"

The cat sprang to the carpet as Miss Gorringe crossed the room to her desk.

"Sir Bernard's daughter—she's working at Farley Research Centre, where Scobie was. She went out with the expedition, but stayed on the ship when the rest went overland. And there was a man called Corbyn, a photographer, as my information goes, they were engaged."

"Cosy situation."

"Yes."

"The others, now—I know about Dr. Taplow and his private zoo. Parish?

She was turning her files.

"Professor Parish is at Harwell. Physicist. Fifty-three years old, bachelor, Socialist, atheist. Charles Moss——"

"Explorer, yes, the fidgety type. Now that the verdict's in, I'd like to see what these people think of it."

"You think they'd tell you?"

One can find out things, Gorry, without being told. And as a rule, women are easier. You say Gregg's daughter works at Farley—what does she do there?"

"She's on the design side. That's a tricky opening, Hugo—she'll have been heavily screened about Scobie's death."

"Quite true. I'd talk to Mrs. Scobie, but it's too early yet, she's only had a week alone."

"Try this man Corbyn, the photographer——"

"Where does he fit in exactly?"

"Exactly, I can't find out yet. He's elusive. The engagement between him and Joanna Gregg was broken off, I know for certain. Shall I trace him for you?"

"Yes, Gorry, please."

He leaned against the edge of his desk, frowning for a moment then: "Taplow—you told me he's retired. Old man?"

"Sixty."

"Lives?"

"In Surrey. Grey Gates, Amberly, Surrey."

"Family?"

"None with him. Manservent who looks after everything, including the animals."

"He'll be on the phone?"

"Yes." She checked on him. "Amberly 505."

"Brief sketch?"

"Dr. Clive Taplow, sixty, unmarried or divorced—not sure on that I'm afraid—biologist, anthropologist, Liberal, no definite religious convictions publicly. No close relatives. Friend of Gordon Scobie's and fellow-member of expedition to Antarctica."

"Right."

He picked up the telephone. "What's my introduction, Gorry?"

"None, except your a slight acquaintance with Scobie."

"It'll have to do." He spoke into the phone. "This is Carlton 2330. I'd like Amberly 505. Please —Amberly Surrey."

He waited.

The telephone rang.

The room was large, L-shaped. Along the main walls were bookshelves, filled. Books too large for the shelves were on a table near the door. Taplow was standing by the french windows. They were wide open, and the soft air of a summer night moved against his face.

He called: "I'm out, Jackson. Gone away, ill, otherwise unobtainable——"

"Yes, Doctor."

Jackson had been cataloguing books. He was a short lop–sided man with a bland face and good eyes. His hands were large and knotty. One of them lifted the receiver and the bell stopped.

"Hello?"

On the line a voice said: Dr. Clive Taplow?"

"No Sir, Dr Taplow's engaged."

"Will it be possible to speak to him, later to-night?"

"I'm sorry, sir, it's fairly late now. Can I have a message?"

There was a pause.

"There's no message, thanks. I'll write to him."

"Very good, sir. Shall I have your name?"

"It's not necessary, but it's Bishop."

"Mr. Bishop, Sir, thank you. Good-bye."

He put down the telephone.

Taplow said from the french windows: "That thing rings too often, and I've never heard of Mr. Bishop. If he rings again I hope you'll tell him I'm dead, and get the Post Office to come and collect their fidgety instrument."

He was annoyed with telephones, annoyed with the night, annoyed with the verdict of Gordon's death; but people would soon forget, and with any luck, remember him for his work. "You can get to bed, Jackson, if you fell like it. I'm going to look at the beasties, and then turn in myself."

"Yes, Doctor." Jackson stood by the door. "I checked temperatures in snake-house , mid-day. Everything normal."

"I'm still not satisfied with the thermostat. If it breaks down again it's going to kill off the two cobras, and we can't afford to lose them."

Jackson waited. Taplow stood for a moment breathing the scent of roses in the warm night air. "Good night, Jackson."

"Good night, sir."

He went out of the room.

For five minutes, Taplow remained where he was, watching the first glow of a moon come creeping across the gardens.

He thought, idly: I worry too much about the beasties. I suppose everyone worries too much, about something.

He moved suddenly, and crossed the lawn outside, walking down the gravel path, passing the three big cages where the monkeys were. He could hear one of them chattering in its throat, and the faint acrid smell of them reached him. It was, for all its malodour, a smell he loved. He loved these animals, more than most others. If a man weren't careful, a monkey could break his heart.

The long low shed was black in the faint moonlight. He stopped, opening the door. His shoes grated on the concrete inside. From the other end of the shed he could hear the slight tremor of the thermostat, pulsing steadily. The sound relieved him.

Warmth, greater than the warmth of the summer night outside, was against his skin, doubly reassuring him.

He lifted his hand, switching on the lights, and walked a few paces over the concrete floor, and had no premonition, not even a fleeting second of instinctive fear before the thing struck, lashing against him.

A cry left his throat, the hoarse, dry sound that is driven out of a man by terror.

3rd

MOVE

"YES—YES, I've got that." Miss Gorringe made another note. "All right, Freddie, I'll tell him. Good-bye." She put the telephone down, and went into the morning-room.

Bishop was finishing his coffee, still in a dressing-gown. A fresh copy of *Autosport* was on the table. Without looking up he said:

"There'll be some tough opposition at Le Mans. Three Ferraris, four Alfas, and the Mercedes works-team. And there's the Cunningham. If our Jags put up the same show as last year, they—"

"Hugo," she said.

He glanced up.

"What now?"

"Can I have a cup?"

He took the lid off the pot and peered in.

"Two, if you like."

She poured herself some coffee and said: "Freddie's just rung through. Dr. Clive Taplow died last night at his home in Surrey." She took a spoonful of brown sugar.

Bishop tilted back in his chair.

"What happened?" he asked.

"There's a snake-house, in the grounds. Part of the little zoo I told you about. Last night he went there, to check a thermostat. A black mamba was out of its den, and it struck him; he lived five minutes."

Bishop got up slowly and put the magazine on to the chair. First morning sunlight was just pouring over the roof of the mews-cottages opposite. It winked on the breakfast things.

"I see," he said.

She stirred her coffee.

"Where do we go from here?" Miss Gorringe asked.

In a moment he said: "It must have happened soon after I rang him up. Mustn't it?"

"Fifteen minutes after, at eleven o'clock."

He said nothing for a while. She drank her coffee, waiting.

"It looks as if we might be right, Gorry. Scobie and Taplow were both on the Antarctic expedition. It leaves Sir Bernard Gregg, Charles Moss and Professor Parish."

"There's Joanna Gregg, and the photographer, Corbyn."

"But they stayed on the survey-ship, they didn't go all the way."

"The girl is your best bet. She'll have been screened about Scobie, but not about this one."

He nodded. "Can you fix me up?"

She went back into the long room. "I'll try." She checked a telephone number, and dialled. Miss Gorringe had many friends. It was her job.

From a vast shed near the main runway, came the sound of a jet under test. It was a thin scream, gusting out minute after minute, slicing knife-like across the tarmac and the fields beyond. When it stopped, the ears seemed to expand, and the silence was groggy.

Joanna crossed the main hall of the technical block and started up the shallow stone steps to the drawing-offices above. A man was coming down; tall, lean-faced, in a perfect suit. He said:

"Good morning, Miss Gregg."

She stopped.

"Good morning. I'm sorry, but—"

"My name is Bishop. I came to see you, if you

can give me a few minutes."

She didn't smile. Today she felt numbed. She had known Clive Taplow since she was at school; he had been her father's best friend.

"Yes, Mr. Bishop, if you'll come with me."

She led him along a passage, into a small compact office. There were drawing-boards, instruments, a huge window, a bowl of roses, her desk, a telephone, charts on the wall. She said: "Please sit down. Have you been checked?"

He sat down. "I have. It took over an hour."

"That was quick." He watched her as she slid some papers into a drawer. She was slim, tight-limbed with quick movements. "You must be a V.I.P. Are you?"

"Yes, if that means very impudent and persuasive."

He looked at the picture on the wall opposite, a water-colour in a light wood frame. A ship, among ice-floes. Why did she still have it, on her wall? Gorry said the engagement had been broken off. Just interest; nothing sentimental.

"I haven't got long, Mr. Bishop. How can I help you?"

She sat down behind her desk. Her tone was crisp.

He said: "I came to talk briefly about two people. One fell out of a train. The other died of snake-bite."

She had a good poker-face. Only the dark eyes changed, and took on pain.

She said nothing, but looked at him steadily.

He said: "When I heard the bad news—last night's—I thought of a connection between these two tragedies. Professor Scobie and Dr. Taplow were friends; but it was their fellow-membership of the expedition, two years ago, that seemed more significant."

In a moment she asked blank-toned: "Of what?"

"I came to find out if you might know. You went as far as the mainland supply-base with the rest of the party, and you know them all: Sir Bernard, Charles Moss, Professor Parish, Professor Scobie and Dr. Taplow. And of course Max Corbyn, the photographer."

Light from the big window cast half her face in shadow. It wasn't a beautiful face; it was intelligent, with fine eyes and a lovely mouth; a face with thoughts in it.

"Mr. Bishop, who are you?"

He would have liked to watch her face for longer.

"A man called Ripton has written several books. *Study of Mental Process, Post-script to Mendel, Dynamics of Physical Fear*—"

"I know the first one. I suppose most people do. You write under the name of Ripton?"

"Yes."

"You're interested in these tragedies, as a writer?"

"Not solely, no. I'd had the privilege of meeting Scobie. He was to have dined with me, the night after he died."

Her voice lost its brittleness.

"You knew Gordon?"

"Slightly. That was my loss."

She combed back her short brown hair with a sudden habitual movement of her fingers.

"I'm feeling . . . out of my depth, a little, today. Those two men were friends of my father's, and my friends too. I don't quite see how I can help you."

"If you'd rather, I'll go now."

She smiled quickly. "No, don't go." The smile changed her face, warmed her voice. "You've taken a lot of trouble, finding me here. Why didn't you phone me, at my home?"

"I wanted to look round here."

"They let you?"

"Yes. Not everywhere, of course. It's a breath-taking kind of place, Farley."

She left her chair and stood by the window, looking down at the runways and the group of sheds. An engine was running up again, but its sound was faint, here.

"A little like a bee-hive, yes," she said absently. "We work twenty-four hours a day, and sometimes a bee goes up, and we watch it. Monotonous and exciting, sometimes mixed."

She turned her head and looked at him, as if for the first time.

"You'll have to ask me simple questions, if there's anything I can tell you."

He got up and stood near her at the big window.

"When Sir Bernard came back with his party from the South Pole in 1952, he said they'd found their objective. He didn't say what it was."

"No."

"But it was a big one, a big objective." He put it as a question, a supposition. She was silent. His voice came again gently. "And now it's a big secret."

After a moment she turned her head, looking away from the scene outside.

"I believe that's right, yes. And you believe it's got something to do with the tragedies. Don't you?"

He nodded.

"It seems very likely," he said. "One couldn't very well overlook a theory like that, even if it's wildly incorrect. Probably you've thought about it yourself."

"Yes, I have. It's—odd, hearing it from you."

He drew a breath. "As far as you know, Miss Gregg, the big secret—if one exists—is now shared by three people, and no one else. Can I say that?"

"My father never told me what he found. I knew he'd found something, across the ice. When they came back, they were silent, reserved, held-in. But I've never been told, and nor was Max Corbyn. I know that for certain."

"And it's unlikely that your father told anyone else—anyone who wasn't with the party—another friend, or another scientist?"

"Yes, I'd say unlikely. Almost impossible."

She moved away from the window, looking down at her desk.

"I won't keep you," he murmured, "any longer."

She watched his face with an expression that was meaningless to him, detached.

"I don't know why I've told you as little as I have, Mr. Bishop. I should have referred you straight to my father. I don't think he'd have told you even as much."

He smiled cleanly.

"You told me because you trusted me. That was because I'd managed to get checked-in here, which showed I was pretty flawless, and because I happen to have written a book or two about a subject that interests you—or you wouldn't have read the first one I mentioned. It gave us something in common, and that makes for trust—a psychological sequence, by the way, that I've always thought dangerously ill-founded."

His voice was gravely amused at her expression. He said quietly: "And you've been thinking along the same lines, about this theoretical big-scale secret. You can't get your father to talk on the subject. He shuts up. Stop me if I'm wrong. So it's nice to talk to someone about it, even a stranger."

"Yes," she said slowly, automatically. "Something like that."

He turned to the door, and stopped, looking at the picture.

"I expect Corbyn painted that?"

She turned her head. "How did you know?"

"The initials, M.C., in the corner."

"Yes. It's the *Snow Goose*, the ship we were on. He painted it from memory. I always thought he was a talented artist, but my judgment's not really—"

"He 'was'?"

She smiled faintly.

"He's not dead. We were engaged, at that time, and now we're not. I suppose I tend to think of him in the past-tense."

He said gently: "One always does, for a time." He glanced back at the picture. "Where is he now?"

On her desk, a buzzer sounded. Before she answered it she said: "I don't know. Somewhere in England."

She put down the switch and said into the speaker: "Just a minute, please."

Bishop said:"I'll go now. It was very kind of you to give me your time, and your help." He opened the door. She crossed towards him.

"Only five minutes, and not much help. If you're near Sloane Square this evening, will you ring the bell?"

"I should like to, but I hear Sir Bernard works at home, as well as at the laboratories—"

"He does, only too often. I'm trying to persuade him not to, so that the invitation's partly . . . a device."

He inclined his head.

"I shall be happy to be of service."

Her eyes were frank.

"Only partly a device."

"Then I shall be happy to come. Good-bye."

Frisnay was sitting in a corner, away from the bar. He was drinking beer. He saw Bishop as soon as he came in. Bishop looked round, and came over. He sat and said:

"I saw you come in. Finished?"

"Apart from homework," Frisnay grunted. "Have a beer."

"In a minute. What's the situation at Grey Gates, Amberly?"

"Taplow's house . . . I was down there, today. Spoke to a man named Jackson—he looked after Taplow."

Bishop was watching a girl who was perched at the bar. She had come in with someone. He liked the way she crossed her legs, and the poise of her head. He thought for a moment about Joanna, and thought he would perhaps ring her bell, this evening. He said in a moment:

"What's Jackson like, Freddie?"

"Rugged type, self-educated and proud of it." He drank some beer. "Why?"

"I'm just interested. What did you find out?"

"One particular thing seemed useful. I'll tell you, if you want to know."

Absently Bishop murmured, "Yes, I'd like to know."

"It seems you have a thermostat, when you have a snake-house, to keep the ghastly little bastards warm." He shuddered slightly. "The one down there had been giving a bit of trouble, and Taplow was worried about his cobras. If they chill off, they die, and they're expensive." Ruminatively he added: "I don't like snakes, much, they're too long."

Bishop got a waiter to bring him some beer.

Frisnay said: "Apparently it wasn't Dr. Taplow's habit to visit the snake-house last thing at night, before he went to bed, but it was pretty certain he'd go there *last* night, because he'd been worried about that thermostat, for some time. Let that sink in, Hugo."

He paused. "Jackson showed me over the place. It's got monkey-cages, nearby. The monkeys were screeching like hell. Jackson said they 'knew', about their boss being dead. It's a most unnerving place, Grey Gates."

Bishop smiled gently. He had once dropped a lizard into Frisnay's desk, at school. Frisnay had thrown a fit. He didn't like things that crept, crawled, swung on trees or lived in holes in the ground. All he could stand were humans.

He said: "I asked Jackson what happened last night. He said he heard a sort of shout, and came running out to the snake-house, and found Taplow with a black mamba, trying to fight the thing off. Jackson killed it with a stick, and tried to squeeze and suck the poison out, but it was too late. Mambas are about the worst you can find—they come as quick as a whip and the bite goes in deep. You die in about four minutes, in agony."

His eyes looked strained. He said: "Charming thought, isn't it? I asked if Taplow had said anything coherent, before he died. Jackson said no."

Bishop studied his beer. "How did they get on—he and Taplow?"

"Very well, from the way he spoke of him. They

both loved animals—it takes all sorts, I suppose—and most animals loved them, he told me.
He said even the mamba didn't really know what
it was doing . . . He sort of forgave the thing, in a
horrible way. I feel like another beer."

Bishop got him one, from the bar.

"Freddie, how did the thing escape?"

"Jackson couldn't explain. He said Taplow
must have failed to fasten the catch of the mam-
ba-den, the last time he was in there. All the
snakes are deadly, and it was the rule that only
Taplow should attend them. If anything went
wrong, he wanted to take all responsibility."

"Almost as if he'd had a premonition."

"Yes. Jackson said that. He said the mamba
must have got loose earlier in the afternoon,
and been lying on a beam over the doorway.
It's a favourite trick of theirs—to drop on the
victim from above. Cheerful thought."

He drank a lot of beer and said: "The point
that's most interesting is this. I asked Jackson
what else he could tell me, that might throw
any light on Taplow's death. He said that last
evening, about seven, he went to a place across
the village to fetch some books for Taplow. Colonel Grayson's house—Grayson runs a nice public library. While Jackson was there, a question
arose about a particular book: should he bring it,
or not? So he rang up Dr. Taplow, from Grayson's

house. And Taplow wasn't alone."

Bishop waited. In a moment he had to ask:

"What exactly d'you mean, Freddie?"

"When Jackson had left home, the Doctor was alone, and there was no talk of anyone calling. But when he was on the phone to Taplow, Taplow apparently said something to someone in the room with him—some remark about a book. Jackson heard him clearly." Slowly he said: "When he got back, Taplow was alone again, and he didn't mention that anyone had called. Natural enough—people come and go—Taplow has friends in the village; but Jackson said he thought he'd mention it. I didn't stress the point. I don't know how much I trust him, to tell the plain truth."

"Think this unknown caller might be dreamed-up?"

"That could be. Look at the situation, Hugo: the thermostat in the snake-house has been giving trouble, so Taplow goes there to check up on it. The catch on the mamba's den hadn't been properly fastened. Result: a death."

"Has Jackson any motive for organising a fatal accident, and putting you on to a false trail with this unknown caller story?"

"Not as far as we know, but we're checking fast. And we've tested for finger-prints—tumblers—ashtrays—any sign that there was really someone visiting the house last evening. I'll be getting results any time now. But you see what we've got, don't you?"

Bishop said: "Yes. A man talking to Scobie, on his train. A man calling on Taplow, last night. Both unknown."

"If Jackson's not lying."

"Of course." He finished his drink. "When you're ready, I'll drive you home. I'm working on a theory that could fit in somewhere, and it's too hot in here."

They went outside to the grey Rolls-Royce. Bishop opened the windscreen. The street was warm after the heat of the day.

Frisnay said: "Why doesn't this museum-piece fall into dust?"

"Because it's a kind of mechanical Father Thames, and if you want to be plaguey rude about it you can plaguey well walk."

Frisnay got in with a grunt.

"Theory," he said when they were moving away.

"It's this. I've talked to Joanna Gregg—daughter of Sir Bernard Gregg, whose cheque was found in Scobie's pocket when—"

"Right."

"And she's been thinking along the same lines as I have. We think the two tragedies might have a common factor: the 1952 Antarctic expedition. Sir Bernard Gregg has said that their objective was reached, but he never said what it was."

"He tell the girl, his daughter?"

"No." He turned the car towards Kensington. Theatre-traffic was beginning, along Piccadilly. "It might be a big secret, Freddie. Big enough to cause two deaths."

Frisnay said nothing for minutes. His wooden face seemed to watch the traffic. Bishop stopped the car outside his flat.

Frisnay said at last:

"There's a chance, I suppose, of some connection. You've seen Joanna Gregg. Who else?"

"No one. I telephoned Taplow last night, a quarter of an hour before he died, but Jackson said he was engaged."

"Apart from Jackson, then, you were probably the last man whose voice was heard in that house, even over the phone."

"Probably."

"Can't leave it alone, can you . . . "

"What?"

"Death. You ask them to dine; you ring them up. They die."

"What a charming sense of the morbid you have, Freddie."

"You going to see anyone else? Parish, Moss, Sir Bernard?"

He got out of the car and put one foot on the running-board.

Bishop said: "Yes. And possibly Max Corbyn.
He's a photographer and a bit of an artist who
was engaged to Miss Gregg, two years ago. Engagement was broken off. He didn't go all the
way with the party, but stayed on the ship."

"Where is he now?"

"I asked Joanna. She doesn't know. Some–
where in the country, she thinks."

"Know anything about him?"

"Nothing. I've asked Gorry to trace him, if she
can."

Frisnay said: "Tell her we'll save her time. I'll
let her know results. Who are you going to see
next?"

"Sir Bernard, in a few minutes."

"He's given you an appointment?"

"No. His daughter has."

Frisnay dipped one eyelid and said: "Oh."

"Yes, she's attractive Freddie."

"I know—your tone took on a permanent-
wavelength. Tell me what you find out, during
the dalliance." He took his foot off the running-
board. "Thanks for the lift, and the beer."

" 'Bye Freddie."

The grey limousine went away, turning left
towards Hyde Park, then right, through Knightsbridge. Bishop rang the bell of Number Twelve,
Collingwood Court, Sloane Square, at five minutes to nine, and waited.

Sir Bernard was standing near the windows, looking out at the small lawn, where dusk was settling. The set of his shoulders was brooding, unrelaxed.

Joanna brought Bishop into the room.

"Daddy, this is Mr. Hugo Bishop. Mr. Bishop—my father."

The two men studied each other. With a shade of dryness to take the edge off, Gregg said:

"I'm disturbed to see you, Mr. Bishop."

"Sorry about that, sir. For me it's a privilege."

"For me it's a bit of a nuisance. I can say that, because you're half my age—"

Joanna said: "My father was going to work this evening. He's annoyed with me, not you."

Gregg moved heavily across the room.

"You'll have something to drink?" he said.

"No thank you—"

"I'm going to make coffee," the girl said. "I expect you'll join us in that."

She left them, with a glance at neither.

"Sit down, Mr. Bishop. I sounded rude. I'm sorry."

"I don't like disturbing your work." He liked Gregg's face. Except for warmth in his eyes, it was as hard as a brick.

"It's my daughter's deliberate design, I don't doubt; but she brow-beats me for the best, of course. She tells me your pseudonym is Ripton.

I've a high regard for it."

"Thank you sir."

"I've had the time to read only one of your theses, and I disagreed with about a third of all it said. The rest was brilliant." He wandered back to the windows, and turned to face Bishop. "You know Joanna well?"

"No, I've met her for the first time, today."

"She's cussed. She doesn't let me work." He had said it half to himself.

"When distinguished men overwork themselves, people who really care for them have to step in. They must. But you knew these things before I learned to talk."

"And forgot them, while you've remembered."

"I'm too often reminded, sir. These days, people are living on the edge of their nerves, and sometimes it's not easy to keep their balance. Professor Scobie was a tragic example."

Gregg stared at him for some seconds, and then nodded.

"Yes. You've read the reports, of course."

"Most people followed them, but only Dr. Taplow followed his example."

"An odd thing to say, Mr. Bishop."

"Is it sir?" The light from the standard-lamp flashed across his wrist-watch as he slowly got up, standing by the hearth. "I've a theory, but possibly it's wrong."

Sir Bernard moved closer to him.

"I should like to hear it," he said.

Bishop said: "I don't believe Professor Scobie killed himself. I don't believe Dr. Taplow died by accident."

The silence drew out.

Without strain to his tone, Gregg said:

"No?"

"I believe they were both murdered, by something on their minds."

He paused, watching the old man.

"Go on if you will."

"I believe that three other men in the world know the name of this abstract murderer. Charles Moss, Professor Parish, and you, Sir Bernard."

In a moment: "I see your line of reasoning, of course. We were all members of the 1952 expedition. But how do you mean these two were murdered, by something on their minds? What manner of thing?"

Bishop moved about, his hands behind him.

"Pressure. Enormous, killing pressure. The thing that usually sends a man to suicide. But in this case it might have been pressure exerted from outside them, by someone else. Perhaps deliberately—"

"A quite horrible conception."

"They died, horribly."

"Most people do, Mr. Bishop. May I say that I

think your theory is like a third of your brilliant book. I disagree with it utterly. After all, these poor devils were friends of mine—I knew them well. I've had theories, too . . . less macabre than your own, and much more plausible. But even mine didn't help me. I have to accept the verdict of the coroner: I think it right, and I've knowledge to go upon. With Dr. Taplow, the finding might be different. It would be a terrible way out, for the bravest man, to invite the attack of a deadly snake."

Bishop nodded. "I agree, sir. But I think there was pressure there, before the thing struck. Murderous pressure."

"You make it sound melodramatic, perhaps deliberately, to invite comment. But you might be right. Have you suggested this theory to the police?"

"Yes."

"Wise of you. They don't care much for theories, I know, but it might help them in their present inquiry. And if they prove you right, I shall respect your intelligence all the more. If these men hadn't been good friends of mine, the idea would be stimulating, as a morbid puzzle. As it is, I find it painful. You'll forgive me if we talk of something else."

"Of course. I shouldn't have broached the subject. We were rather led into it."

Sir Bernard smiled faintly.

"With some adroitness, Mr. Bishop. I admired that, too . . . "

Bishop didn't smile.

"There's one question I'd like to put to you, sir. A very brief one."

"Yes?"

"You made a discovery, two years ago. Perhaps a big one. You shared it with four others. Two have died. There are two left alive—and yourself. Have you considered that you might conceivably be in danger of death?"

"No, I have not. The idea's absurd. You mustn't try to apply theoretical process to cold fact . . . not, at least, in matters of life and death."

"It was stupid of me, Sir Bernard. And I apologise."

"My dear fellow, there's no apology asked. But we'll drop the subject, please."

"By all means."

4th

MOVE

AS MISS Gorringe came into the room she heard the smack of the pellet going into the ping-pong ball. The ball fell, rolling across the carpet.

Bishop said: "Hello," and put the ball up again. He stood back with the air-pistol.

Miss Gorringe shut the door and said: "Hugo, is it necessary to put the ball on top of a valuable Venetian vase?"

"Of course." He aimed. "If it were put on top of an old china jerry, I shouldn't have to be so accurate." He fired. The ball span down. "And I am very accurate. Note."

She stood farther away.

"Did you see Sir Bernard tonight?"

"Yes. He dismissed all dramatic theories, contemptuously. I'm half inclined to think he's perfectly right."

"What's he like?"

He put a new pellet in the gun and levelled it.

"A very good type, Gorry. That's where the girl gets her character from. I like them both."

"For different reasons."

He fired.

"For different reasons."

She picked up the ball. She said: "If the Princess Chu Yi-Hsin finds these bits of lead about, she might eat them. I do wish you'd do something else."

"She's got more sense, and I'm out of practice."

"You never carry a gun."

"Gorry darling, why don't you go and knit some rusty wire-netting or something genteel, instead of nagging at me?"

She sat down at her desk with a sigh.

"Did you ask him if there was really a secret?"

"Who?"

"Sir Bernard."

"No. I suggested it. He didn't deny anything. I even implied that there was a kind of murder going on."

"There's more than one kind of murder?"

"There are millions. All fascinating. But these might have been simple and direct. Remember what Freddie told me: there was a man seen talking to Scobie on his train, before he died. There's Jackson's story of a man at Grey Gates, before Taplow died. It could have been the same man."

"Nice idea, but sounds wide. What about the motive?"

He sent the ball spinning and she ducked. It skated across her desk.

He wandered about after it and said: "The motive could be the secret of the expedition—the secret that Gregg didn't even tell his own daughter. The man might want it, desperately enough to kill for it."

He stood the target up again. It was full of punctures.

She said: "Could it be one of the ship's crew? Or the photographer, Max Corbyn?"

He said: "It could. And by the way, Freddie told me you needn't waste your time. The Yard's going to have Corbyn traced."

"I wish them better luck than I've had."

"Freddie's going to phone, as soon as he's found him."

"If he's not—"

The door-bell sounded, from the hall. She said: "I'll go. Cease fire, for pity's sake, and let me out."

He stood the ball up and paced back, slipping

a slug in. There were voices in the hall, Gorry's and another woman's.

In a moment the door opened. The slug hit the ball and it split, flying apart.

"Hugo, someone to see you."

"Oh."

Miss Gorringe showed the woman in. She was a slight-built ash-blonde with the tension of a cat in the way she moved. She was about half Bishop's size.

Miss Gorringe said: "Miss Johns." She went out and shut the door.

Miss Johns looked around the room.

"I hoped I'd find you in."

She spoke softly and firmly, and did not smile.

"I'm glad you did, Miss Johns. Will you sit down?"

"Thank you."

She dropped a mink stole over a chair and curled up, deftly. "You're expecting someone else?"

"No. Why?"

"The gun."

"Oh." He put it down. "No, I was just mucking about. What will you drink?"

"Gin and French. Thank you."

He moved to the sideboard. "We haven't met before, or I should have remembered."

"No." Her voice floated softly in the long room.

"I'm vaguely connected with someone else you haven't met before—but would like to. His name is Corbyn."

He came back to her. "Yes?" She took her drink.

"Thank you. Here's how."

"Cheers."

She looked round the room, more slowly this time.

"I like your den. It's too enormous for intimacy, and the range of period's pretty wide, but I like it."

"A tribute to Einstein. The scene is the Universal Now. But we were talking about Corbyn."

She smiled with white small teeth.

"You're pressed for time?"

He said: "No, but if I don't get to the point fairly fast, you'll have had time to sum me up very thoroughly, and that'll put me at a serious disadvantage."

She crossed her legs, making news of an old trick. The lamplight sheened across her stockings.

"Does your guard always fly up when a stranger calls at night, Mr. Bishop?"

He sat on the floor like a tailor and sipped his drink.

"Beautiful strangers never call at night, to comment on the furnishings."

"There's something lovable about your icy

69

calm." She looked at him for a moment longer and then said: "I heard you'd become interested in two recent deaths. Professor Scobie's and Dr. Taplow's. And want to locate Max Corbyn."

"You're well-informed."

"I don't know how many million telephone-wires there are spread across London; but it's surprising how voices carry, even on closed circuits. If you want to talk to Corbyn, I can give you his number."

He said: "That's nice of you, but—"

The telephone had begun ringing.

"Do excuse me."

He got up and answered it. He said: "Yes. Yes, that's right—he promised to tell me." There was a long pause. "And the number—?" He made a note on a pad. "Thank you. Perhaps you'd tell him I'll be along later, if he's still there. Yes—goodbye."

He put down the receiver and came back to his drink where he had left it on the floor.

"I'm so sorry, Miss Johns. You were saying—? Oh yes, you could give me Corbyn's number."

"That's right, if you want it."

"It's Belgrave 3892, isn't it?"

Her voice went hard.

"How long have you known where he is?"

"Fifteen seconds. They've just rung up to tell me."

"Who are 'they'?"

"You probably know their number, too. It's Whitehall 1212."

She sipped her drink deliberately, watching him.

"Scotland Yard's looking for Corbyn?"

He said: "Well, not any longer, it appears."

She looked down at her glass.

"Mr. Bishop, I've heard something of your reputation."

"Not all, I do hope."

"They say you have quicksilver qualities. Just when one has one's finger on you, you're suddenly somewhere else."

"That makes me sound rather like a lemon-pip."

"More formidable than that, I think. Hugo Ripton Bishop, isn't it?"

"So you've looked me up in the Winkle-monger's Who's Who."

"No, but I've seen your books, and I imagine it's you who's done all the summing-up, since I came in here."

"Appraising, shall we say, of an enchanting profile, an exquisite scent—"

"You like it? It's called Music of Roses."

"It suits you, almost."

"Almost?"

"Roses . . . suggest innocence."

She got up impatiently and said: "Hugo—I can't

call so cold-blooded a pagan by the name of Bishop—I think I'll just say what I came here to say,
and then go."

"I'm immeasurably saddened."

She said: "I wanted to warn you. You don't
realise you're moving into a situation that's as
gentle as gelignite."

"The alliteration's pretty but the sense is
absurd. Give my compliments to Corbyn and say
sorry, but I'm not scared."

He watched her intently, deliberately. Her
breathing was quicker but her voice almost as
soft.

"It wasn't Corbyn who sent me. I came here
for my own reasons."

"I'm glad you did. I've enjoyed it. I wish it
seemed to be mutual."

"It is, Hugo. You're a good host; you don't per-
mit awkward silences."

"You'll have another drink, before you go."

"Thanks, but no."

Her hand was cool.

"You don't seem very domesticated, Hugo, but I
hope you know how to remove gelignite-stains."

He showed her through the hall, and said good
night. When Miss Gorringe came out of her room
she found him leaning against the front door,
with his hands in his pockets.

"What now?" she asked.

"I'm counting ten."

"Instead of swearing?"

"No. Miss Johns has just left. I want to see where she goes."

"Why not follow her?"

"I'm going to. She has ears, built-in. They work."

He opened the door gently, and stood on the step. Along the mews, the woman's footsteps came faintly over the cobbles.

He murmured: "Might phone you later, Gorry."

She closed the door for him, quietly.

Mrs. Cobb came in.

"It's for you, Miss Joanna."

"Thank you, Mrs. Cobb." She came into the hall, and took the receiver.

She said hello.

"That sounded just like always . . . "

She frowned quickly.

"Is that—Max Corbyn?"

"So you still remember my voice. How are you, Joanna?"

"Very well." She said it coolly. "And you?"

"Oh, the world goes round. Could I see you for a few minutes?"

"When?"

"Now."

She hesitated. He said:

"It could be fairly urgent. Nothing sentimental, Joanna."

"Where are you?"

"At Trent's Hotel. I could pick you up, if you like, and—"

"No. I'll get a taxi. Say in about ten minutes."

"Fine. In ten minutes. Au revoir . . . "

She hung up and stood thinking. The house was quiet. From the Square, the sounds of traffic came faintly. His voice had sounded the same. He would look the same. But everything was different.

She put on a dust-coat and got a taxi outside the house.

Corbyn was waiting on the steps of the hotel, his head bare, his air casual.

"Joanna," he said, and took both her hands. She studied him. He was the same, yes: taut-looking and easy, a paradox with a too-handsome face.

"It's a long time, Max."

"Yes."

He took her into a small lounge and got drinks.

She said: "I didn't know you were back in London. What are you doing now?"

"Oh, covering a sob-angle series for Twentieth-Century Mirror—close-ups of weeping widows—"

"You're more cynical than ever."

"Not in the least. Let widows weep, but don't take pictures of them doing it. I don't like exploiting grief to boost circulation, that's all."

"Then why do it?"

"They pay big, and a man's got his price. They let me keep my principles, and the wolf from the door. And what about you—still drawing aeroplanes?"

"Yes." She asked for a cigarette and he lit one for her. "I was talking about you, yesterday. A man who called at my office admired your picture of the *Snow Goose.*" It was odd, sitting here with him, so long after the wonderful days, and the hellish row that ended them. It was like talking with a mirror that had no third dimension.

"Did he want to buy it?"

"M'm?" She smiled suddenly without humour. "That picture isn't like its creator. It hasn't a price. It's a keepsake."

He made his eyes soften but she saw the effort. He said: "But it can't mean anything now."

"No. Keep-sakes never do, really, when you work it out. The man who admired this one is called Bishop."

"I've heard of him."

"Yes?"

"Slightly peculiar fish, isn't he?"

"I find him a slightly likeable fish."

"Oh sorry . . . he's a friend of yours?"

She looked down at her shoes.

"Yes."

He waited, but she didn't go on. He asked:

"How's Sir Bernard? I should have inquired much earlier."

"He's fit, but overworking."

"Have these affairs worried him, unduly?"

"It's been a shock, for most of us."

"Ye-es." He watched some people coming in. A woman was talking very loudly with a distorted accent. "I rang Charles Moss, and old Parish. They didn't seem anything more than—just shocked."

She glanced up. She had to wait till the woman stopped talking.

"I don't think I follow, Max."

He said: "Maybe I'm imaginative, but Scobie and Taplow were two men out of five, weren't they? Only those five knew what was discovered on the survey, and now there are only three. Let's not fool ourselves: they found something pretty important, out there. When they came back to the ship they wouldn't say a word. There was an atmosphere, quite unmistakable. And since then, nobody's had a clue as to what they found."

He dropped ash from his cigarette. "Unless your father's told you?"

"No." She spoke cooly, as she had on the telephone. "I just forgot about it, as I assumed he wanted me to."

"Yes, of course."

Steadily she said: "You told me it could be 'fairly urgent' that I should meet you here."

"Yes. You see Joanna, a lot of people were very interested in that expedition—scientists, journalists and so on—it was carefully organised and beautifully equipped. Charles Moss saw to that."

He leaned forward with his elbows on his knees, concentrating. "And I think there are some people who have refused to forget—unlike you—that a discovery was made . . . and deliberately hushed-up."

In a moment she said: "Well?"

"Unless I'm wrong, darling, it's very simple. Someone wants to know the secret, because it's a big one. Big things are usually valuable: there's a price on size." His mouth drooped cynically. He asked: "Did they try to get it out of Scobie and Taplow? Have they used pressure of any kind? In fact did those two have to face a choice—to give up the secret or their life?"

More loudly he said, turning to her, "Or was the choice made for them?"

Her eyes were steady. Only her voice faltered.

"You're talking about murder."

"Of a kind. You see why I told you it might be urgent for us to meet. I think your father should be warned. He'd listen to you, if not to me—"

"Warned?"

"Joanna." He laid a hand on her arm. "Five men found the secret of—shall we put it—Area X. Two have died. Surely the others should be made to realise their situation, because it's rather a fearful one. Don't you think?"

She watched her cigarette. The loud-voiced woman had stopped talking and started drinking. A dance-band was playing, in another room.

"Max, a moment ago you asked me if I knew the secret of the expedition—if my father had told me. Did you hope I knew, and would tell you?"

After a few seconds, and with only a shade of rancour he said: "That is known as a back-hander—"

"It's nearly two years Max, and people change. I don't know you any more. But I'll apologise, and go."

He stood up, the movement easy, over-casual.

"I'll see you into a taxi," he said. He was very polite.

"Please don't bother."

She stood in front of him, quiet and straight. "Sorry, Max. You wanted me to warn my father, and I've mistrusted you. But Gordon and Clive are dead, and I'm unnerved."

"But of course you are." It was too nicely said.

"I think you may be right. They may have died because of something they found, out there in the South. I've been connecting things, myself, and so has a friend of mine. That makes my back-hander worse than ever, and I'm going because I think you'd rather I did. Not for anything else."

He smiled without expression.

All he said was: "Good night."

She had the commissionaire get her a taxi and went straight home, torn between wishing she had stayed longer with Max, and wishing she hadn't come at all.

"Where did she go? Or did you lose her?"

"M'm?"

"Christine Johns."

"Oh. I followed her as far as her hotel."

He lit his pipe again. It kept going out. It was blocked, and he'd run out of cleaners.

Gorry asked: "Which hotel, Hugo?"

"Trent's. That's where Max Corbyn's putting up."

Gorry's colourless eyes widened.

"Is that so?" she said.

"That is so. People might have begun to fit in; on the other hand the arm of coincidence is notoriously elastic."

Unintentionally he blew out a shower of ash

and sparks from his pipe, unblocking it too well.

She murmured: "Sir Walter Raleigh should have been decently hanged, like Guy Fawkes."

"Was Guy Fawkes hanged?" He stamped out the last spark. "So her name's Christine . . . "

"Yes. She announced herself as Christine Johns. It sounds rather nice, but she's not very, is she?"

"It depends what you want. She offered it to me, until I went quietly into deep-freeze." He put new tobacco into the white bowl. "While I was looking at Trent's Hotel, I saw my sweet Joanna, getting into a taxi outside—"

"Joanna Gregg? She'd been to see Corbyn—?"

"Or Christine. Or both. Or the arm of coincidence is as aforesaid. But it's all good stuff . . . no rubbish. It's the people in a case that make things happen, and they're forming a sizeable queue."

Miss Gorringe was going to say something when the telephone rang. Bishop reached across for it.

"Yes?" he said.

"Freddie here. Care to come round?"

"Your flat?"

"No, my office."

Bishop looked at the time and said: "You told me you'd knocked off, except for homework."

"Except in theory old lad, my office is my home.

A p'liceman's lot is just a bed of nettles."

"Poor old bucket, never mind. There's always the pension, and the thought of seeing me again in five minutes."

Freddie grunted. "I'll be here."

Hugo rang off and said to Gorry:

"It looks like blowing up into quite a night." He went into the hall and called softly: "While I'm gone, at any time, if Miss Johns delivers a parcel, put it in the fridge and retire smartly to Stoke Poges or somewhere distant."

"Comforting," murmured Miss Gorringe, but the door had shut.

Frisnay was looking fresh. He looked fresh when things went wrong, and the work was tough. When there seemed to be a gleam of daylight in his job, he got worried, because it wasn't natural.

He said: "Don't sit down. We'll look in at the laboratories. Smith has some facts."

As they walked along the passage and down the stone steps, he added: "I believe they're very negative, but they're facts, the food of life."

He pushed open the green door and went in with Bishop. From the far end of a bench came the soft rush of a Bunsen. Its flame bloomed like a blue crocus. Two men were working quietly in a corner, dipping plates. Smith was near the ventilator, a withered quiet man with a stoop and a tattered lab-coat.

Frisnay went up to him and said:

"Well, old cock?"

In a moment Smith looked up gently and said: "Ah. Just a minute."

He went on swirling crystals round a dish, as if mesmerising himself, and at last put it down to stand. The Bunsen burned on with a long-drawn never-ending breath. He got some papers from a drawer in the bench and looked at them and said in a melancholy way:

"Specimen A. Thread of cloth. Found on doorpost of snake-house, Dr. Taplow's home. Not from jacket or coat belonging to Dr. Taplow, nor Clifford Jackson."

Frisnay said to Bishop: "We took samples, from the lot."

Bishop nodded.

Smith said mournfully: "Thread is from black and grey Harris tweed cloth, probably overcoat, because of atmosphere deposits, locality London. Coat is about ten or twelve years old."

He stopped, as if someone had switched him off.

Frisnay said: "Can't be more than fifty thousand coats like that in London, can there—black and grey Harris tweed . . . "

Smith said: "No, but there are eight million people in London, so we've narrowed it down a lot."

"Specimen B," said Smith. "Short brown hair. Belongs to monkey, likely from India, not Africa. Beast in good health."

Bishop smiled. Frisnay grunted.

"Specimen C. Found on post of snake-den, marked 2. Thread from coat similar to Specimen A. No variations."

He turned the papers back-to-front. "Prints left me this for you, Inspector. No finger-prints except for Dr. Taplow's, Clifford Jackson's and your own."

"Clum-sy . . . " Bishop grinned.

Smith said: "Glove-prints found on handle of French doors leading out to snake-house from library. Imitation pigskin, fairly new. Three identifying marks: broken thread of seam and two small jags. Microscope would confirm."

He put the papers back into the drawer. "Duplicates follow."

Frisnay stood for a moment thinking, then said:

"Thank you, Smith. Time you went home."

"Time?" echoed Smith vaguely.

"He never thinks about time," Frisnay said as he led Bishop back to his office. "We think he died, years ago, but his ghost's invaluable."

They sat down and Bishop said:

"D'you keep pipe-cleaners, Freddie?"

"No."

"Dammit, they're cheap enough."

"I don't use a pipe."

Morosely Bishop put his *meerschaum* away and said: "Then you should. Make a man of you. So all we've got is a ten-year old overcoat and an imitation pigskin glove."

"It's better than the hair off the behind of an Indian monkey in good health," said Frisnay.

Bishop didn't say anything for moments. Then: "You seen Jackson again today, Freddie?"

"For a few minutes, yes."

"What was he doing?"

"Cataloguing the library."

Bishop said: "He hasn't wasted much time."

Frisnay began sharpening a pencil. "I don't see what you mean."

"Suppose we've got a big secret. Just suppose. And it's the mainspring of these two affairs. Suppose that. Taplow might have put it on paper, and slipped it into one of those books in his library."

Frisnay got down to the lead and went cautiously with his penknife. He said amiably:

"Oh, quite. He might also have written it down on a Chinese cigarette-paper and stuffed it into the old Japanese egg-timer in the kitchen."

"Dear Frederick, you've got a wonderful head.

Why don't you have it connected? I'm only trying to see things from Jackson's viewpoint, if he was after the secret."

"So you don't think much of his intelligence ... "

Bishop got up and wandered about and subconsciously looked about for something long and thin made of wire, to unblock his pipe with. He said:

"Oh coconuts, Inspector. You've no vision. I'm going to see Jackson myself. I think it might be interesting."

He stood in front of Frisnay's desk and added: "D'you know a girl called Christine Johns?"

"I don't think so."

"You should. Face like a Botticelli angel, figure like Venus only with arms, but socially a disappointment."

"When did you meet her?"

"Tonight. She tripped seductively into my place without an appointment, and said that Scobie and Taplow were just part of an almighty explosion that hasn't gone up yet, and went smartly away in an aura of gin and French. And her scent is called Music of Roses."

"Oh, God help us all," said Frisnay.

"I just wondered if she were somewhere in your files—Impossible Persons Bureau."

"I've never heard of her."

"Oh." Dreamily Bishop said: "Her address is Trent's Hotel."

Frisnay hooded his eyes and moved his pencil. It had a nice new point.

"I'll check on her," he said. "Let me know if she calls again."

"You'll probably hear the blast. Her lipstick's called Glamorous Gelignite. I'm going, Freddie."

"God bless you, little brown brother. Sorry we've nothing big for you."

Bishop went to the door.

"Never mind, but I'm disappointed. When you phoned, I thought things were working up to a nice noisy night." He opened the door. "D'you actually sleep here?"

Frisnay looked at the time.

"I'm waiting for some stuff to come in from Operations. Have a good night's sleep, and think kindly of the guardians who watch over the peace of your city."

When Bishop turned into Whitehall, Big Ben chimed eleven. He drove West, through thinning traffic. For five minutes he concentrated on the pedestrians, and after he had picked out seven black and grey Harris tweed coats he gave up and drove easily, idly, through Knightsbridge to King's Road.

Miss Gorringe was on the telephone, in the long room.

She said: "Oh, just a minute please—he's coming in now."

She gave the phone to Bishop. He asked her: "Who?"

"Joanna Gregg. Nervous."

He said into the phone: "Good evening, Miss Gregg."

Joanna hesitated.

"It's Mr. Bishop speaking?"

His face blanked off. Her voice was strung-up badly.

"Yes," he said.

"My—father's just had a message. A note. It isn't signed. It just says, 'the secret, or your life.'"

Quietly he said, "I see. Well, I'll come round, if you'd like me to."

"I—would, rather. But it's late, and—"

"Five minutes. Good-bye."

He put down the phone and said to Miss Gorringe on his way out: "Sir Bernard's got a threatening note. It's not going to be a dull night, after all."

5th

MOVE

THE GREY Rolls-Royce pulled up outside the house near Sloane Square. Bishop got out. As he climbed the steps, the front-door opened, Joanna stood there.

"I saw you stopping," she said. "Come in."

She took him into the drawing-room. "My father's still talking to the police, in his study."

She was wearing a turquoise house-coat that she must have slipped on to come downstairs in. He had a brief second-thought. She was beautiful, not only the other things.

"He called the police in, did he?"

She nodded. She looked cold. Not cold: chilled.

"As soon as he found the note, yes. He's been working late, in his laboratory at the hospital."

She looked round nervously. "Do sit down—we'll have a drink?"

"I won't, but please go ahead."

"I don't really want one. It was—nice of you, to come so quickly. I'm not sure why I rang you."

He offered her a cigarette, and lit it for her. He said:

"I'm glad you did. I'm interested in this rather startling affair, and—it's nice to see you."

She looked at him quickly and away. He said: "Where did Sir Bernard find this note?"

"On the bench, in his laboratory, this evening. He went back there after dinner, and the note was lying near his instruments."

"And that was all it said: 'the secret or your life'?"

"That's all."

"It's absurd." He perched on the arm of a chair. "We assume the 'secret' is the one we've always suspected—the discovery made on the expedition. The note implies that if your father doesn't give it up, his life's in danger—"

"But how can he give it up, if he doesn't know who left the note?"

"Precisely. In any case, the wording alone is ridiculously dramatic. Does he take it seriously?"

She clasped her arms together. The wide sleeves of the house-coat hung down. "Not really, but he rang the police right away because he doesn't like people snooping about in his laboratory while he's not there. His work might have been tampered with."

"Of course. How long have the police been here?"

"Half an hour—"

"More than one man?"

"No, just an inspector."

"His name's Frisnay?"

She nodded. Her eyes were less worried now. "Yes. You know him?"

"Slightly. We used to chuck ink-pellets at each other during Algebra to relieve the boredom, several decades ago."

She smiled. "You were at school together? And still friends?"

"Yes, although we still chuck the odd ink-pellet, metaphorically."

They heard voices in the hall.

"I think he's going," she said.

In a moment Sir Bernard came into the drawing-room.

"Oh, Mr. Bishop—didn't know you were here—"

Joanna said: "I telephoned him, to ask him what he thought about this."

Gregg moved about restlessly. "M'm—I think we should leave things to the police. I don't like people going into my laboratory and I don't like practical jokers. I'm extremely annoyed, as I told the inspector."

"You think it's a practical joke, sir?"

He rounded on Bishop.

"Do you know the exact wording of this note?"

He hesitated. Joanna said:

"Yes."

"Then you see why I can't take it seriously. If it means anything at all, it means—"

He heard the telephone ringing, in the hall.

"I'll go, Daddy—"

"No." He waved her aside, and went into the hall, leaving the door open. Taking up the phone he said: "Hello?"

He recognised the voice of Parish. Parish said:

"Bernard, do you happen to have received a message, of any kind? Anonymously?"

"What? Yes, I have. How did you know?"

"I've received one, as well."

"The devil you have." Gregg's tone lost a little of its impatience, took on caution. "Where did you find it, Parish?"

"It was put into my letter-box." His voice sounded bleak and out of its depth.

Gregg said in a moment: "Look here, we'll have a talk about this—the three of us, Charles as well. He might have had one, too. Come for dinner tomorrow evening."

"Couldn't we meet earlier? In the morning?"

"My dear fellow I've not the time, and in any case there's no urgency. I've just spent half an hour with a police-inspector and he told me not to worry. The same goes for you." With the droop of weariness gone from his big shoulders, he seemed to tower over the telephone in his hand, crushing it. "I think it's some damned fool playing a joke in poor taste, Parish, but we'll certainly discuss it, in private. I'll get hold of Moss, and ask him along."

Parish didn't sound reassured, but he didn't persist.

"Very well, Bernard. What time?"

"Say six-thirty."

In a moment he said good-bye and came back to the drawing-room, closing the door sharply. Almost as if it were Parish's own fault he said: "Professor Parish has had a similar note."

"Yes?" said Bishop.

Joanna glanced at him. She asked her father: "Has he told the police, too?"

Gregg stood brooding.

"M'm? I don't know, my dear. I shouldn't wonder—he's a nervous man." Half to himself he grunted: "So am I, I suppose. Damned infuriating nonsense."

Bishop watched him. He thought he was whistling in the dark. Probably it was the anonymity of the note that aroused his impatience and his contempt.

He said: "Well, I must turn in. Please excuse me."

Joanna stubbed out her cigarette and looked up at Bishop when the door had closed.

Softly she said: "He's worried. All that is bluster."

"I wondered."

"And Professor Parish will be worried too. Father's quite right—he's a nervous kind of man."

"Yes? He works at Harwell, doesn't he?"

She nodded. "Yes, he's a nuclear-physicist."

"You know him quite well?"

"He was one of the expedition; I met him then."

Bishop offered her another cigarette, but she shook her head. "I—still feel I shouldn't have brought you out. I feel slightly foolish."

Gravely he said: "There's no need to. You look very lovely."

She was surprised. Her eyes focused on him, as if she had to register what he had said.

"Thank you." She said it slowly.

He turned away, and stuck his hands into his pockets. It had been wrong, it wasn't the right time. He had said it without thinking.

Hesitantly he asked her: "Are you going to worry about this message? Going to sleep all right?"

"Few things worry me, at night. I switch off."

"Good." He turned to face her. "Before I go, can I ask something?"

"I don't know, do I?"

"Not very difficult. Have you seen Christine Johns tonight?"

In a moment she said: "I don't know anyone called that."

"I'm sorry. Or Max Corbyn?"

She raised her level brows.

"Yes. I saw him this evening." He said nothing. "Did you know I had?"

Odd-voiced he told her, "If I'd known, I shouldn't have asked you. It would have seemed like some kind of trap, don't you think?"

She came closer to him. There was more colour in her face and she smiled faintly.

"I don't quite know what country we've got into. I'm sorry, I must seem slow-witted."

Her mouth was in shadow; the lamp burned almost behind her. He looked at her face for a moment and then turned away deliberately and said: "Not a bit. I'm feeling my way." He studied the Renoir copy over the hearth. It caught the light well. "Don't try to understand my half-formed ditherings, Joanna. I'm having to talk about serious things, and I'd rather . . . just talk. If you want to, tell me what happened, when you saw Max Corbyn."

She took a cigarette from a box and flicked a table-lighter. He heard her movements behind him and when he turned to face her she was watching him, still with a faint smile touching her mouth.

"I'm beginning to understand you, Hugo, just a little. It gives me confidence, when I need it most. I'm very grateful."

"What did Corbyn say?" he asked bluntly.

She really smiled. She said: "A few minutes ago, I would have misunderstood your brusqueness."

His eyes smiled. He tilted his head. He asked:

"Did he say anything important, about this double tragedy?"

She looked away. "Yes, he did." Her voice went crisp again, as it had been in her office, at Farley. "He rang up, out of the blue, and asked if we could meet. I went along to his hotel and he warned me that my father was in danger. He believes in some way that whatever killed Gordon and Clive, it was something to do with the secret."

Bishop's chin lifted alertly.

"So he's working on our theory too?"

"I don't know about working on it. He—also tried to find out if I knew the secret, myself. If my father had told me. I'm sure I'm not wrong about that. I pretended I was, and apologised, and left."

"Why?"

"I suppose I just wanted to go. Max has changed. I—I'm not easy, in his company, any more."

Bishop moved near her.

"Did he warn you about your father's danger—or try to scare you?"

"I don't know."

"It could have been either?"

"Yes."

"Is he a friend of yours, Joanna? I mean now?"

"No."

"Then I can ask—does he seem short of money?"

"No, but he's money-conscious, as always."

"He's just come back to London?"

She said, "I think so."

"Has he got in touch with Charles Moss or Professor Parish?"

"He said he phoned them, when he heard the news about Dr. Taplow."

Bishop waited a moment and then said:

"Are you afraid of Corbyn?"

She looked up. "Odd question. No."

"Uneasy?"

"Yes, I'll meet you halfway. He's changed—or I have—or we both have. People do. He made me angry, confused. But now it seems he might really have been wanting to warn me, not just scare me."

"Because of this anonymous note?"

She nodded.

"You've seen the note, Joanna?"

"Yes. It's typewritten." She shrugged slightly. "I can't say whether Max sent it, or not. Or why he should."

"There are lots of reasons."

She asked in a moment: "Who is Christine Johns? Was that the name you said?"

"She's a rather brittle young lady who came to me with a chip on her mink-covered shoulder."

"When, Hugo?"

"Earlier this evening. She said that these two deaths are simply the trigger-spring of a very big bang. She was also kind enough to suggest that if I didn't stand back a few yards I'd get my eyebrows singed."

"Did you take her seriously?"

"Not very, because I've got fireproof eyebrows."

"Talking to you is wonderful for me," she said suddenly. "It—eases everything off."

Seriously he said: "You're a bit bothered, aren't you, about this threat to your father?"

She nodded.

"Yes, underneath." Rapidly she went on, "He could have a dozen notes like that, and I don't think I'd worry, because there are people who haven't the wish or even the wits to hurt a fly, who put their complex into a note and send it to someone anonymously—it doesn't matter to whom. Sorry to quote your own writings, but they fit the case, if—"

"If it weren't for Scobie . . . and Taplow."

"Yes, that's just it. They make rather a terrible difference. The note could mean something, after what's happened already."

He felt for his pipe, remembered, and lit a cigarette instead. He didn't like them, but kept some for friends.

He said: "People are making grim prophecies, all round. Corbyn, Christine Johns, the anonymous notes—"

"Is there any connection between those two?"

"There could be, yes. After she'd left my flat, I followed her. She led me to Trent's Hotel—"

"Where Max is staying . . . that's why you asked me if I'd seen him. You saw me there."

"Outside, yes. It just occurred to me that . . . "

She smiled. "Of course. It would have occurred to me."

He put his half-finished cigarette out and said:

"You must go to bed now, or you'll be tired for tomorrow. And you're not going to worry?"

"No. I might do some thinking, but I shan't worry. The police are handling this, and there's you."

She stood in her straight way, hands behind her, and looked at him in silence for a few seconds. "Good night Hugo," she said.

He moved his glance from her eyes to her hair, touching her face with it, her mouth. She didn't look away. A slight shiver passed through her body. He said softly:

"Good night, Joanna."

He got his gloves; she went with him into the hall, and opened the front door, looking out. Between the Gaymer Hotel and the opposite building, she could see a crack of Sloane Square, with buses crossing and lights burning brightly.

She looked down, across the steps.

"Hugo, I like your car."

"Honestly? People call it a mobile museum, but with forty-five horse-power it's highly mobile, so I don't give a cuss."

He touched her hand lightly, and went down the steps.

"May I phone you tomorrow, Joanna?"

"Please."

"I may not have much to tell you—"

"But phone, anyway."

"All right." He crossed the pavement. She called softly:

"Hugo."

He turned and looked up at her. She was framed in the light oblong of the doorway. She was looking past him, to his right. She said:

"Can you see that man over there?"

He looked round slowly. A man stood in a doorway, watching the buses go by. Bishop said: "Yes."

"I think I've seen him before."

"In the same place?"

"No. Somewhere else. I recognise the way he stands."

Bishop watched the man who stood a hundred yards off. The man's face was turned a little in their direction, towards the house; but in the patchy light of the streetlamps it wasn't possible to see his eyes. He might be watching the house, or just the traffic.

Her voice floated coolly down.

"I expect it's just my nerves."

He nodded. "That could be. Go in and give them a rest. I'll check him as I go by, and if he doesn't seem right, you can leave him safely to me."

He got into his car, and started up. She gave a little wave and went into the hall, closing the door. He got into second gear, turning left across the corner, and pulled up alongside the doorway where the man was standing. Bishop had never seen him before.

He let the engine idle, and called across the pavement:

"Can you tell me which way out of the Square leads to Knightsbridge?"

The man remained where he was, motion-less. He had a red, square crumpled-looking face under an old cap. He called out:

"You want to go across t'other side—down Sloane Street. On'y a couple of minutes, then."

"You know your London," Bishop said.

"Should do—I'm near enough on my own door-step, here."

"I see. Well thanks very much—good night."

"G'night."

Bishop drove away quietly, turning into the Square and going slowly round to the far side. At the beginning of Sloane Street he pulled up, and got out of the car, and walked through two narrow roads and a mews, coming out at a point from which he could see the man in the doorway, and the Greggs' house.

The man was still there, and from this clos-er vantagepoint Bishop could see clearly enough that his eyes were watching the house.

It was difficult to know what to do. It was not midnight yet, and he had some more work to get through before he went home. He couldn't stand about here, marking time.

He went back through the mews, turned into Sloane Square almost at once, and saw a beat-man pacing past the little theatre-club. He went up to him.

"Evening, constable."

"Evening, sir."

"I—er—just wondered if you'd noticed the chap standing in a doorway, in Collingwood Lane. He seems to be interested in Collingwood Court, though one can't be certain."

The constable said: "I've passed him once, sir. If he's still there when I go round again, he'll be moved on."

Bishop nodded. He said: "So everything's under control. I should have known."

"That's what we're for, isn't it, sir?"

Bishop went back to his car, drove as far as Knightsbridge Tube-station, and went into a telephone-box and dialled his own number.

Miss Gorringe was still up. She answered in two rings.

"Gorry—Hugo. Just to say I probably shan't be back till the early hours. Any messages come in?"

"Not a one. What's the score?"

"Oh, nothing decisive."

"Where are you going now?"

"Down to Amberly, Surrey."

"What are you going to do there?"

"Oh, just amble. See you in the morning. I'll bring your breakfast in, as an illustration of one of those little things that make life worth—"

"Hugo."

"Yes?"

"If you're going to break into the snake-house, or—"

"I wouldn't break into the snake-house for a pension—"

"But you'd do it just for the hell of it. Have a care, that's all I ask. 'Night Hugo."

The drive took thirty minutes over good roads and through nil traffic. The world had gone to bed. A few lights still shone from buildings; a few taxis stood at their ranks; here and there a policeman walked; the trafficlights were set at green along the main roads; then the buildings lessened, and suddenly it was country, and quiet, on the other side of midnight.

He drove through the village, rounding the market-cross and keeping on until he saw the gates, grey and stark in the flood of the head-lamps. He doused them, and put the car on to a wide grass verge, turning the side-lights off.

He got out, sniffing the air. It was sweet and cool. Here in the green places there was little to hold the heat of a long day, as there was in the city.

An owl came swooping, not far from him, and vanished into gloom and grass. The thin dry scream of its prey sliced into the silence, its echo pricking his spine. Born in a city, he was not used to natural inevitable death, as tiny as this one.

He crossed the grass and skirted the grounds of Taplow's house, moving methodically towards the rear. On his right, now, he could make out the great skeletons of monkey-cages. Below them, and more solid, were long sheds. One of them must be the snake-house. He thought of Taplow, and the black mamba, and Freddie murmuring: "They drop, from above. Charming thought, isn't it . . ."

He moved left, into the vast lee of the house. There were french doors, their panels glinting faintly in reflected moonlight. He got a feeler-gauge from his pocket, and tried first with the thick twenty-five-thou'. It was too stiff; the doors joined with hardly a crevice. He worked for fifteen minutes, trying the twenty and finally the fifteen-thou'. It snapped, but had done its job, just. Quietly he opened one of the doors.

The gloom was intense, inside, for the moon was on the far side of the house. Somewhere a clock ticked. There was no other sound but his own breathing.

The pencil-torch sent a thin beam across the library. The highlights on furniture came up, gleaming on each side. He went across and sketched in the main room with the moving beam, painting it out of the dark. Two long tables, a few brown-leather chairs, a glass case containing specimens of some kind, and shelves of books. More books were piled on the floor, and there was a wide gap in the shelves. Jackson was still cataloguing: there were papers and two pencils on one of the tables, and a title-list.

The torch moved down. He read the first few: *History of the Termite . . . Reaction to Stimuli in Lower Apes . . . Biological Synthesis . . .* This was Sternberg's; he had read part of it, years ago.

He moved across to the shelves, and began slipping his fingers edgewise between the books, separating them one by one so that when he took them down there would be no sound of hard cloth against cloth.

He had moved a dozen by the time the voice sounded from over by the door.

"Don't move."

The room-lights came on with a glare.

Bishop didn't turn round. He said:

"All right, if you say so."

6th

MOVE

JACKSON STAYED where he was for a moment. He had a thick blue dressing-gown on. He held a gun. It was very large.

Bishop turned round slowly and looked at him. "Evening, Jackson."

The man said in a rough hollow voice: "So you know my name. I don't know yours."

"Never mind, let's not be too formal. That's one of the heaviest six-chambers I've ever seen."

Jackson said: "Probably. I've never used it for indoor games, yet. I've stopped a lion with it, though, like it had hit a brick wall. So don't be silly. What're you looking for?"

Bishop was turning on the balls of his feet, with a slowness that began making them ache.

He wanted to face the french doors. It was a shocking big gun.

"Can you guess?" he asked Jackson.

The man spoke sharply. "Come on—what are you looking for? Quick now."

"The same thing you're hoping to find, perhaps."

"Look here," said Jackson, and came a few paces into the room with the gun steady as a rock in his big hand, "you're in no position to argue the toss with me. I want an answer, quick."

Bishop said: "If you mean you'll shoot if I don't answer, it doesn't make much sense. Dead men are notoriously oyster-like."

For thirty seconds they looked at each other. Bishop was now facing the french doors, and had edged back an inch or two, so that he could use the shelves behind him as a spring-board, to give him a good start. Not that there seemed a chance in all hell of winning a race with a bullet that big.

Jackson was first to break the unnerving quiet.

"All right, we'll see if the police can get it out of you."

Bishop was moving his left hand back, feeling for the edge of the shelves to know where they were.

"Keep still," Jackson said without heat. "I've shot lion with this, but never a man. It'd make a change."

He moved steadily across the room to the telephone.

"They don't hang you for killing lion, Jackson."

He picked up the receiver. "Be self-defence, wouldn't it?"

"But I'm unarmed."

There was no point in talking, but it was easier to think, without the dead silence in here.

"I'm not sure," Jackson said. "Just keep your hands where they are, d'you mind?"

Bishop heard a voice faintly on the line.

Jackson said: "Get me the police, please. Emergency."

There was a pause.

Bishop asked: "Jackson, how did you know I was down here?"

Jackson said nothing.

"I didn't make a noise, did I?"

"Not a sound. You were very good. A professional, I'd say. But there's an alarm, see. A quiet one, right by my bed. I like to come down and receive people like you—personally." He said more loudly into the phone: "Police? Ah—who's speaking? Well listen, this is Cliff Jackson here, from Dr. Taplow's place. Yes. I've got a man here, been breaking in. Come along and pick him up, d'you mind?"

Bishop watched. Jackson hadn't looked away from him for a second. His stare was constant, like a cat's. He said into the phone: "I will, don't worry. I've got him safe. Right—'bye."

He put down the receiver, feeling for its rest, not glancing down.

"That's fixed up," he said. "They shouldn't be long."

Bishop leaned idly against the book-shelves, looking round the room, taking in objects at the edge of his field of vision. The only useful thing seemed to be the candelabra, in the middle of the room. It was a low-beamed ceiling, and the crystals weren't much higher than his head. He was about two yards away.

Jackson was three or four yards away to his right, and between the two of them was one of the long tables. The telephone stood at one end of it. It was a very heavy-looking table, and would probably take a long time to pick up, even if he could get across to it. And to get to it, he'd be going right into the bullet-path. That would be silly.

He said easily: "You like to come down and see people like me personally. So that you know if we're just cracking the Peter or . . . searching these books. Tell me if I'm wrong, Jackson."

"It makes n' difference what you're doing. The charge'll read the same."

The tension had gone out of Jackson's tone. The police were on their way. They shouldn't be long now.

"Unless there's a slip-up," said Bishop. "The man—for example—who came here on the night Dr. Taplow was killed . . . didn't wait for the police to arrive. Did he?"

In a moment Jackson asked:

"What man?"

"The one the Doctor spoke to, in this room, when you were on the telephone from Colonel Grayson's place." He waited, then said gently: "Or was he just a figment of your imagination?"

Thinly the man said: "Who the hell *are* you?"

"Tiny Tim." He was getting worried. Even Freddie couldn't help him, if the police found him here. He had broken in, and that was that. The law didn't like it, and he respected the law.

"You seem to know a hell of a lot about this house," said Jackson. It sounded a little as if Jackson was getting worried, too. "Was it you here, that night, then?"

The candelabra glared with light, across Bishop's eyes. He had begun, unconsciously, staring at it, thinking about it. If the thing went out, perhaps he stood a chance of going out too, without a lead poultice on his spine.

He couldn't trust Jackson not to shoot. He couldn't even trust him to shoot low. He felt very uncomfortable, and his feet ached with tension.

He said evenly: "It might have been me, that night. It might have been anyone. Once your story is accepted, the imagination has a free rein."

The two words dropped like stones.

"What story?"

"That when you telephoned from Grayson's house, you heard Dr. Taplow speak to someone in this room. Something about a book, wasn't it? But there's only your word for it. People might otherwise think there were only the two of you here, that night. Dr. Taplow, and you. And the black mamba. Except for your story—"

"It's God's truth."

In a moment Bishop said: "I almost believe you."

"I don't give a damn if you do or you don't. I've made me statement to the p'lice and there's an end to it."

His diction was slipping. Frisnay had said he was a self-educated man. So he was getting rattled. Bishop liked that. He liked people getting rattled. It made them do silly things.

He said slowly: "The police . . . I'm glad you've reminded me. On their way here, aren't they . . . "

"They are, an' not so far—"

"Then I haven't got long. Although I didn't come here to steal, I realize that technically I'm a felon. Is 'felon' the right word?"

Jackson said sharply: "It'll do, for the sake o' politeness."

"And I don't want the inconvenience of arrest, so—"

"That's a shame, isn' it?"

"So if you don't object, I'll be getting along—"

"You move . . . " It was hissed out. "You move, that's all, you bastard!"

"Yes, that's my idea, Jackson. If—"

Headlights came sweeping across the ceiling and for a second they were lined-up with the windows and Jackson stood in their glare, so Bishop pressed very hard against the bookshelves and left them with an upward lunge like a goalkeeper going to meet a high one. There wasn't much you could do with a five-bulb candelabra because there wasn't time to knock them out one by one to the percussion-music of bullets. All he could do was to bring the whole thing off the ceiling in one go.

He did that, and for a moment lost himself in a mass of glass fragments and an explosion that deafened him and left him with his ear-drums singing and a hot kind of splash against his face. In all the mess he thought he heard the whine of the thing go by very close.

Jackson was shouting because he was very worried and wanted the police-car to come round this side of the drive instead of going on to the front of the house where nothing much was happening, but they probably couldn't hear him shout, and they'd take a second to wake up to the idea of shots banging out at the rear of the house.

There'd been three so far, and apart from the hot splash against his face Bishop hadn't reserved any for himself, but on the floor and in the dark it wasn't easy to remember exactly where the open french door was, and he didn't want to guess at it and throw himself against a wall instead. That was how you stopped lions.

A voice was shouting "Jackson!" somewhere inside the house. They'd got in, somehow, hearing the shots and thinking there was an emergency on.

Jackson bellowed to them and fired again and the flash blinded him but Bishop wasn't looking that way, and he could just make out the oblong of the french doors, lit for a split-second by the flash. The bullet coughed into the carpet and chewed up woodwork. Bishop thought that if he stopped one of those things it wouldn't go through him, it would be too big, it would pick him up and throw him against something far away.

He flung an armful of glass towards the flash and got up and ran like a horizontal plummet for the pale oblong, and hit his shoulder hard as he went through into the night air. Jackson fired again and Bishop automatically counted "five" as the bullet smashed a panel and sprayed glass against his neck before he was clear.

He dodged right and then left and hit bushes and went on through them, and number six went ploughing across the leaves with a ripping-calico sound. It would take a few seconds for Jackson to load up, so the worst seemed to be over. He ran across a hundred yards of clear lawn and rose-beds and found a massive black hedge six feet high and solid-looking. He began climbing it like a wall, and was halfway up when the boughs gave under his weight and flung him into a ditch on the other side. He looked both ways along the road like a good boy should and saw the faint grey hump of the Rolls-Royce not far away. His direction-finding hadn't been too good but at least he was within sight of transport.

He ran hard and felt the wind against his face. His face felt stiff and one eye was very moody, but he got to the car all right and started up just as headlight-beams flooded out across the drive of the house.

The road was narrow and the car was wide but he got into third with a rising surge from the engine and picked up lights in the mirror before the cross-roads. He took the left turn, well out on a controlled slide as the two tons of metal tried to ditch and then failed as he put his foot down and drew her straight.

The lights came again, sliding across the mirror, but the grey saloon was up into the sixties now and moving into her stride. Before the next bend the clock got round to eighty and then the needle fell like a stone as the brakes came on.

He doused all lights after noting the terrain, and swung the car between a rotting post and a barn, leaving rubber on the road and a shriek of friction on the air.

It was vital that he turned round and looked at the policecar as it went by, because Jackson might be on board and he might not.

It went by very fast, with two peaked-caps in front and a man sitting in the back and leaning right forward to see through the screen. That would be Jackson. It would be all right to go back past the house and find the main London road, without any shooting. That thing would stop Rolls-Royces, too.

He reversed carefully and drove back, passing the house and reaching the wide smooth arterial. Then he began moving very fast until the suburbs came, slowing him. Once, when he looked fully into the mirror, he saw a red-coloured rubbish-heap, and knew it must be his face.

Miss Gorringe said petulantly:

"You promised to bring my breakfast in. I was

looking forward to it, all night. I couldn't sleep for thinking about it."

He was sitting behind his desk, brooding.

"I clean forgot, Gorry. We'll make it tomorrow, instead."

She looked at him hard and sat down on the davenport and said: "Where was the party?"

He was scribbling on a pad. In a minute he looked up.

"M'm?"

"Party. What location?"

"I don't remember any party." Morning sunlight was spread all over his desk. Miss Gorringe gave the elegant feminine equivalent of a grunt. She said:

"I've sent your suit to the cleaners, but God alone knows what they'll do with it. It looked as if you'd dipped it in woad. I take it you don't actually want a transfusion?"

Bishop sighed. "Gorry darling, it's your job to be inquisitive and you do it splendidly, but don't do it about me. All I want you to do is to send twenty-five pounds in cash to Clifford Jackson, Grey Gates, Amberly, Surrey."

She reacted with her eyebrows. "In cash?"

"Cheques are traceable, and I've spent the night incognito."

"Are you paying Jackson for information?"

"Nothing so unworthy. I happened to wreck a

117

candelabra on my way out of the house—"

"How in hell did you do—"

"By ill-chance," he said with heavy patience, "I caught my hand against it as I was waving good-bye."

"Twenty-five pounds won't buy a new candelabra, if it was a good one."

"It wasn't. I'm being generous, if anything."

Miss Gorringe crossed reluctantly to her desk and sat down.

"What shall I put it down as, Hugo—the money?"

"Life-insurance."

He picked up the telephone as it began ringing and said: "Yes?"

A girl said: "Inspector Frisnay is in now, if you'd still like a word with him, Mr. Bishop."

"I should. Thank you."

In a moment Frisnay said: "Good morning, Hugo."

"Freddie, I understand there was a bit of trouble last night, down at Dr. Taplow's place."

Gorry was watching him hard. There seemed to be no structural damage to his face, but there had clearly been a lot of glass flying about, and his hair was parted on the wrong side, which meant he was covering up alterations. The thought sickened her that he might have killed himself, and it wasn't as easy as it should

be just to sit here and look at him and realise
that he obviously hadn't.

Frisnay's dry accents reached her, but unin-
telligibly. He was saying to Bishop:

"You 'understand' there was trouble? That's
quick of you—I've only just been told myself."

"I'm a very understanding kind of cove. What
I wanted to tell you, in the name of our long
and miserable friendship, is that you're going to
waste your time if you go poking about at Grey
Gates looking for whoever it was who made the
mess there. It's a dead-end, brother."

There was a pause. Tightly, Frisnay asked:

"Bishop, what d'you know about this thing?"

"Enough to warn you, quite sincerely, that it
has no bearing on other inquiries you've made
there, or on Taplow's death. I'd hate to think of
you on a goose-chase when certain knowledge
of mine could save wear-and-tear on those gar-
gantuan galoshes—"

"Now look here, I've got a tough day on my
hands and—"

"Freddie, just let this sink in . . . Don't—follow
it up—until we meet. That's a word in your ear
from the deeps of my golden heart."

Again Frisnay paused. Then he asked:

"This straight, Hugo?"

"As a die."

"All right. But you know I can't lift a finger for

you, if you've made any mistakes?"

"Yes, Inspector, I understand that."

"As long as you do. Now I'm busy—good-bye."

"Good-bye, you rusty old bucket."

He put the telephone down and Miss Gorringe said:

"You appreciate that it practically amounts to corruption, Hugo."

Impatiently he said: "It practically amounts to sticking my neck out for the sake of Auld Lang Syne. If I hadn't phoned him, they would never have connected the affair with me."

He sat back in his carved chair and stared morosely at the Chinese ivory water-carrier on his desk. The tiny old man had been carrying his water across this desk for years and had never spilled a drop.

"Did you learn anything at Amberly last night? Apart from self-preservation?"

"No. That's why I feel like an unmade bed this morning. I wasted my time. There was a damn burglar-alarm, and I didn't even think of checking the door for the contacts. Serve me plaguey well right, I suppose."

"What were you going to do there?"

"Browse through Taplow's books. But Jackson came in and said it was rather late, so I let myself be persuaded to leave." He did a quick sketch of Jackson's face on the pad, didn't like it, and drew a better one. He murmured:

"Jackson didn't make a slip, when I was talking to him. Either he's straight, or he's a first-class actor, in which case he wouldn't have been working as a factotum for a retired biologist. What I'm more interested in is the note that someone left in Sir Bernard Gregg's laboratory last night. A similar one was put through Professor Parish's letter-box. They're having dinner tonight, with Charles Moss, to talk the thing over."

"Has Moss received a note, too?"

"I don't know. I should say he might have."

"Will Joanna be at the discussion?"

"I doubt that. She's an intelligent woman with a responsible job at a top-secret research-station, but her father hasn't trusted her with the big secret yet. I doubt if he will now—"

"Certainly not now that it's become deadly to know."

"Quite. I'll ring her this evening, after dinner. She might have heard something by then. So might I."

"From what source?"

"Various. I'm going to do some wandering about during the day, and tonight I think I'll call on Professor Parish."

"Why him?"

"Because I can't learn anything from Sir Bernard, and Charles Moss was the only nonscientific member of the expedition, so that even he might not be in full possession of the facts."

"But you won't get them from any of those three, Hugo. If Joanna can't be told, no one can."

"I'm not so much after the secret. I want to know why it's become deadly, after two years, suddenly. A man dies. Within a week, another man dies. It's a killing pace."

He took a pipe-cleaner from the dozen new bundles that Gorry had put on his desk, and cleaned his *meerschaum*.

She said: "Shall I make an appointment for you to see Professor Parish?"

"No, Gorry. I'll just drop in on him after he got back from Gregg's house. He'd never agree to an appointment as late as that, but it's no good seeing him before he's talked things over with Gregg and Moss. He might be in a very different frame of mind."

"He might not see you. He doesn't know you."

"I'll edge one foot into the doorway, metaphorically. It's the only way, this time."

Sir Bernard led his guests into the drawing room.

"There you are, Moss—you take that chair, and you can stretch your gammy leg out."

Moss nodded and sat down. He was a wiry-looking man with a brown skin and bright eyes, built like a catapult, always ready to go. Even sitting in the armchair he seemed to be shooting halfway out of it, on impulse.

Gregg had known him for a long time. He had often thought Moss was probably the least happy man in the world. He was always halfway to somewhere else, afraid of staying where he was, afraid of being bored and lonely. He even went halfway to meet death, because he was afraid of that too. Sir Bernard asked him:

"How long is it going to be in plaster?"

Moss looked at his leg.

"Another week, if I don't kick the stuff off in a fit of fury."

Professor Parish hadn't spoken yet. He spoke now. He said:

"It's always infuriating, mending a bone."

He said it almost dutifully. Parish always knew the right thing to say. Sometimes he didn't know the right thing to mean.

Gregg said to Parish: "Another brandy for you, of course."

"Well, I—"

Gregg nodded. "Good," he said. He saw to Parish's glass.

"It'll make him feel more cheerful," said Moss lightly.

Parish glanced at him. They had been friends

for years, but it was not a friendly glance. He and Moss understood each other as well as two very different kinds of person ever can, but perhaps that wasn't very well.

He told Moss: "I hope I don't seem to have been a wet-blanket." He spoke half to his host, and Gregg said with a warm growl—

"Of course you don't, my dear Parish. You're a little disturbed. We all are. But we're less honest than you—for some absurd reason we pretend we're not."

He gave him the brandy.

"Thank you, Bernard." He added, "And the fog's been getting inside me, you know. I hate fog." Since late afternoon, the fog had come down like a lid on London: not a cold, bleak, gray winter-day fog but a humid, unseasonable Turkish-bath fog that left one dripping and inert.

"You're not drinking, Bernard." Moss was watching him.

"No. I shall be putting in a spell at the laboratory, later on." He squared his wide shoulders and said: "Well, gentlemen, we shan't be disturbed in here for a while. Suppose we look at the situation for a few minutes and see how it strikes us."

He looked at Moss. Moss nodded very briefly. Parish said with a slight effort: "Very well, Bernard."

Gregg began quickly, to kill the silence before it took on tension.

"Each of us has received one of these notes. I found mine on the bench in my private laboratory last night. Parish had his put through the letter-box. Moss was handed his by the porter at the Runway Club this morning: the porter said he found it on his desk."

He paused. "Please correct any mistakes I might make. We want to see this matter as clearly as we can. Now these notes have all been given to the police. Their wording is identical. I am told they were produced on the same typewriter."

Moss glanced up. This was news to him. Bernard had been more closely in touch with the police than he or Parish.

"Technically, the matter is now out of our hands, and in the more capable hands of Scotland Yard. But between these four walls... there is the subject of the notes. The secret. And I think we need concern ourselves with only the one simple question."

He looked down at his shoes and there was a pause. Both men were watching him now. He finished carefully:

"My own reaction is perfectly straightforward. The question is—what is yours?"

He looked up at Parish first. Parish hesitated.

"Our reaction to these notes?"

Gregg nodded. "Of course."

Moss said readily—"As far as I'm concerned, whoever sent those things is going to have a tough job on, if I see him coming."

Gregg turned back to Parish.

Rather irritably Parish said: "Yes, Charles, but that qualification is important, surely. 'If we see him coming.' How do we know we shall be given the chance?"

The silence lasted two or three seconds.

Moss said: "You're not at all happy about this, are you?"

Shifting his hands impatiently Parish said, "Can one feel 'happy' when Gordon and Clive are both dead within the last ten days? If the sender of these notes was in some way responsible for the death of those two men, how can we be sure of 'seeing him coming,' when *they* couldn't?"

"You believe," said Gregg slowly, "that their deaths were connected with the—er—discovery we made in the Antarctic?"

Parish did not hesitate. "On the face of it there certainly seems to be an alarming coincidence, if there's no obvious connection. Did Scobie have a note? Did Taplow?"

Moss glanced at him seriously. This had never occurred to him.

Gregg conceded: "They might have, of course,

and might have decided not to disturb anyone's peace of mind."

"All right," said Moss energetically, "suppose we don't get any sleep, for worrying over this thing. Is it so vital, after all this time, that we hold on to the secret, in the face of what's already happened?"

"Vital?" said Gregg sharply. "Good God, man—"

"I don't mean we should simply throw it to the public, of course." Moss was really halfway out of his chair now. "But it's becoming a pretty big responsibility, and I don't care for responsibilities—on this scale. I don't know that I'm qualified to look after it. Why not simply give it to the Government and relieve the load on ourselves?"

After a moment Gregg said quietly, "We agreed otherwise, Charles, out there."

"Out there, we were five men cut off from the world. We stood on the Polar cap, and the whole world was North. That gave us a queer kind of perspective. We were alone, remote, isolated. And in our hands there was a discovery that I do admit looked just too big to tell another living soul. So far, we haven't. That was what we agreed—"

"But now we're back in civilization," nodded Parish quickly. He felt pleased and surprised at the good sense shown by Moss.

Gregg said shortly: "The argument is inadmissible. The situation has not changed."

He looked steadily at them in turn.

"Except," said Moss, "that there were once five men with the secret. Now there are three."

It wasn't a statement that required embroidery. He left it.

Gregg moved about, heavily, the squareness gone from the set of his shoulders.

"We merely conjecture that Gordon and Clive lost their lives because of this appalling knowledge we hold. If we are to agree with the coroner's verdict—and if we don't, then we should have said so, in a public court, at the right time—poor Gordon committed suicide. Clive was the victim of tragic circumstances. A deadly reptile had made its escape, and it struck him instinctively. That's tragic enough, in all conscience, but is it without precedent? Wild beasts are dangerous, and they sometimes escape."

Moss placed his plastered leg more comfortably. The movement was impatient. Parish sat very still and said:

"I would agree, Bernard, but for these threatening notes. They *do* change the situation, radically."

With sudden contempt Sir Bernard said: "They were sent by some idiot who wishes to create a disturbance by implying that there was foul play, and that he was responsible. After every murder of nation-wide interest, the police are plagued with a number of cranks and unbalanced confessor, either because their minds are twisted into odd religious channels, or because their poor damned lives are so deadly dull that they'll even reach out for the notoriety of public trial on a sensational scale. I suppose there are other motives, and all unreasonable—"

"But are we certain?" Moss cut in. He leaned forward with a jerk. "Are we so certain they were sent by a screwball? If anyone's lurking about laying an ambush for me, I don't mind taking him on. I've got out of far too many tight spots to worry about an anonymous note. But *if* someone wants our secret so badly that he's resorting to subtle, cold-blooded killing, then frankly I think the police ought to clean this thing up themselves, and I think we ought to help them by handing over the secret to the authorities and letting them look after it. After all, are we qualified to guard a discovery as big as this one?"

"But you must—" began Gregg.

"With all due respect—" said Parish at the same time.

They both stopped. Gregg said:

"Yes, Parish?"

"I just felt that with all due respect to you, Charles, this idea of someone laying an ambush is perhaps a little too simple. Your life has taught you to think in terms of hot blood and quick action. A—a man, a gun and a lion form the kind of triangle you're accustomed to. Dangerous—intensely so. But hardly subtle. If Scobie and Taplow were murdered—and no one has denied the possibility of indirect or direct murder—then it was done very subtly."

He folded his hands. They had been trembling slightly.

Moss shrugged. "I don't dispute that. But . . . " he left it, uncertain where the argument was leading. He had gone over to Parish's side, and Parish appeared to be in opposition. He looked up as Sir Bernard spoke.

"I think the issue has become clear enough, gentlemen. You are both for handing over this knowledge that we have—a monstrous and evil knowledge, once it's used. You feel we should place the burden of it on to the Government."

No one answered. He looked at Moss.

"Charles?"

Moss shifted about in his chair for a moment, but in the end said:

"I think that's a reasonable scheme, yes."

Gregg looked at Parish.

"Reasonable," nodded Parish, "and sensible."

"Very well, gentlemen." His voice had gone tired. "It would be foolish of me to say I can't see why you should propose such a move. Quite possibly I shall one day feel grateful to you for forcing the issue—God knows I've too much work on my hands to welcome added worry." Almost formally he wound up: "But we should meet once again, don't you agree, before we finally take the step?"

Reluctantly Moss said: "All right, but it'll be nice to get rid of this load as soon as it's practicable, now that we've decided." He didn't like decisions that went on being decisions. They lacked their own conviction.

Parish put his thought into words, and added to it.

"Yes, Bernard." He tried to get the relief out of his tone. "We don't want any dangerous delay, for the sake of just sitting on it. And meanwhile I feel we should be very careful. I've never seen myself as a coward, but I don't regard the deliberate taking of risks as very intelligent—" he broke off and added hastily—"present company excepted, Moss, of course. You are a professional cheater of death."

Moss said lightly: "Retarded adolescence. I've no illusions about cowardice or bravery; they're the most relative values in the world."

He seemed to be brooding about the decision they had reached, and he had spoken on the surface. He moved his stiff leg again, and didn't look up as Sir Bernard said quietly:

"Then we'll sleep on it, for tonight. In a day or two, at the most, we'll have a final talk, and finally decide. Is that satisfactory?"

Parish hesitated. He would have liked to pick him up on the 'finally decide' bit, because it looked suspiciously like a wriggle. But Bernard couldn't easily go back on things now, without appearing two-faced; and Bernard was not that.

"All right with me," said Moss.

Parish nodded.

"Yes, Bernard."

The silence was awkward. Moss was thinking he hadn't put his argument too well; some of the things he'd said must have seemed odd, even deliberately irrelevant. Parish was thinking that a day or two might be too long. He would be happier when the load was shifted, for good.

Gregg was thinking he'd capitulated too easily. The issue was too big for dealing with in a few minutes' afterdinner conversation. But he couldn't go back, now. He stood in the minority, and that was good enough, and bad enough.

He straightened his shoulders and said:

"So be it. I hope we're doing right."

Bishop moved his right hand stiffly. He had bruised the wrist, last night. He put the chess-pieces beside the chequer-board, and thought for a time.

"Five of them," he said softly to the Siamese.

The Siamese stared at him, looking down only when he moved his hand again to place the white King in the center of the board. "Sir Bernard Gregg, Baronet, chemist, leader of the 1952 expedition."

Twilight was in the windows. The ivory and wine Regency stripes on the walls looked black and white in the darkening room.

Bishop took the four Knights, and set them down beside the King.

"Scobie, Taplow, Moss, Parish."

Thoughtfully, he laid two of them down, the two red ones, on their sides. *"Requiescat in pace . . ."*

The fawn cat moved her head, watching the chequer-board. It was a plaything of hers. She let the larger animal play with it.

The white Queen was put down a few squares away from the main group of figures.

"Joanna." He looked at her for a long time, and her to bring his thoughts back suddenly. On the other side of the group he put down the red Queen and a Rook.

"Christine Johns. Ash-blonde, ice-cold, less dangerous than she believes, but still dangerous." He looked at the Rook. "Max Corbyn. Maxwell or Maximilian? A man with a price, perhaps, on his head."

For half an hour he looked at the ivory figures. Now and then he moved one, as a variation occurred to him in the pattern of the case. Did Joanna know anything about Corbyn that might help inquiries, anything she was holding back for sentimental reasons? Had she ever really fallen out of love with the man?

For ten minutes she stood beside him, the white Queen beside the Rook; then he moved her back, to stand alone, until the board seemed to lack a character.

He picked up a Bishop, and hesitated, then put it down near Joanna. "Why not? She'll never know."

He looked suddenly at the cat. "Have you ever fallen in love, Your Highness?" The cat blinked smugly. "Of course you haven't, you shameless little tart, you settle for a bit of slap-and-tickle on the tiles." He looked back at Joanna. "Nor have I. But sometimes I've felt an odd sensation. Most odd."

The twilight deepened. He turned on the desk-lamp and looked at the time. It was nearly ten, and too early yet.

The cat's fur gleamed in the light of the rose-shaded lamp. Her eyes grew enormous, the narrowed pupils nearly drowned in the luminous blue. She sat humped on the corner of the desk, watching him.

Shadows, cast by the lamp, fell from the chess-pieces like insubstantial cloaks. The two red Knights lay quietly.

"Charles Moss . . . a fidgety man, from what Gorry says. Liable to fly off at a tangent, to do impulsive things. A very brave man. Morally, or only physically? They don't often go together."

The cat's eyes closed slowly, until the door opened and Miss Gorringe came quietly in.

"Ten o'clock, Hugo."

He nodded.

"Give him a few more minutes. Sir Bernard's a good host. What's the address again?"

"Forty-three, Park Mansions." She came down the long room and stroked the Siamese. "So Mr. Bishop is fancy-free tonight."

He looked at the chequer-board, where the Bishop stood next to the white Queen.

"I felt lonesome," he said, "and she was the only one without an escort."

Miss Gorringe said cheerfully: "You're a senti-mental old fool, for a hard-headed young man."

"You can't have it both ways, Gorry." But he was hardly listening.

"You can. You're a double-exposure. Shall I make coffee again—we've had two pots since dinner?"

"Not unless you want some more."

"I don't. I use it as medicine. After last night, I'm staying up tonight, in case they ring up for identification by friends." She had been trying not to ask it, all day: "I suppose that was a bullet, that gave you the second parting in your hair?"

He nodded vaguely. "Yes. I hadn't got a comb." He got up suddenly. "One thing you can do for me, Gorry." With his left hand he dropped a Pawn into a square on the chessboard, to stand alone. "There was a little old geyser watching the Greggs' house, last night. Can we get hold of any photographs taken on that expedition?"

"I'll try the newspapers. They might still have files."

"I'd like originals."

"They might have files of originals. Keystone are always helpful."

Absently he murmured, looking down at the Pawn, "Joanna thought she'd seen him somewhere before. Recognized the way he was standing."

"He might have been one of the ship's crew?"

"Something like that."

She made a note on her desk. He began wandering towards the door. She glanced up and said: "You going now?"

His voice floated back.

"Yes."

"Hugo, if Professor Parish invites you in, go easy with his candelabra. They're very expensive."

He opened the door.

"Very good, Miss Gorringe."

The Park was still under fog, a motionless, clinging fog that took on a tinge of yellow from the lamps along Park Lane. Ten days of heat were ending, and the pressure was down. Tomorrow there'd be storms, and with any luck, rain.

Park Mansions was a Victorian block of chambers to the west. Bishop left the car in a side-street, and walked round to the front. On the glass panel over the doors were the numbers 1 to 30. He walked on to the second entrance, and climbed the worn steps.

A porter, as worn-looking as the steps and as Victorian as the building, was reading an evening paper behind a low mahogany desk. He had a period moustache, by neglect rather than training.

"Has Professor Parish come in yet?"

The steel-rimmed glasses were very slightly lop-sided, and he looked as if his head were permanently tilted, listening.

" 'Bout fifteen minutes ago, sir. Number forty-three—lift's over there." He made a pretense of getting up but Bishop said it was all right, he'd find his way.

A cable-strand had parted, somewhere in the lift-shaft, and it made a musical twanging, all the way up to the third floor. The thing sounded all rather unreliable, and he was glad to get out.

Forty-three was at the end of the passage. He walked along and pressed the bell. He heard it ring, inside. He waited. The fog had brought silence, as well as obscurity. There was no sound, even, of traffic outside. There was only the sound from inside the flat. Something had fallen; it was made of glass, and it shattered. The silence came back.

Bishop drew a breath.

"Professor Parish!" He rapped on the door.

Silence. Dead silence.

He looked along the passage. The porter was an old slow man, and might not even have a spare key. And it was an old slow lift, and the glass might mean anything—

"Parish! Are you all right?"

His voice echoed along the passage. There was no answer.

He stood away from the door because there was no handle, just the Yale lock and letter-box, and the first time he hit the door it just quivered, and held. He went at it very hard next time—the lock broke and he half-fell into the room, flinging out an arm to stop himself going down.

He looked round. The light was on. It was a tumbler that had broken. It had fallen from Parish's hand. Parish was sitting at a small writing-desk, in the corner. His face was down against the desk, and his right arm dangled, with the fingers loose, hanging just above the fragments of the broken glass, as if he were trying to point to it.

Bishop went across and slipped his hand inside the man's jacket, flat against his chest. Then he went out, and along the passage, to telephone.

7th
MOVE

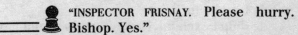 "INSPECTOR FRISNAY. Please hurry. Bishop. Yes."

Frisnay came on. Bishop said:

"Listen Freddie. Five minutes ago I called at Professor Parish's flat here in Park Mansions. There was no answer to his bell but I heard glass breaking, inside. I took a chance and broke the door down. If you hurry, you'll find he's not quite cold yet."

"Mean he's dead?"

"I mean he's dead. I've just rung treble-nine, so there'll be a prowler-car here any minute—"

"What phone are you on, Hugo?"

"Not Parish's, don't worry. Nothing's been touched."

"I'll be over," Frisnay said, and rang off.

Bishop put three more coppers into the box and dialled again. He waited. From the telephone-closet he could see a window, across the passage, a window with bars and frosted glass. On the other side there was a long diagonal shadow from corner to corner. That would be the fire-escape, running down from the floors above. There was another shadow, a thicker one, and for an instant he thought it had moved.

Miss Gorringe came on the line and he went on watching the thicker shadow.

"Hello?"

"Hugo. I'm at Park Mansions. Parish was dead when I broke in."

She didn't exclaim. Her eyebrows would have gone up a fraction, that was all. He said:

"I've contacted Freddie at the Yard and he'll be on his way here now. I want you to telephone Trent's Hotel the moment I ring off. See if Max Corbyn's there. It doesn't matter what you tell him—make it a wrong number—all we want to know is whether he's there. Check?"

"Check."

"I've not phoned Joanna Gregg yet. I told her I would. After you've rung the hotel, try her number, and ask if she'd care to drop round to our place in half an hour. I know it's a bit late but try to persuade her—and don't say anything about Parish, that's important."

"Right, Hugo. Does—this one look like murder?"

He remembered the broken tumbler, the writing-paper on the desk. He smiled sourly.

"No, Gorry. It's like the other two: it doesn't *look* like murder. When I broke in—"

He stopped speaking. Gorry said:

"Yes?"

He said: "Just a minute."

There wasn't any mistake, now. Against the frosted glass of the window across the passage the thicker shadow was moving, going down.

"Good-bye sweetheart," he said and dropped the receiver and went out, turning left along the passage and finding a narrow door. It was locked but the key was in it and he turned it, opening the door and going out on to the iron fire-escape.

The fog was in his lungs within a second. He stood quite still and strained his eyes, downward. Maybe he could just make out a movement down in the gloom, or maybe it was tricks. But there was a vibration coming along the iron rail, and it was real, it wasn't tricks.

He went down the ladder two steps at a time, trying to land with his feet quiet. At the bottom he stopped dead and listened. Footsteps were pounding off across the concrete yard. He turned his head slowly, trying to get a bearing by sound.

When he'd fixed it he ran very hard over the concrete and nearly pitched into a wall, skating off it and running on towards a glow of light. He stopped and listened again. There was nothing, this time.

The glow of light became a hazy flush, spreading across a big area, and when he went forward he found he was on the pavement of the road running past the front of Park Mansions. Someone was going by. Bishop said:

"Did you see a man come out of here just now?"

"Man?"

"A few seconds ago."

A trilby hat, a tired face, a newspaper under an arm.

Bishop said: "It doesn't matter."

"Some trouble, is there?"

"No, there's no trouble." He walked towards the second entrance. "No trouble at all."

Two constables were up on the third floor, one of them standing inside Parish's room, the other in the doorway.

"Evening," Bishop said. He leaned against the wall of the passage and felt for tobacco. He was quietly furious about missing the thicker shadow down there, but he'd seen it, and that was something. They could do with even a shadow, this time, to work on, somehow.

He lit his pipe. When Frisnay came up in the

lift with his sergeant he looked round the rooms
and sent the two radio-car men back on patrol.
Bishop nearly told him about the shadow, so that
the two men could make a search. But what was
there to search for?

Frisnay said: "Keep the passage clear of people, Sergeant, if any come along." A little woman with a dressinggown on was hovering about
near the lift, looking anxiously at the two constables who were on their way down.

Flack went out and Frisnay said to Bishop:
"Well, Hugo?"

"I thought I'd call here to see if I could get anything useful out of Parish. I rang this bell and
heard a glass break, inside. So I broke the door
in."

"You had an idea, then?"

"Of finding him like this? No. Not really. But
Scobie's dead and Taplow's dead, and that left
three. Now there are only two."

Frisnay listened. His face was like a blank hard
wall. His eyes were frozen, unblinking. Bishop
said, "It's killing them off very quick, right?"

Frisnay turned towards the dead man again.
He said:

"My God, yes," in a quiet empty voice.

In a moment he asked: "You touch anything?"

"Felt his chest, that's all. Then I went out to
the phone."

Frisnay was mooching about the room now. He said:

"It looks like suicide, doesn't it? Sitting at the desk, writing-paper in front of him, pen near-by—just going to write the usual messages when the poison in the tumbler beat him to it and the tumbler fell down and broke." He looked down at the pieces. "Never mind, there's a drop left in the bottom piece, for analyzing."

He straightened up. "That's what it all *looks* like."

"Too clearly," said Bishop.

"See anything else, unusual?"

"Yes." The police-doctor came in just then with another man, and Frisnay spoke to them. He turned back and said, "What?" to Bishop.

"I've just chased a man down a ladder."

Again Frisnay said sharply: "What?"

"When I was phoning, I saw someone on the fire-escape, and went out and followed them down. No future."

Frisnay said: "How long ago was this?"

"Five minutes—"

"Description?"

"None. Sorry, Freddie—"

"The bloody fog of course." It wasn't often Bishop had heard him rattled. He was rattled tonight. There were only two green bottles, now, hanging on the wall. "Certain it was a man?"

"No, but I'd bet on it. Footsteps sounded heavy."

Frisnay muttered: "On the fire-escape." He crossed the room, avoiding the police-doctor's crouched figure, and stopped. "This door leads out to the ladder. Could have been coming away from this flat, yes?"

Bishop said: "Yes. He would have passed the window where I saw him, on the floor below this one. If he'd started from here."

Frisnay looked at the door. The key was in the lock, and the lock was home. The fittings were rusty. Rain had got at them, down the join. He said:

"This door hasn't been opened for a long time and it's locked on this side, with the key still in. So it was just Houdini's ghost you saw, or someone who'd got out on to the escape some other way. Not from inside this room. But we'll be checking for prints. Life's full of surprises."

He turned round. Bishop said:

"The door I broke down was also locked from the inside, Freddie . . . "

Frisnay went into the bathroom and the lavatory and the kitchenette. In a moment he came back.

"Windows are all fast. The damned lot. And you can't do much if you climb out of them anyway. They don't lead out to the ladder, there's a long drop."

He gazed at Bishop for a little time and said gently: "It certainly looks like suicide, and the more it looks like it, the less I think it was."

He looked very bright-eyed and fresh. The going had got very bad. He began talking to the other two men who had followed the doctor in. He said: "Check everything twice. Don't miss a speck of dust. This door, especially. Get lamps on the fire-escape—a man went down there recently. I want dirt from his shoes." Holding himself very tautly he said wooden-faced: "If his breath's still on the air I want it analyzed for ectoplasm because either he's a ghost or he's smarter than we are and I never like to believe they can be that."

Bishop was standing by the door. Frisnay said: "You going, Hugo?"

"Unless you want me to stay."

"No." Frisnay shook his head. He looked down at Professor Parish. "No. I may want to ring you—be there?"

"Yes, Freddie. Or if I'm not, there's Gorry."

He went out and along the passage. He felt sour. He should have got that shadow, but Freddie had been very nice. It was the bloody fog.

Miss Gorringe said crisply: "I rang Trent's Hotel but Corbyn wasn't there."

The main lights in the room were burning, and the two reading-lamps. The Siamese was prowling round the walls very slowly, sniffing at things, flexing her sensitive whiskers against familiar surfaces as if she suspected something. She was like a barometer, registering atmosphere. The atmosphere in this room tonight was electric and she reacted. She always did.

Bishop was standing in the middle of the room looking at nothing.

"He wasn't there. Did they say where he'd gone?"

"They didn't know. They said he'd left the hotel about an hour ago."

"That doesn't mean he was near Park Mansions but it means he could have been. We can chalk up another straw."

She said: "Joanna Gregg is coming. She sounded curious—"

"You mean odd or puzzled?"

"Puzzled. But she didn't hesitate about coming."

"Did she ask why you'd phoned?"

"No." Without any change of tone she said: "A summons from my lord Bishop is scarcely to be ignored by slinky women."

Vaguely he said: "She's not slinky. She's nice."

He watched the cat. The cat walked on hot bricks, all round the room.

He said, "Gorry, I'm becoming a two-legged kiss-of-death, aren't I?"

"Which means?"

"Scobie was to dine with us, but he couldn't make it. I phoned Taplow's house, fifteen minutes before he met the mamba. Tonight I rang Parish's bell, and heard the glass fall out of his hand."

Miss Gorringe looked at him.

"Don't worry. Don't get psychical, late at night. You go round looking for trouble, you're bound to find it. But I think I'll be out, the next time you phone me. For reasons of health."

They heard the door-bell ring. She started, very slightly.

He said: "So you're jumpy too." He went across to the door. She said:

"That'll be Joanna. I'll go to bed, but my things'll be all laid out ready like a fireman's. Just let a gun off or something and I'll be available."

Crossing the hall, he tried to get the edge off his nerves. He was going to have to break things gently, and all he felt like doing was just breaking things.

He opened the door. Joanna said:

"Hello." Her eyes were slightly wide, questioning.

"I hoped you'd want to come." He tried to get

warmth into his voice. With her hand touching his for a moment, it was easier.

She came into the long room, quiet and straight-footed. He thought it was very important, the way women walked. This one proved it beautifully.

"Sherry," he said. He wasn't going to take no, whatever she decided. It would help, with the raw edge.

Steadily she lit a cigarette for herself while he got the drinks. She said: "Something bad's happened, hasn't it?"

He looked across at her, and said nothing until he gave her the glass.

"Yes. Professor Parish died, this evening."

Her tone went pitching up as she said: "But it's not true—he was having dinner with us only a few—" and she stopped, and stared at him without any expression. A shudder came. As if from a long way off she finished slowly: "But it happened after that, did it?"

He nodded. "Quite a long time after. It was about a quarter past ten. At his flat."

She leaned back against the arm of a chair. A drop of her sherry spilled. He took out a handkerchief. She said absently: "It doesn't matter, thank you." She swallowed, and asked him: "What happened, Hugo?"

"It looks very like suicide. But appearances are

deceptive. In this case, they might even have been faked."

He touched her arm. "I'm sorry, Joanna. I know how you feel. Not long ago, Scobie was to have been my guest for dinner, just as Parish was yours, tonight. It makes it all rather personal and close—"

With a short almost ugly laugh she said: "What a macabre link, between you and me . . . "

Turning away he said briefly: "It's not the only one. It's just the least pleasant."

"Hugo . . . there's only my father left, and Charles Moss, now."

He didn't know how to put it, as an answer. There wasn't really an answer to be made. She'd said it as a statement and it was true.

She said slowly: "You think it was this discovery, on the expedition, that began these ghastly tragedies. Don't you?"

He nodded. "Yes."

Her face was drawn, her eyes empty.

"It's killing them, one by one."

"It seems like that. For some time I thought it might be pressure on their minds: the strain of not talking, of keeping this deadly secret of theirs. But now I'm not sure."

"You're not sure." She echoed it dully, having to hear the words again to understand them. "What do you think now?"

"I think there's a direct menace involved. A person, a man. Just before Gordon Scobie fell from the train, there was a man seen talking to him in the corridor, but nobody knows who it was—"

"Yes, the police told my father—"

"The night when Clive Taplow was killed by the snake, there was someone in the house, while Jackson was away on an errand. Jackson has told this to the police. Nobody knows who it was."

She was listening intently, watching his face.

"Tonight," he said, "I followed a man down the fire-escape in Park Mansions, a few minutes after Professor Parish died. But I lost track of him. We don't know who it was."

She said nothing. She just watched him.

He said: "But he was there, all right. Just as the others were there. In each case there's been this half-seen, indescribable, unknown man near the scene of death. We might be forgiven for believing it's the same man, every time."

She remained motionless, and then seemed suddenly to realize there was a glass in her hand. She drank a little from it and put it down, spreading her hands flat against the arm of the chair behind her, looking up at him almost as if she were at bay.

"Why is he doing it, Hugo? If there's a man, if

it's not just a coincidence."

"I don't like a triple coincidence. A single one is bad enough. I think he's doing it to protect the secret of the discovery, to confine it to five men . . . then four . . . then three . . . until it's in the possession of one man only, one man in the whole world. Then he'll ask him for it, and kill for the last time—"

"It's incredible—it's not—"

"Joanna, the secret is very big. We already feel that. In the last fifty years we've seen discoveries that have rocked our minds, changed the face of the earth, involving millions of pounds, millions of people. None of them has ever been controlled by one single man, because these discoveries were made in the heart of civilization, and enormous resources were needed to develop them. This one might be different. It was made in the deserted wastes of the icefields. It can easily be that it doesn't require development, on any scale."

He finished his drink and stood for a moment looking at the ceiling. "If all this is right, Joanna, we don't have to ask why your father and his team decided to say nothing when they got back. Because it can't be a good secret. It must be a very bad one. And they don't want to let loose. And they're paying for that, with their very lives, because they think it's right, and think it's what they should do."

He put out a hand suddenly and spoke hard—
"Look at these men, their characters—fine men,
and brilliant, and not all of them young, but
strong enough to go out there and face hazards
that have killed others, and strong enough to
come back and do what they think is right."

There was a little silence. She said:

"We've been thinking, so much, along the same
lines."

"You probably know a little bit more than I do."

She said: "No, I doubt it. My father never men-
tions the expedition. He doesn't have much time
to talk to me anyway, because I'm in my job and
he works pretty well day and night."

"I asked Miss Gorringe to ring you for two
reasons, tonight. One was that I said I'd phone.
The other was so that I could ask you if you
could help me, by telling me anything you feel
you can, about the dinner-party, and about what
was said."

"This evening?"

He nodded. "Naturally you'll know best how
much to tell me, and how much to withhold—"

"Hugo, I can't help. I don't know anything. I
wish to God I did. At dinner the talk was general, and there was not the smallest reference to
these affairs. After dinner my father went into
the drawing-room with Charles and Professor
Parish, and I was tactfully left out."

"Did you see Parish leave, later?"

"Oh yes, quite early."

"About what time?"

"I think about half-past nine. Charles Moss went with him, in a taxi, because of his leg."

Bishop said: "His leg?"

"He broke it, not long ago, and it's in plaster now."

Bishop moved slowly towards his desk. "May I smoke my pipe?"

"Of course, do."

He filled the *meerschaum* bowl. On the desk, the chequer-board was still holding the little ivory figures, and Joanna was still in his care.

He said casually: "How did he break his leg, d'you know?"

"Not exactly, no. In the country, a few weekends ago, I believe."

"Bad luck. An active chap like him. Must be most annoying. They left about nine-thirty, then. How did they seem?"

She came across to the desk, her arms clasped one across the other.

"They seemed all right," she said. "Quite cheerful."

"It's not easy to think back . . . is it . . . when one of them's dead now."

"No. It's very hard. One baulks."

He struck a match, standing away from her as

he lit his tobacco. He asked in a moment: "Is your father working again, tonight?"

"Yes. He won't listen to me. He'll be at the laboratory for another few hours, still. He phoned the house, soon after ten, and—"

"Why? Was he worried about anything?"

"Oh no, he often phones me for a reference in various books he keeps in his study. That's what he wanted tonight."

"He sounded quite normal—didn't seem to be worried about the discussion?"

"No." She smiled gently. "He'd forgotten about it. When he's working at this pressure his mind's like an arrow, and it never swerves."

"So Parish couldn't have given him any intimation about what he was going to do. Or we'd better say, of what was going to happen."

"No. None." She sat down in the big carved chair. "I can sit here?"

"It suits you."

"No, it's too impressive, but very comfortable. You play chess, often?"

He turned away and refilled her glass and his own, saying:

"Not often. Sometimes." She wanted to talk about ordinary things, just for a minute. Chairs, or chess, anything not to do with death. But it was going to be difficult, because of the two red Knights who were lying down.

He came back and put her sherry near her on the desk.

"That's not the tag-end of a tricky battle. The figures represent people. You father's the white King."

She leaned her arms along the edge of the desk, studying the chess-board with a child's quiet. "And his four friends," she murmured. "Who's the red Queen?"

"Christine Johns, the brittle young lady I told you about. I've put Corbyn next to her, as they're staying at the same hotel."

"The Pawn?"

"He's the little man who was watching your house last night. Not sure he should be there at all."

"You said you'd check up on him. Did you?"

"Yes. I drew blank—never seen him before, couldn't place his voice. A policeman had his eye well on him, so I left him alone."

"He was just my nerves."

"That's possible, but we're still checking on him, with photographs."

Her face was in repose, now, with the strain gone. She was just quiet. The lamplight fell across her clear brow, casting the shadows of lashes against her cheek. He watched her from the little distance; she didn't glance up. For a moment he had stopped thinking about death, and was not aware that his pipe had gone out. There was a peace in the room that would be hard to break.

She scarcely broke it, with her soft voice.

"And the white Queen?"

"Yourself."

"And next to me?"

"My namesake." It couldn't be left like that. "You looked a bit lonely, by yourself."

She didn't glance up, even now. There was a faint smile in her tone. "Thank you. I feel very safe. Don't move me, will you?"

"All right."

With a rough movement he struck another match, and put it to his pipe.

"Shall I go now?" she asked.

"Not unless you want to."

"I don't, specially." She leaned back in his chair, away from the desk, looking up at him. "I don't mean specially. I'd hate to go, for a little while." Without a pause she said, "I wish we hadn't met, like this. Don't you?"

With unconscious bitterness he said, "I've got used to meeting wonderful people in rather terrible situations. The two seem to go together. But yes, I wish it had been different, this time."

She was watching him frankly. "I know so little about you, don't I? And these rather terrible situations in your life—"

"Not in my life, in others' lives."

"And you've got used to other people's tragedies?"

"You begin to think you have. Then suddenly you realise that you're on new ground, because the people are new, and you see the same old tragedy for the first time again, through their eyes. And sometimes when their eyes are very beautiful, it makes the business worse."

She looked down. She said coolly:

"Yes I see. Of course it must."

He turned and stood by the windows. A taxi was going by, along King's Road. The fog was lifting, slowly, and there was only a pale halo round its lights.

From behind him she said:

"Now I must go."

"I'm sorry."

She got up, smiling to him. "Thank you."

"I'll drive you home."

"No, I'd rather walk. I want to think."

"Sure?"

"Quite sure."

He went down with her to the mews.

"Joanna, I feel I rather began boring you."

She didn't smile. She said: "No, Hugo, you didn't. I just began wanting to stay so much that I thought it better to go. Fairly quickly. Good night."

Her mouth was cool as he kissed her. For an instant the pressure of her hand on his arm grew insistent, then she stopped herself. Without saying any more she walked along the mews, and he watched her until she had gone.

He came back in a little while, and sat down at his desk, thinking about her. But it was no good. They were both caught up, and when they met to talk, they had to talk about death. Later, if . . .

He put his pipe down, with controlled patience, and let it go out. The figures stood silently on their black-and-white squares. Carefully he reached out, and touched the third of the Knights, and laid it down beside the other two.

8th
MOVE

THE NEXT morning there was a call from Frisnay, soon after breakfast. He told Bishop:

"Various items. You ready?"

"Yes."

"There were dregs of poison in the broken tumbler at Park Mansions, and death was by that poison."

"Type?"

"Stuff called fluocyn, quick-acting. If it was suicide, it looks as if he might have chosen it carefully, so as not to hang things out."

"You think it might be suicide, Freddie?"

"I don't think anything, yet. Point two: the door to the emergency-ladder hasn't been used for months, and there were no finger-prints on the handle. There are no finger-prints anywhere in the place, except for Parish's and those of the woman who cleans the flats. She co-operated with us. We've found nothing, Hugo, except on the handle of a cupboard door, in the main room."

Bishop held the earpiece closer and concentrated.

"Yes, Freddie?" he said.

"On the handle of the cupboard door there are distinct glove-prints. They're identical with those we found on the french doors at Taplow's house in Amberly."

Gently Bishop said: "Really."

"How much can we rely on glove-prints? Not much. But there's one thing our experts are prepared to swear: the glove that opened the french doors in Taplow's house is the glove that opened the cupboard door in Parish's flat."

In a moment Bishop said: "That's very good."

"No, it's not very good, but it's something."

"If you could have combed that train of Scobie's for prints, you might have found the same glove."

"We could believe that. It's the thinnest clue I've ever struck in a case involving three deaths, but once you've got a clue, things quicken. That's all for now, Hugo."

He rang off. Bishop sat thinking. His shadow-

man was really coming up, taking shape. He'd
made the same mistake twice. He should have
wiped the handles, or thrown away the first
gloves and bought a new pair. So he was human,
and could make mistakes.

When Miss Gorringe came in he said:

"Gorry, there were glove-prints in Parish's flat.
They match the ones down in Amberly."

"So."

"Freddie's very pleased. It's the first start."

She pursed her mouth, standing halfway down
the room, looking very cool in a linen suit. A
paper was in her hand.

"Has Freddie seen the advertisement, too?"

He asked: "What advertisement? He never
mentioned one."

She came down to his desk and opened the
paper and spread it out for him.

"Personal column." She had marked it with a
pen.

It was a two-line insertion, right at the bottom. It said: *Who wants the secret of the snows?*
That was all it said. There were no initials or
anything.

He read it again. He said: "I wonder . . . "

"You think it's a trade-advert from a travel-
agency or a ski-manufacturer? They wouldn't
use a box-number. I think there could be only
two people in the world who put that in."

Bishop got up slowly and kept his eyes on the newspaper as if he were hypnotised. In a moment he said:

"Sir Bernard Gregg, and Charles Moss."

She nodded.

"Check. They want to back out, before it's too late. They're prepared to give up the secret, before their turn comes."

"Not Gregg, no. No, Gorry. I've only met him once or twice, but he's no backer-out. I can't say, about Moss." He picked up the telephone slowly.

Miss Gorringe said: "The number's Whitehall 1212."

"That's my Gorry, always a jump ahead."

She went across to her desk and sat down. She felt pleased with her morning; it had got off the mark in no mean manner.

Bishop said into the phone:

"Inspector Frisnay, please. Mr. Bishop."

He glanced across the room and said: "Gorry, where does Charlie live?"

"Charles Moss, the Runway Club, Kensington High Street."

Frisnay came on the line.

"Yep?"

"I have a flash for you. It comes to you by courtesy of Miss Vera Gorringe, M.A., who sits here expecting a rake-off from the Assistant Commissioner."

"Give her my love," said Frisnay, "that's all she'll get."

"There's an advert in this morning's personal column of *The Times*. It might also appear in other papers but we've not checked. Have you put an advert in?"

"Have I?" asked Frisnay. "No."

"It's addressed—in effect—to the man who killed Scobie, Taplow and Parish. The message is: *Who wants the secret of the snows?*"

"Again?" said Frisnay.

He repeated it. There was quite a long silence. Freddie was trying to decode it on the spot. Bishop didn't think it was in code.

"Hugo."

"Yes, old lad."

"Either Moss or Sir Bernard could have put this in."

"That's right. Or you. That's why I rang you straight away, to ask."

"Ye-es, you mean we might have inserted this as coming from either Gregg or Moss? Too slim a chance. If the right man sees it, he'll be damn careful how he answers it. What's the box-number?"

Bishop read it off for him.

"Right. We'll put someone on it. There's another point of course—Professor Parish might have put it in, yesterday or the day before. But we can't ask him." There was another silence, then he said: "I'll be letting you know. Please tell Miss Vera Gorringe, M.A., what I said."

Bishop rang off.

"Freddie offers his love. He says it's all you'll get."

"What's he think, Hugo?" She was too interested to be facetious.

"Same as we do—plus the possibility that Parish might have put the advert in ... a little on the late side."

She nodded. "Yes, it could have been Parish."

He wandered about for a while and then said:

"I think I'll see Moss. It's time I did. What sort of place is the Runway Club?"

"It's controlled by the people who run the Sky-high Club, with the accent on ex-R.A.F. and flyers generally, but the Runway's a better proposition, mainly residential. People who live too fast to settle in any one place put up there from time to time. That's all I know."

"Fair sketch." He went out. Before he closed the door Miss Gorringe said:

"I hope you find Charles Moss in good health, when you ring his bell. . . ."

The grey Rolls-Royce went sliding quietly among the traffic, crossing Exhibition Road and turning left. Above the streets the sky was just a wide flat glare, with the sun trying and failing to filter through a skin of milky cloud. There was no trace of fog left, but the air was electric, still.

He thought: Gregg didn't put it in. Moss probably didn't. It wouldn't fit their characters. Neither was a man to back out. Don't know about Parish. Moss might give a clue there.

The traffic-lights flicked green and he went away, moving into Kensington High Street. He pulled up near the Tube to ask a news-vendor. The man pointed and told him where he had to go.

The Runway Club was a square white concrete building, functionally ugly until you went inside. Inside there was a lot of quiet good taste, and a bright-looking steward.

"One can park, outside?" Bishop asked him.

"Oh yes, sir. Long as you're well tucked-in, you know."

"Good. I think Mr. Charles Moss is staying here."

"That's right, sir. What name please?"

"Mr. Bishop."

The man went to the small telephone switchboard in the corner, and plugged in a lead, saying cheerfully: "Better now that fog's gone, eh sir?"

"Much better," said Bishop. He looked at the

lift, beside the main staircase. There was a lot of wrought-iron and gold paint about, and a big indoor vine growing in a pot. He thought it looked a very nice place.

"Now what's happened to our Mr. Moss?" The man was fidgeting with the telephone-leads.

Bishop said: "He's not answering?"

He looked at the back of the man's neck.

The man said:

"Not yet, no."

Bishop counted five and said:

"I don't think I'll waste any more time down here. I just think I'll go up and—"

The man said into the mouthpiece brightly— "Ah, Mr. Moss? Mr. Bishop to see you, sir."

Bishop unclenched his hands slowly. The man said into the phone:

"Very good, Mr. Moss."

He tugged out a lead and said: "Will you go right up, sir?"

Bishop said yes. He went towards the stairs. The steward called: "Number nine, Mr. Bishop, first floor."

"Thank you," said Bishop.

He found the room and pressed the bell-push. In a few moments Moss opened the door. Bishop had seen photographs of him. He said:

"This is good of you, Mr. Moss. You don't even know who I am."

Moss brought him inside and gave him a nice smile.

"But you're wrong. I've heard a great deal about you, Mr. Bishop. What to drink?"

Bishop said: "Hello," to Christine Johns, who was standing in a corner, looking at some gramophone records.

Moss said carefully: "Chris, this is Hugo Bishop. Bishop—Christine Johns."

She smiled very metallically, with a visible jangle of nerves. Bishop thought that was odd, because Moss obviously knew they'd already met, and when the steward had phoned just now, Moss would have told her who was coming up. She should have been poker-face by now. She wasn't. She was too bright and friendly for words.

She said to Moss, "We've met, darling."

"Oh. Good."

She said, "Only once."

Bishop smiled pleasantly. He said: "But memorably, to the music of roses."

Moss looked slightly out of his depth, and was anyway impatient to catapult himself at the little ritzy drinks-bar in the corner.

"Whatever you're having," said Bishop.

"Well actually I'm on Pernod."

"Excellent."

Moss poured some out. "Water?"

"No, neat." He took the glass. "Thank you."

Moss swung his stiff leg in a half-circle and sat down.

He said: "Pardon my blasted bread-poultice."

"It's on the mend all right?"

"Yes, but it's a slow job. I decide to shoot myself, every night, like they do horses. Fortunately I haven't a gun. You also know Joanna Gregg, don't you, Bishop?"

The change of subject was jerky, with no warning.

"Yes," Bishop said. He looked sympathetically at the stiff leg.

Moss nodded. "That's right, she mentioned your name only last night, over dinner."

Christine's voice came clearly across Bishop's left shoulder.

"Hugo knows practically everybody, darling. Though very few know him."

Moss smiled. "That so?"

"Yes," said Bishop. "I'm constantly coming across people unexpectedly." He glanced at Christine. She was looking very nice this morning, in a plain black Dorville sweater and pencil-skirt. Her face still seemed a fraction worried but her smile was wonderful as she said:

"But Charles and I are old friends. I'm often here."

"I was merely generalising, of course." Her smile nearly cracked. He asked: "How is Max?"

"Max—?"

"Corbyn." She was overdoing the innocence, badly. She said:

"I don't honestly know. Should I?"

"I understood that you and he were ... old friends too."

Moss said easily: "So Corbyn's in town? I didn't know."

Bishop raised a careful eyebrow.

"You didn't? How odd."

"Why odd?"

Bishop sipped his Pernod and then said: "Well Joanna told me she'd met Corbyn, a few nights ago. And she happened to mention that Corbyn had phoned you, recently. But of course there's some mistake." He tried to look foolish but it didn't work very well because he wasn't feeling in the least foolish, he was feeling right on his toes. Christine was so jumpy that all he had to do was give her the wrong question to get the right answer.

"Certainly there's a mistake." Moss was perfectly cool. His faint smile was warm and amused. "I've not seen the man for months."

"Actually," Bishop murmured, "he said he phoned you. He didn't say he'd seen you."

"Nor have I heard from him, by telephone.

173

There is, as we agreed, some little mistake." The smile didn't go.

Christine said: "It can happen, Hugo, even to the most intelligent people. Charles darling, don't get up, but can I help myself?"

"Course."

She brought her glass across to the diminutive bar and mixed some gin and bitters.

Bishop admired her poise. She'd been such a long time, getting it back. He said to no one in particular:

"Who wants the secret of the snows?" He sipped some more of his drink. His glance had flicked from Moss to the girl.

Moss looked vaguely puzzled. Christine didn't even look round. Moss said:

"What secret, and what snows?"

"I was quoting from an advertisement in *The Times* that appeared this morning, in the personal column. That was the exact message." He looked at Christine. She had turned round from the bar and was leaning with her hip against it. Her body was nearly perfect. He said: "I wondered if you could help me. I wondered if you'd seen the message, and knew what it meant."

He felt slightly awkward, having to force things like this. She didn't know anything about it, because she looked quite at her ease, and she was a bad actress.

She said: "Sorry, Hugo. I can't help. It sounds like one of the usual cryptic messages in personal columns."

"Usual? Cryptic?"

"Yes. You know, 'Jim—thanks for chocolates received safely—Mary.' Usually means a consignment of Sten guns has reached Algiers without any trouble at the border."

"Oh yes, I see. You think this message means something quite different?"

"My dear, why should I know? I don't ship Sten guns to foreign parts."

There was a short silence. Moss broke it casually.

"Bishop, I'd be a fool to say I don't know what the devil you're talking about. If I'd seen this message in the paper, I should certainly have wondered about it, too. I understand you're very interested in the three tragedies that have occurred recently. You've also let your imagination go to work, and on the right lines, I suspect. Frankly I'd like to hear what *you* think about the advertisement."

Bishop perched on the arm of a chair facing Moss and said:

"I think that either Professor Parish, or Sir Bernard Gregg, or you yourself had it put in the personal column."

"I see. And that's why you're here now."

"Yes."

Moss shifted his leg a few inches and leaned forward and said: "Well perhaps I can help you, if only by saying that it wasn't my doing. I can't of course vouch for the other two, certainly not for poor old Parish."

Bishop said: "Well I doubt if Sir Bernard's developed cold feet."

Moss shook his head. "I'm dead certain he hasn't. He'd see 'em hanged first."

Bishop said gently: "I hope he does."

Moss looked up at him seriously. "There's something in that. You've gone quite deep into this thing, haven't you?"

"Yes, but my feet are still a long way from the bottom."

He finished his Pernod.

Christine moved her hip. She said, slightly bored-voiced:

"I suppose I've a vague idea of what all this is about, have I?"

Bishop smiled nicely. "I'm certain you've got a very good idea." He put his glass down on the end of the bar. He said: "Now I must go. That was all that was on my mind."

"I envy you, Hugo. There's so much more on mine. Not that it surprises you."

He said: "On the contrary."

Moss gave a short laugh, looking up at them.

"I must say you two don't seem very much in love."

"We find ourselves," said Bishop cheerfully, "on both sides of a fence."

She said: "And the one thing that worries us is that we each think the other one's going to jump off first. But we're still good friends, in a murderous kind of way."

Near her elbow, the telephone began ringing. Moss turned his head and said: "I can't blasted well move, much. Take it, will you?"

She picked up the receiver.

"Yes?" She looked at Bishop, listening. Then she held out the receiver. She said: "It's for you."

"For me?" He glanced at Moss. "I'm sorry, I—"

"My dear fellow, help yourself."

Bishop took the receiver. He said: "Yes?"

"Hugo?"

It was Gorry. He said: "Speaking."

Miss Gorringe said: "There's been a call from Sir Bernard, and I've telephoned Farley Research. No one has seen Joanna, since she left you last night to walk home."

He was looking at the bottle of Pernod, on the little bar. Light from the window gleamed on the long bottle. He looked at it for a little time and then said:

"I see. Anything else?"

Christine turned her head and looked at him.

His voice had sounded like dry steel. On the line, Miss Gorringe said:

"No. Except that I've phoned Freddie."

"All right. Good-bye."

He put down the phone. The heat of his hand had left a moisture-smudge on the black bakelite. He looked at Moss.

Moss said: "Something serious?"

"Yes. Joanna Gregg hasn't been seen since eleven o'clock last night."

Moss didn't move. He said quietly, "Oh God . . . "

Bishop said: "Yes."

9th

MOVE

DETECTIVE-INSPECTOR Frisnay nodded, holding the phone.

"Yes, sir. We're going ahead with it now." He paused. "I will, sir."

He put down the receiver and made a click with his tongue. He called out very sharply: "Flack!"

The door opened like an echo. Sergeant Flack came in. Sergeant Flack's face was as wooden as his chief's, permanently expressionless; but he always seemed just about to express something. He never did. He said: "Yes sir?"

"They're turning the heat on, upstairs. Joanna Gregg. We're taking priority action. Missing Persons are on the job but we're checking too, as cover."

He shifted a folio on the desk for Flack to pick up.

"There's a batch of her photographs. We want fifty copies right away for circulation. Find out if the beat-men saw her last night anywhere between Cheyne Mews and Sloane Square. Try taxi-drivers in that area—hotel-porters—the coffee-stall in King's Road and the all-night garage across the road—anyone who might have been about as late as that.'"

Flack put the folio under his arm. Frisnay said:

"Report at once with the slightest information no matter how thin it is, and keep in constant touch with Missing Persons. And don't neglect a lead simply because you know they're following too. This is a double-check."

"I get it, sir."

Frisnay got up. "I'm going round to Cheyne Mews now. Mr. Bishop was the last person to talk to her, as far as we know. If you can bring along a few rush copies of those pictures when you come, all to the good."

Flack went to the door and opened it.

Frisnay said: "We've got to be very good. We might save a life."

Flack looked at him once, said nothing, and went out.

The grey saloon drifted slightly over the cobblestones and pulled up outside Number Ten,

Cheyne Mews, immediately behind the black police-Humber. Bishop got out. Frisnay was standing on the doorstep. A driver and observer were sitting in the Humber. The booster whirred faintly in the luggage-boot; a call was going out to Base.

Frisnay said: "Good morning, Hugo."

"Any leads yet, Freddie?" He sounded very held-in.

"No, but we're throwing big mountains about on this job. What are the facts?"

"Joanna left here about eleven-fifteen. I came down to this door with her, to see her off. I'd offered to drive her home, but she said she'd rather walk. I didn't insist." He said it with a slight sag of anger in his voice.

"You feel she'd any special reason for wanting to walk?"

"She said she wanted to think. I assumed she meant alone." He looked along the mews. He said: "I saw her go out of sight. Round the corner, by the lamp." She had walked very beautifully, even over the cobbles, in high heels. Very straight. Alone.

Frisnay said: "So she turned to the right, into King's Road, towards Sloane Square."

"Yes."

"She seemed normal?"

"Except for Parish's death on her mind. She'd

only just heard about it, from me."

Frisnay looked at him hard and said: "It's no use my asking you to tell me absolutely everything. I don't think you'd hold anything back, whatever it was." Bishop was watching him blank-faced. "But she was talking to you in your flat, just before she became missing. You can't throw any light on this, can you?"

In a moment Bishop said: "Please don't be a damn' fool. I'd move heaven and hell to find her."

Frisnay nodded, and looked away.

"Then that's all right."

"What's the official view?" He kept his voice even. It had got a little bit out of hand.

"She might have had an accident, followed by loss of memory. She might have decided, for some reason of her own, to leave home for a while. But we think, officially, she's been grabbed."

"To put more pressure on Gregg?"

"It'd be reasonable, as a motive."

He put his hands into his side-pockets. "What are you going to do, Hugo?"

"I don't know. But something. As soon as I can get a line."

Frisnay turned away to the police-car. "When you get it, let me know, or get Operations on treble-nine. We're all one big happy family to-day."

He got into the back of the Humber and it drove away.

Bishop went upstairs. Miss Gorringe was ripping open a big envelope. He brushed his hair back and looked at her and said: "Freddie's just left. He's on edge."

"Aren't we all?"

He said nothing. She gave him a quick glance and said:

"Don't worry, old boy. We'll find her."

He gave a slow cracked smile.

"Yes, Gorry."

She took out glossies from the envelope, spreading them across his desk.

"Pictures of the *Snow Goose* and personnel. They were taken just after she docked at Southampton, back from the South."

He looked down at them reluctantly. These wouldn't help him find her. He asked:

"Where did you get them?"

"Channel Syndicate. I said we'd return them when we'd looked them over, but there's no actual—"

"Yep," he said suddenly.

She glanced up at him. He said: "This man in the top row third from the left." He turned the picture sideways. She looked at it. He said: "Have you seen him before, Gorry?"

"No."

"I have, the night before last, watching the Greggs' house."

"He's the man you checked?"

"Yes. It doesn't tell us much, except that a member of the ship's crew has turned up two years later to watch Sir Bernard's house—"

"Hugo, he might have been watching Joanna."

"My God," he said softly. "You could be very right." He looked at the other photographs. "See if you can get his name from Channel Syndicate— might have been captions used—and send this one to the Yard, Criminal Records and Central Office."

He straightened up. "If this man was watching the house, the night before Joanna became missing . . . "

Gorry was going to the door.

"I'll hurry this picture along. You want the car for ten minutes?"

"No."

She went out. He crossed his fingers, and hoped to God.

A man was putting a tyre on, near the row of petrolpumps.

He'd got one edge on, and he was jumping on the other edge with his shoes working rhythmically round. He looked like a monkey in a rage.

Bishop went up to him and said:

"Were you working here last night?"

"That's right. Till twelve, any rate."

"I'm trying to find out what's happened to a friend of mine. She left my place in Cheyne Mews about eleven-fifteen—."

"Young lady in a blue coat, sir?"

Bishop said: "Yes." He waited.

"No, I never seen her. They've been askin' me, twice in the last few minutes. Police." He looked curiously at Bishop. "Missin', is she sir?"

"Yes." He thanked the man and walked on. There was a cab-rank, not far from the Square. There were five cabs in a line. A driver was sitting in the first one, cleaning his nails with an old penknife.

Bishop said: "Were you on this rank last night, after eleven?"

"Eh? No. I went off at nine. It's Bob Mills you want to see, him or Sam Thompson, like I told the other chap."

He looked critically at his nails.

"The other chap—a policeman?"

"That's right. Plain-clothes." He looked briefly at Bishop. "Like you," he said succinctly.

"Thanks."

As he turned to go along the rank, the driver said:

"Mills an' Thompson get back here soon after

185

twelve, 'bout an hour's time. Ask them, I should. They was both on."

Bishop nodded, and crossed the road. The coffee-stall wasn't open yet but a rattling of crockery came from inside. He rapped his knuckles on the big wooden flap. A voice came, muffled.

"Not open yet, chum!"

Bishop called out that he wanted to ask something. In a moment the flap opened halfway up and a big man with a tobacco-stained moustache peered out.

"What say, mate?"

"I'd like to ask something."

"Oh-ah?"

"Were you here last night, about eleven?"

"Every night, 'cept Sundays. Why?"

"I'm trying to find someone who's missing. A young lady in a blue coat. She might have gone past here, walking."

"Ah." The man went on dumping cups into a big tin basin of soapy water. "You the p'lice?"

"No. I'm a friend of hers, but the police are also checking-up."

"I see, yes. Missin', eh? Blue coat—walkin'. Nice-lookin', dark girl?"

Bishop said steadily: "Yes, dark hair, blue eyes, light snakeskin shoes and handbag—"

"That's right, yes, I remember. Tell you how I know."

He began wiping cups. Bishops said: "Yes, tell me."

"*If* it's the one, o'course. I see a young lady come by 'ere, must've been gone eleven—well gone that—an' I see a car stop, over there by the furniture shop." He pointed with the cloth in his hand. "I thought, 'allo-'allo . . . looked like pick-up, you know what I mean?"

"What happened," asked Bishop tonelessly.

"She gets in the car, but it was a woman drivin', I was wrong, see?"

"They drove off?"

"Eh? Tha's right."

"What sort of car was it?"

"Ah. Well it was red. Not red—plum-coloured, you know. Woman drivin'."

"Saloon? Drophead? Open car?"

"S'loon. Nice little car—sporty-lookin'."

"What make?"

"Oh, I dunno much about that, see. Very smooth-lookin', all streamlined—British, I know it was British, know that much—"

"Healey? Bristol? Jaguar?"

The man shook his head. "Now I can't say, chum. Sorry. But sporty-lookin', and stream-lined. Quite new—good polish."

A little man with a basket of fruit came up and asked for tea. The man inside said: "Well, I'm not open, mate, but you look thirsty." He got a cup of tea. Bishop said with a quiet insistence:

"Which way did it go, the car?"

"Er—off that way, t'wards the Square."

"The driver—what was she like?"

"I never see 'er, plain—"

"Young? Old? Dark? Fair?"

"Now it's no good, mate, is it—I could say she was young or I could say she was old. I think 'er hair was light-coloured, but might've been white, or blonde, see? That's all I can remember, straight."

The other man with the basket was looking at Bishop and blowing on his tea. Bishop said:

"Well you've been a great help. I appreciate it."

He folded a note and handed it up.

"Oh, that's all right, you keep it. If I've done any good, I'm 'appy, see?"

Bishop put the note away. He said: "You've done a lot of good. You may have saved someone's life."

He walked away. The two men looked after him. The one in the coffee-stall dropped a dirty cup into the soapy water and said: "Well, blimey . . . "

The little man said: "Eh?"

Across the road, not far from the three long windows of the furniture-store, Bishop went into a telephone-box. He dialled Scotland Yard Operations Room. When they came through he said:

"Hugo Bishop. I've been asked to send in any information of Joanna Gregg."

"Please go ahead, Mr. Bishop."

It was Sergeant Wainwright. Bishop said:

"I've been told by the man who runs the coffee-stall in King's Road, fifty yards from Sloane Square, that a girl in a blue coat was picked up after eleven last night by a woman driving a plum-coloured, streamlined, new British saloon car."

Wainwright was using shorthand. Bishop heard him murmuring it down. He paused a few seconds and said:

"As a guess I'd say it was either a Bristol, Healey, or Jaguar, from his description. Woman driver had 'light-coloured' hair, might have been white or blonde. Car drove off towards the Square. No other known details."

When he heard Wainwright stop murmuring he finished: "You'd better send someone along to question the coffee-stall man—I'm not police-trained."

"We'll cover it, sir."

Bishop was looking through the glass panels. He could see the coffee-stall from here. Before he put the phone down he said: "No, don't worry. It's being done. I can see them from here."

He came out of the box and stood for a few minutes watching the plain-clothes man talking to the proprietor. He was trying to believe that by sheer luck he'd picked up a lead, and was trying to think where he'd seen a plum-coloured saloon recently. Somewhere, very recently, he'd seen a saloon like that. He stood looking at nothing. He thought of the names of British cars from Alvis to Wolseley, and then went over them backwards, trying to keep plum-colour in his mind. He stood there for fifteen minutes and then suddenly turned into the kiosk again and dug up three more coppers. The number was in the book. He dialled it.

"Runway Club—good morning."

Bishop said: "Good morning. This is Mr. Bishop."

"Oh yes, sir?" The man remembered him. He said:

"When I left you this morning I put a scribbled note for Miss Johns behind the windscreen-wiper of her car, but I was in a bit of a hurry and I might have made a mistake. I left it on the green Riley that was parked outside."

"Green Riley," the man said. "No, sir, that's Major Stewart's, that one—"

"I knew I'd got it wrong, when I had time to think. But Miss Johns' car was there somewhere—"

"Yes, sir—she went off in it not long after you left here yourself."

"What car has she got, d'you know?"

"Now that I can't say for sure, Mr. Bishop. It's plum-red, with silver wheels, but what kind it is, you're asking me. I know it's red because she's got a handbag to match—"

"It's a saloon, isn't it?"

"That's right sir, yes—"

"Well never mind, the message wasn't very urgent. I'll phone her at the hotel—she'll be back there by now if she left for there—"

"If you want to leave a message with me, sir, in case you don't manage to—"

"No. I'll find her. Many thanks."

He said good-bye and put the receiver down slowly. There were a lot of red cars in London—cherry-red, plum-red, all kinds of red. A lot of saloons, new ones, British. It was a very thin chance, and it would be very silly to start feeling happy.

The door of the box banged behind him as he went out and crossed the road. The man in the coffee-stall had plenty of coppers, yes. He said: "I've just had a plain-clothes man, askin' me about that car. Told him the same as what I told you. I 'ope you find the lady."

Bishop took the coppers.

"Yes," he said. He went back to the phone-box and had to wait five or six minutes until a girl came out. There was a lipsticked cigarette-end lying along the slots of the ashtray and the warm sickly smell of cheap scent in here, very unlike Music Of Roses. And the lipstick was darker, and less—

"Trent's Hotel?"

"Miss Johns, please, if she's there."

"Yes, sir—what name please?"

"Coddrington." He was looking at a beer-advertisement across the pavement. It said Cool Customers Drink Coddrington.

He waited. In a moment she said:

"Hello?"

"Christine?"

"I'm Christine Johns, yes." Very guarded. "Who's that?"

"Hugo."

"They told me Collington, or some name—"

"I wasn't certain of an audience. Christine, you should listen carefully to this. The police are working very hard on a certain case and I happen to know something vital. Frankly I don't feel like helping you, but it might suit my book. If you come round to my place right away, you stand a fair chance. If you don't . . . you don't."

She said: "I've no idea what you mean. It's gibberish. If—"

"Then forgive my troubling you. Good-bye."

"Hugo—just a minute—"

He put down the receiver, and got three more

coppers, and dialled Cheyne Mews. When Miss Gorringe came on the line he said:

"Listen, Gorry. I can't be sure, but it's likely that Christine Johns will call on us within the next ten minutes or so. If she does, ask her to wait for me. I shall arrive precisely two minutes later. Check?"

"Check. What situation, Hugo?"

"Situation is that she'll probably take the direct route from Trent's Hotel to Cheyne Mews—via Sloane Square. I hope to get her car identified by someone who saw one like it in that area last night."

"Is this a definite lead, Hugo?"

"No, but it's a lead of some sort. No time for more—'bye."

He went out of the box and breathed in some fresh air on his way back to the coffee-stall. Three or four men were standing round drinking tea and buying cigarettes. Bishop stood near the long narrow door. It was open, to let air in. He filled his pipe, looking absently at the traffic that was flowing in from Sloane Square. From here, he could just make out which stream was entering the Square from Sloane Street. If she came, she'd be in that one.

He got his tobacco burning and walked across the end of a side-street to the cab-rank, and said to the first driver:

"Stand by for me, will you? I'll be five minutes."

It was the man who had been cleaning his nails. He said:

"Any luck yet, with the lady?"

"You can never tell. You'll be helping me to find out."

"I'll pull up a bit, off the rank."

"All right."

He went back to the coffee-stall. He said to the man with the stained moustache:

"I don't give you much peace."

" 'Ow's it goin' now?"

"I don't know, but you can tell me. In a minute or two there might be a plum-coloured saloon coming past here from Sloane Square. It might be the one you saw last night. Think you could recognise it?"

The man thought about this. He was more interested now than he'd been before. It looked as if they were getting somewhere, this gent, the police and himself. He said:

"I'll do me best, but the colour might be a bit diff'rent in daylight, see. Cup o'tea while you're waitin?"

"Make it coffee and we'll do a deal."

While the man was getting the coffee he looked at the traffic, moving his head slightly now and then to line up his vision with small details that were all he could see, behind a bus, a taxi, a van—knock-off hubs, the tip of a bumper-bar, a wing-antenna, a driver's hand. A Jaguar came by, but it was metallescent-blue: an A.C. coupé: a Lea-Francis, but black: a Talbot, but not new. From the nudging pack of cars he tried to select this one colour, and shape, and type, before it went by too fast, and the chance was lost.

The cup of coffee was in front of him. He stirred it with the spoon on the string, without looking away from the road.

The man said: "Not 'ere yet, eh?"

"Not yet. Might not come at all."

A bus thundered out of line and turned past a parked van, blocking his vision completely. When things cleared, he saw a red saloon, a Bristol. He said:

"Look. That one?"

The man leaned across the counter, frowning. The Bristol went by neatly, changing down as the bus slowed. Christine was at the wheel. She didn't glance their way. Bishop said curtly: "Well?"

"Well, I'd near swear, I'd near swear—an' she's a blonde, eh?"

Bishop put down a ten-shilling note on the counter and said: "Take it or leave it, you've earned it this time, chum."

He walked over to the taxi and got in.

"Cheyne Mews."

The Bristol was three cars ahead, but it didn't matter. They didn't want to follow it. She'd lead them to Cheyne Mews of her own accord.

He lost sight of the plum-red saloon just before they turned off. In the wide cobbled mews there was another car, Frisnay's. The Bristol had gone straight on.

Bishop got out and paid the taxi off and went over to the police-car and said to Frisnay:

"I sent in some information, about a car—"

"They passed it on to me, yes—"

"It's due here now, but—" he broke off. In a couple of seconds he said tightly: "Of course . . . she saw your car standing here, and panicked."

"What the hell," said Frisnay. Bishop got in quickly and slammed the door and said—"Owner's name is Christine Johns, Trent's Hotel."

Frisnay said to his driver: "Go there."

They moved off with the rear wheels spinning a fraction over the smooth cobbles. Bishop said: "I've got the number of the car."

They swung out of the mews into King's Road. Frisnay said:

"Martin, give me the phone."

The observer reached back with it. Frisnay had to lean right forward to get it to his ear.

Martin opened the contact. Frisnay said into the mouthpiece:

"Hello JK, hello JK. Wanted for questioning: Christine Johns, driving dark-red saloon—"

Bishop leaned beside him. He said quickly and quietly: "Bristol, number TJB 3898."

"Dark-red Bristol saloon, number TJB 3898— three, eight, nine, eight—seen vicinity Cheyne Mews few minutes ago. Converge Chelsea area and search. JK-5 Over."

The speaker crackled.

Hello JK-5. Message understood. JK Over.

"Hello JK. Car might be going to Trent's Hotel, Bayswater. Check up there. Action-call please. JK-5 Over."

Hello 5. Action-call, sir. JK Out.

Frisnay passed the phone back to Martin and settled in his seat. They were going along Sloane Street, overtaking patchily on the horn, just taking the lights at amber.

Bishop said: "It could all be wrong." He told Frisnay about the man at the coffee-stall. "It might not have been her car, last night. But she's panicking, for certain: I rang her just now and said the police were on her tail, and she—"

"You *what?*"

"I had to get her to my place, quickly—"

"That was the hell of a way to go about it—"

"Sorry, but I was pushed."

Frisnay grunted.

"Well, you got on to her before we did, and they make their worst mistakes when they panic."

When they pulled up at Trent's, Frisnay got out, leaving Bishop in the car. There was no red Bristol anywhere. There was a black Wolseley across the road, with two uniformed men on board. They sat like statues, watching the hotel entrance.

Frisnay came out and said: "No go. She's not been back. I've put a man in the lobby, just in case." He climbed into the car and sat there looking keyed-up. "Martin, have you got any ideas?"

The observer turned half-round in his seat.

"She'll have gone to ground, for certain, sir. With an action-call out she couldn't have got more than a mile away without dodging and doubling—they'd have closed in, before now."

Frisnay grunted and looked at the driver. "Hoskin?"

Hoskin nodded a big, steady head. "She'll still be in Chelsea, sir, with the car somewhere out of sight."

Frisnay drummed his fingers on his knee for a time and then said: "All right, back to Chelsea."

He said to Bishop as they drove off: "We've had a call out for Corbyn, too. It's time they pulled him in. If Johns has had anything to do with grabbing Miss Gregg, it might have been on Corbyn's orders."

They slid down through the Park, unobtrusively, deceptively quick. A location-call came through and was answered. There was nothing else. They were hitting blank, all over the place.

Bishop said: "I should check up on Charles Moss, while you're about it. Christine's a friend of his."

"That so?"

"She was there at the Club, in his room, when I saw him this morning."

"We've got a man on the Club, and another one on Sir Bernard's house. They're the only two left . . . What were you doing with Moss?"

"I asked him if he'd seen the advert, or if he'd put it in. I think the question was a surprise, but he's not a bad actor. Christine Johns is as readable as an open book, and nothing registered when I mentioned the subject."

They sat in silence until the car turned along Knightsbridge. Then Frisnay said:

"We'll pick something up, soon. We've got tabs on people, we've got two action-calls out, we're double-checking with Missing Persons. We'll pick up something."

Bishop murmured: "Whistling in the dark?"

"Blazes. I'm just telling you, son."

They neared Chelsea and Bishop said:

"Put me down at the Hospital, will you Freddie? St. Marks."

"You going to see Sir Bernard?"

"Yes."

"Going to be difficult. Works like a fiend."

In a moment Frisnay told his driver to pull up. Bishop got out and said through the open window: "If Joanna's been hi-jacked, it must have been done to get the secret out of her father. Because that's the key to the whole thing. Has Gregg had any word from the kidnapper yet?"

"So far, no word. But he's passing it straight to us, the moment it comes in."

"Fair enough. Did you get a picture from Gorry?"

"Yes. We've found the name of the man you marked. It's Arthur Bell. No criminal record. We're still trying to trace him, but there's a two-year gap—"

"Two nights. He was the man watching Gregg's house."

"If he stands there again—or anywhere in that street—he'll be picked up the same minute. But if he doesn't, it might just as well be two years. I'll let you know."

"All right, Freddie."

He crossed the pavement. The low thin exhaust-note of the Humber died away. He climbed the shallow steps and went across to the porter's desk. The porter was a small man with a leathery face and wide brown eyes. Bishop didn't say anything for a moment. It was quite a pleasant shock.

" 'Morning, sir."

"Good morning," said Bishop carefully. "I—er know Sir Bernard doesn't like interruptions, but I should like to see him for a moment, if that's possible."

The man put his head reluctantly on one side. "Very doubtful, you know. What name?"

"Bishop."

"Mr. Bishop. You haven't got an appointment I s'ppose?"

"No."

The man hadn't moved. He stood like a wall.

"That makes it very awkward, you know."

"Does it? You were more helpful the other night, when I asked you the way. Your name's Arthur Bell, isn't it?"

With indifference the man said: "That's it."

"And you were one of the ship's crew that went on the '52 expedition, to the South."

Bell's eyes watched him steadily. He said:

"Can I see your credentials?"

"I've no credentials. I'm not the police."

"Then I'm not bound to answer any questions, am I?"

"Not in the least, but it doesn't really matter,

because I seem to know the answers anyway, don't I?"

Bell said nothing. His eyes didn't shift, once. Bishop said: "Perhaps you'll be kind enough to ask Sir Bernard if he could spare a few minutes."

"He doesn't like being disturbed when he's down in the labs, but if you'll take the responsibility—"

"By all means."

"Very good." He moved at last. "I'll tell him you're here."

He was away five minutes, and seemed faintly surprised to see Bishop still waiting.

"You know the way, Mr. Bishop?"

"I'll find it."

"I'll show you. We can't have people wandering about in this place, you know."

He led the way along a passage and down steps, and left Bishop at the door of the laboratory where Sir Bernard worked.

He greeted Bishop calmly.

"You've some news, Bishop?"

He looked tired, with the weariness of endurance rather than of fatigue. He did not look hopeful.

"I can't really say that, sir, but the police are following a lead that looks promising. I know that sounds vague and optimistic, but the signs are good, I know personally."

Gregg leaned against the high polished bench, and slid his hands into the pockets of his white lab-coat.

"There's no indication that Joanna has come to any serious harm?"

"None at all. Have you had any message, or threat?"

"Threat—?" He looked up slowly.

"If Joanna's been kidnapped, we should expect a message from those who did it—"

"Yes, of course, quite—the Inspector mentioned that. No, I've had no message."

"It's not possible, sir, that she might have stayed somewhere overnight—of her own free will—and been delayed this morning? I mean without letting you know?"

"Few things in this life are impossible, Bishop; but in view of these tragic events we're all concerned with, it would seem cruel of her, surely, not to reassure me. If she were able."

"Of course. We just have to think of every conceivable answer, and—"

The telephone at the end of the wall-table was ringing.

Sir Bernard said: "Excuse me one moment." His walk to the telephone was that of a man resigned. He lifted the receiver. He said:

"Yes . . . "

Bishop was watching him. His voice changed

as he said: "Indeed." It had changed to quiet anger. "You will please tell me who you are." For a moment he turned his head and looked at Bishop, and gave a slight nod. "I demand to know your name, and—"

Bishop ran and hit the swing-door and went through and up the steps in two leaps, sprinting along the passage to the main hall of the building. Bell was near the porter's desk. Bishop grabbed the main telephone and dialled three nines. Bell was asking what the matter was. Bishop didn't answer. He was aware of Bell's face held near his own—"Is Sir Bernard all right, damn you?"

Bishop said curtly: "Yes," and the line opened and as Bell ran off along the passage he said: "Exchange, there's a call coming through to the laboratories here—St. Mark's Hospital—Carlton 3776—it's vital you trace it before they ring off."

He waited. They told him:

"There's no line open just now but I'll try tracing and ring you back at that number."

"Please. They'll have used a phone-box, but we might as well make sure." Bell was walking back along the passage. Bishop said: "Get me Scotland Yard, please, while you're there."

Bell came up and watched Bishop with a long steady brown-eyed stare.

"Police—can we help you?"

"Bishop here. I'm at St. Mark's Hospital. Sir Bernard Gregg has just had a phone-call from someone unknown. I think it was about his daughter. They're trying to trace the call but I don't think they'll be lucky. If you'll contact Inspector Frisnay by radio, I'll wait here for him."

"St. Mark's Hospital. Right, Mr. Bishop."

He put down the phone. Bell began saying something but it rang again at once.

"Yes?"

"Carlton 3776?"

"Yes."

"We can't trace that call, sir. It was from a public call-office. I'm sorry."

Bishop thanked them and rang off.

Bell said: "So you are the police. Why didn't you say so in the first place?"

Bishop turned away and went back to the laboratory. Gregg was leaning against the bench again, as if he had never left it to answer the telephone.

"Well sir?"

Like a gramophone-record Gregg said: "I was told that my daughter is safe, but that her continued safety lies in my own hands. I was given . . . certain instructions."

Bishop dug his hands into his pockets. They were clenched. It was difficult, not being able to do anything. Hellishly difficult. He heard Gregg saying steadily: "Of course I was expecting some such message."

"Doesn't make it any easier, does it, sir?"

"No. No, it doesn't." He looked up as he heard footsteps, and for an instant Bishop saw him go right over to the defensive, his eyes, the set of his face. For this instant, even Sir Bernard was afraid of the things that had come to Scobie, and Taplow, and Parish. There were only the two of them left, now. He and Moss.

Bishop turned and saw Frisnay coming in with a sergeant. He looked questioning. Sir Bernard said:

"You've been quick." Relief was in his tone. There was nothing to be done, but the police were here. It made a little difference.

Frisnay said briefly: "I was in this area. It was Mr. Bishop who was quick. Now this phone-call, Sir Bernard?"

The sergeant stood near the doors. Bishop was pacing. Gregg had scarcely moved. He said:

"I am told my daughter won't come to any harm, providing I co-operate." A faint grim smile touched his face. "That was the word . . . 'co-operate'."

"You were given instructions, sir?"

"Yes."

Frisnay waited. In a moment Sir Bernard said, "I was warned particularly not to reveal them to the police. Quite naturally—"

"I must advise you to ignore that, sir—and we're fully aware of the situation. We don't want Miss Gregg hurt, any more than you do."

Bishop came to a standstill. Frisnay was very light on his feet. He stood almost literally on his toes. He wanted to go, to get moving. It depended on Sir Bernard.

"I realize that, Inspector. Only a fool wouldn't. But it's . . . a closer thing, for me. She's—" he shrugged, and made his decision. "I was told to wait outside the little stamp-shop where Carter and Vale Streets make a crossroads—"

"In Pimlico," Frisnay said, wooden-faced. "What time?"

"At nine o'clock tonight."

"Are you to take anything with you, sir?"

"Nothing."

Frisnay sent Bishop a glance and looked back at Gregg and said: "What sort of voice was it, sir?"

"Difficult to describe. Difficult even to say whether it was a man's or a woman's. They were distorting their voice in some way. Its pitch was neither high nor low—"

"Any trace of accent, sir?"

Gregg raised his brows, listening again to the voice on the telephone. He said in a moment: "No, Inspector. It was an educated voice, with no particular accent—"

"It wasn't familiar to you, even for a second?"

"No, it was not. I'm afraid that I was so intent on the message that—"

"Yes, that always happens, and they know it." He looked down at his shoes. "Sir Bernard, what is it they want, in exchange for your daughter's safety?"

"Some knowledge that I have." His voice was empty. Without this knowledge, his life would have been much simpler, and there would have been more time for his work.

Frisnay said: "The same knowledge that was shared by Professor Scobie, Dr. Taplow and Professor Parish, before they died. And is now shared with only one other person: Mr. Charles Moss. Is that quite correct, sir?"

"Quite correct, Inspector."

Bishop had begun wandering again, along the bench, keeping a careful distance from it so that his elbow shouldn't brush against equipment. Sir Bernard's work was fighting cancer, so that there was a lot of good going on, in this bright-lit, semi-basement room, with its charts, and microscopes, and chemicals. It would all stop, down here, if they got Sir Bernard, because there weren't so many men in the world who worked with such resolute drive, and they were on something else.

Some man, some crawling, sickening louse

of a man, was waiting to trip Sir Bernard in the dark, as he had tripped the others. It was a thought that wouldn't easily let up.

Frisnay asked quietly enough:

"Are you prepared to give up this knowledge, at nine o'clock tonight, Sir Bernard?"

Gregg hit the edge of the bench with the flat of his hand and swung his head up and said: "I don't know, I don't know, until I've had time to think. They could do what the devil they pleased with me and they could take their souls to hell before I gave in. But this is Joanna. I don't know, I can't say what I'll do at nine o'clock tonight."

Frisnay put his hands behind his back, and said very reasonably, "I know how you feel, sir. By God, we all do. But I'd like to advise you again."

Gregg said nothing. He waited. His hands gripped the edge of the bench and their blue veins criss-crossed the pallid skin.

Frisnay said: "Be at the rendezvous tonight, and leave the rest to us."

Tonelessly Sir Bernard said: "I was warned that I must go there alone. For her sake."

"Take a second opinion, sir. I think it'll be biased, on your side, and on Miss Gregg's."

He was looking towards Bishop. In a moment Gregg said: "You mean ask Mr. Bishop?"

Frisnay nodded.

"Yes."

"Well, Mr. Bishop?"

Slowly Bishop said: "With an absolute under-standing of what this means to you, sir, and biased as I am where Joanna's safety is con-cerned, my advice would be the same as the Inspector's, if you felt in need of it."

Frisnay stared at a lamp above the bench.

Sir Bernard said: "I am in need of it, Bishop. I value your advice, and I'll take it." He looked at Frisnay. "I shall be there, at nine o'clock. And will leave the rest to you."

Frisnay nodded briefly.

"I'm glad, sir." He looked carefully at his shoes again. "Of course, I should have had to go ahead with my own plans in any case, because our job is to fight crime, and we can't do that without closing in on it. But we like co-operation. The whole system's built on that, in this country. The police are on the side of the public, and we like the public to be on ours. Sometimes it doesn't work, but mostly it does." He looked up. "Let's hope it works tonight. You won't see anything of us. Nor will the other party. But in case you find yourself worried, or in an awkward spot, you might like to bear it in mind: we shall be there, in strength."

10th

MOVE

LIGHT WAS soft in the long room. On the window-sill, the cat was asleep. The radio was going quietly, short-wave from Italy. It was a new symphony. It had begun ten minutes ago.

Miss Gorringe was sitting near one of the standard-lamps, doing the remains of *The Times* crossword that Bishop had left for her. Bishop was behind his enormous desk, smoking his *meerschaum*, not speaking, listening to the music.

It all looked very domestic, and comfortable. It looked like that for another half-hour, until Miss Gorringe said:

"Eight-thirty, Hugo."

"All right."

He was polishing the lenses of a pair of Zeiss night-glasses, with a yellow duster. She asked:

"Am I to come with you?"

He got up, sliding the glasses into their case.

"Would you like to?"

"Yes."

"Then you're in."

She put the crossword down. It was not often she was able to join him, on active work. There had to be someone here, usually, in case the phone rang, or she had to switch a message for him. And it was easier for one to move about London very fast, than two.

"Are we taking the car?"

He said: "Yes. I've had a look round the area, and picked our spot. It's practically fool-proof. If we get in Freddie's way, he'll cosh me with a steeple."

He turned off the radio. On the window-sill, the Princess Chu Yi-Hsin opened her eyes, and blinked slowly. In the room, the atmosphere had changed, suddenly.

"Hugo, if Freddie makes a *coup* tonight, it can do more than free Joanna. Yes?"

"Yes. If the one who grabbed her is the one who was on Scobie's train, and in Taplow's house, and on the fire-escape at Park Mansions, the whole thing could fold-up tonight."

"But you don't think it will."

"Why don't I?"

"It's in your voice."

He shrugged, tapping the ash out of his pipe.

"I think Christine Johns took Joanna. In which case, I'm doubtful. But she might be acting under orders."

"In which case, she might not squeal."

"Quite."

Miss Gorringe looked at him for a moment. "The main thing is," she said, "that you think we've got a good chance of finding Joanna. You don't care very much about the rest, for tonight."

He smiled briefly.

"That," he said, "is probably the main thing. Yes."

He turned out two of the lights, and looked across to the window-sill. He called softly: "If you want fish, you know where to get it, you fat old baggage."

The cat stood up and preened herself, ignoring him.

They went out, and downstairs to the car.

The moon that had been young when Taplow had died was now almost full. It was already, at a quarter to nine, halfway up the sky, and daylight was still pale over the roofs of Westminster.

The theatres were in, but people were still with their coffee in restaurants, and in Pimlico there was here and there a promenade, or a group on a corner, or people sitting on their steps, their backs against iron railings, talking to neighbours about neighbours going by. It was, in brief, a summer night, with the air still, and the sky clear.

Lights were coming on, from Whitechapel to Knightsbridge, from Brixton to Maida Vale. Along the river, a few boats moved, with only a spread of lazy ripples fanning out astern.

In Hopgood Road, Pimlico, a constable broke his pace and took the telephone-receiver from its box, just on the corner.

"P. C. Whitehead calling from Nineteen Box, taking up position."

At the switchboard in Operations Room, the girl made a tick against a special list and plugged-in a different lead as the light flashed again.

In Pimlico Road, a dark saloon pulled up without a sound. In the luggage-boot, the radio-booster whirred, barely audible. The phone came off its clip.

"Hello JK ... hello JK. Location outside sub-post-office, Pimlico Road, JK-2 Over."

Hello JK-2. Location received. Stand-by. JK Out.

In Vale Street, in Charringford Lane, along the Embankment, East of Battersea, West of Victoria, North of the Thames, South of the Park there were cars pulling up, and men moving, and calls going in, testing, reporting, locating. Waiting.

"Hello JK . . . "

JK answered, and said *Stand-by*.

Watches were synchronised, at five to nine.

The air was still. People's voices carried. Somewhere, two cats fought in a basement area. Someone threw a tin can and the cats darted away, swearing, and met again, and fought again. A taxi passed them.

In Carter Street a quiet grey Rolls-Royce was parked, facing the cross-roads. Beneath a plane-tree, behind the cabmen's shelter, it was nearly invisible, from the South. It had been here ten minutes. The lights were out. On the satinwood dashboard, the clock ticked with a sharpness that silence gave its sound.

Bishop reached up his hand, and unlocked the windscreen-levers. He pushed the screen wide open, and locked it in place.

The clock was at three minutes to nine.

Miss Gorringe said softly:

"Any sign?"

Bishop had the field-glasses resting on the top of the steering-wheel. In a moment he said:

"Sir Bernard's there. Standing alone, between the stamp-shop and the phone-box on the corner."

"Anything of Freddie's mob?"

He spoke on his breath.

"No. Not a sign."

"Trust Freddie."

There was a little silence. It was broken by the chimes of Big Ben, over to the West.

"Want to have a look, Gorry?" His murmur was less loud than the tick of the dashboard clock.

"No. You might miss something."

In a moment he said: "Just in case we can help, get things ready for moving-off." He held the glasses rigid.

She turned the ignition-switch, and moved the gears into first. He put his left foot down, freeing the clutch. The handbrake was off.

He said: "Just standing there, alone. He must be feeling rotten."

The chimes had died away. It was nine, and gone.

" . . . Two people passing him . . . woman with a dog, coming the other way . . . and a man in a mackintosh who—"

Miss Gorringe looked sideways at him.

He said in a moment: "No. He stopped to glance at Gregg, but now he's gone into the phone-box, a few yards away. Thought Gregg was waiting to use it."

In the gloom of the car, he was carved out of

solid, with the night-glasses part of his shape. She waited.

He said: "Coming out of the box . . . man in the mac . . . yes—going up to Gregg, saying something to him . . ."

Miss Gorringe swallowed. Her hands were pressed together.

Bishop murmured: "Now Gregg's going into the phone-box, and the man's walking on."

"Which way?"

"Down Carter Street, away from the crossing. Walking quite steadily . . . not hurrying . . . but if he turns the next corner we'll be losing sight of him—"

He broke off as a sound swelled from behind him. A car went by with a rising rush, its lights flicking on and the exhaust-note whining thinly between the houses.

"There goes the heavy-mob . . ." said Bishop comfortably.

"There's another one shooting out of Vale Street—"

"To pick up the man in the mac—"

"Shall we go?"

He gave her the glasses and pressed the start-er, bringing the clutch in as the engine fired. "Yes, Gorry."

They slipped down the street in the wake of

the police-saloon. Air rushed through the open screen. Reaching across him, Miss Gorringe closed it.

They met the cross-roads and stopped dead behind the police-Humber. Two other cars were sliding to a halt across the road. Men came out of doorways, up from basements, round the corner into Carter Street. All moving slowly, waiting for orders, watching the Humber. Gregg was coming out of the telephone-box and Frisnay met him as the door of the Humber was thrown open.

Fifty yards down the street the man in the mackintosh was standing between two plain-clothes men. Everything looked very quiet.

Frisnay was going down to talk to the man.

Bishop got out and said to Sir Bernard: "Come aboard, sir."

Gregg looked at him, for an instant seeming not to recognise him. Then he said: "Yes. Yes, Bishop. Thank you."

He climbed into the Rolls-Royce, and relaxed wearily in the back seat. Bishop got back behind the wheel. He didn't like Gregg's expression. It looked beaten. That was very unlike Gregg.

Along the street, Frisnay reached the man in the mackintosh.

"May I have your name, sir?"

"Mortimer. I don't understand what's—"

"These are my credentials, Mr. Mortimer. Now will you please tell me what happened, during the last five minutes?"

Mortimer was a thin man with quick eyes, a man who knew his rights, a man who thought that perhaps he was a little bigger than he was. But he was co-operative. For the moment he seemed to be the centre of attraction, and there was no actual disappointment on his face.

"I was simply walking along, minding my own business, and just as I got near the phone-kiosk, I heard the bell start ringing—"

"Someone was calling that number?"

"Well of course—how else would the bell ring?"

"Go on, please," said Frisnay.

"I looked at the gent who was standing near the box, but he didn't seem to have heard it, so I went into the box and picked up the receiver."

He glanced at the two men who had stopped him. There were two others across the road. Nobody was moving. Two or three people who had come walking down Carter Street had stopped, too, and were watching.

"You had no idea who was calling the number, Mr. Mortimer?"

"How should I know?"

"What happened then?"

219

"They asked who I was, and I—"

"Just a moment, please." Frisnay looked at Sergeant Flack. "See if they can trace that call, Flack."

"Right sir."

Only the one man moved, the Sergeant. From lower down the street, from across the road, from the silent cars, the others watched him go to the phone-box.

"Now, Mr. Mortimer, please repeat the exact words the caller used, as far as you can remember them. It's important."

Mortimer nodded and made much of concentration.

"They said: 'Who's that speaking?' I tell them I'm just passing by and heard the bell ringing—I don't give *my* name to everyone who wants to know. They say, 'Can you see an elderly man standing anywhere near the kiosk?' Of course I can, so I says, 'Yes'."

Frisnay was patient. He wished he hadn't asked the man to concentrate. All this might be sheer embroidery, for the sake of sensation; but the facts would fit. This was exactly what could have happened.

"'Well,' they say, 'if his name's Sir Bernard Gregg, will you please ask him to come to the telephone?' So I got out of the box—"

"And give the gentleman the message, and he

goes to the telephone, right?" Frisnay wanted more action. He wouldn't get much standing here with Mortimer.

"How d'you know?" asked Mortimer.

Frisnay said: "What sort of voice was it, on the phone?"

"Oh, sort of—" he fingered his chin. Frisnay waited wooden-faced. "Sort of nondescript—"

"Man's, woman's high-pitched, low-pitched, any accent?"

"I don't know, I can't rightly say—might've been a man's and it might've been a woman's—it was muffled. Not so much *muffled*—kind of *put-on*."

"Carefully disguised, yes quite. You didn't notice anything else out of the ordinary, Mr. Mortimer?"

"If you ask me, the whole thing's out of the ordinary, in fact downright peculiar—"

"Yes, that's right, it is. Thanks for your help, sir. We have your address?" He glanced at the plain-clothes men. One nodded.

"Yes," said Mortimer.

"We'll get in touch with you, then, if we want you again."

"I'm not at home at all hours of the day, you know—"

"Never mind," said Frisnay, "if we want you, we'll find you. Good night, Mr. Mortimer."

He walked back along the pavement, meeting Sergeant Flack.

"No go, sir. Call-box."

Frisnay grunted. "All right. Put a man on Mortimer, just to make sure."

"Yes, sir." Flack went off. Frisnay looked round for Sir Bernard. Bishop called from the car.

"In here, Freddie."

Frisnay went up to the open window and asked:

"You're all right, sir?"

Gregg nodded.

"We'll clear out of this area, I think, Hugo. Follow me, will you?"

He went back to the Humber. In a moment it drove off, running steadily down to the Embankment and turning left, pulling up under the trees. Frisnay got out and climbed into the grey saloon. Gregg said roughly:

"Inspector, who was that fellow?"

"The one who got you to the phone, sir?"

"Yes."

"Nothing to do with it—a passer-by. But I'll check his story with yours, if I may."

"Of course. I heard the bell ringing, from where I stood, but never thought of answering it—assuming it was a wrong number, since no one was in the box. Then that fellow came along, glanced at me, and went into the box. In a moment he came out and asked my name, if it were Gregg. I said it was, and he told me the phone-call was for me personally. I think I hesitated, and then went to the box, and took the receiver. It was the same unfamiliar voice—"

"Neither a man's nor a woman's."

"Quite. It was recognisably the same as before."

Frisnay leaned his arms along the back of Miss Gorringe's seat. In a moment he said:

"What was the message this time, Sir Bernard?"

"They—asked me outright."

Frisnay looked at him.

"For this information?"

Gregg nodded. "Yes. I refused. They then told me that I . . . shouldn't see my daughter again, alive."

Miss Gorringe watched the clock on the dash-board. She was feeling very cold about the voice on the telephone. Gregg said slowly:

"I—I bargained with them, and said I must have more time to consider."

He stopped speaking. Frisnay said gently:

"Yes, sir?"

"They have given me until midnight."

Frisnay seemed to relax. He said: "Three hours more. What happens then?"

"They'll telephone me for the last time, at twelve. They warn me that it's the final chance of saving my daughter."

"Did they say anything else, sir?"

"Nothing at all."

"Suppose for a moment that you'd been pre-pared to give them this vital information, over the phone. Wouldn't it have taken some little time? Would they have been able to understand it? I imagine it's technical, and probably compli-cated—?"

Sir Bernard said:

"No. Two words would suffice."

Bishop was watching his face in the driving-mirror. Miss Gorringe half-turned. Frisnay said:

"They'd understand, from a couple of words?"

"Anyone would."

The silence stretched out until Frisnay said with a slight movement of his hands: "I see. Well, sir, what are you going to do, at midnight? We'll need to know."

"You must advise me again, Inspector. I'm at a loss."

Bishop looked at Frisnay. Frisnay nodded. Bishop said:

"Sir Bernard, if you gave up this information, there'd be repercussions?"

"Enormous repercussions, Mr. Bishop. I think I can say that if my daughter knew the facts, she'd beg me to keep silent, even at the risk of her life."

Frisnay murmured: "Then I can see what you're up against."

"I'm glad you can. If it were money they wanted, they could have it, my last shilling. If this secret weren't harmful, or if I were keeping it for my own advantage, things would be very different."

Frisnay said: "Yes, quite." He straightened up in his seat. "Where are they going to phone you, sir?"

"At my house. I was told to be there without fail, to answer them personally."

"All right, we'll have the wires tapped, and ask the Post Office for special facilities." He looked along the perspective of the Embankment. "If that call was made from somewhere fairly distant, they won't know you had the police behind you, and they'll phone again, according to plan. If they used a box somewhere near, they might have seen some of our chaps, in which case they might panic and scare off."

"They would have mentioned it," said Gregg, "surely, when they spoke to me on the telephone."

"True, yes, they would. If only to show they knew everything that was going on."

He was silent for a minute and then said: "If you don't mind, Sir Bernard, we'll drive you home, and I'll have a few more words with you about this next phone-call?"

Gregg opened the door.

"I'm in your hands," he said.

Bishop got out, and waited until Gregg was safely inside the Humber; then he got back into his own car.

Miss Gorringe sounded flat-voiced.

"Where now, Hugo?"

"I don't know." He lit his pipe, irritably. "It looks as if we'll have to hang about until twelve." His voice pitched up, strangely for him. "It's this damned lack of action . . . "

"We'll try a few things," she said. "Trent's Hotel, for one. Christine won't have shown up there again, because they'd have pulled her in; but you never know what you can find out from hotel-porters—"

"They've already been grilled by the police—"

"I know, but sometimes a pound note works better than a police-card."

He gave in. He said: "We'll try."

They got into gear and turned, moving off quietly along Carter Street, northwards. Miss Gorringe said:

"Hugo, why did they tell Sir Bernard to wait outside the stamp-shop, and not actually in the phone-box? Someone might have been using it, or—"

"They knew the police would have the line tapped and specially rigged, if the box was the known rendezvous."

"But they're going to ring him at his home, and

the line *will* be rigged, this time."

He said: "Yes. That's why I've got a niggling feeling that they won't be phoning at all."

"Then why—"

"I think that when Freddie gets him home, they'll find the place has been broken into and torn apart. I think they're dead certain he'll never give up that secret. It's killed three men already—"

"They just wanted to get him out of the house?"

"It seems a fair theory, unless—"

"Hugo."

"M'm?"

"What was the number of the plum-red Bristol, remember?"

"Er—TJB 3898—"

"Dead ahead of us."

His eyes focused on the saloon they were following.

"My God," he said. "Right in our sights . . . "

He changed down.

"There we are then," said Miss Gorringe. "Bishop's move."

They closed in, bringing the gap down to a dozen yards. The Bristol was steady at thirty, then the white blur of a face appeared for an instant through the rear window.

Miss Gorringe said: "Seen us. Hold tight."

"Man driving, or woman?"

"Man."

"Here we go then."

The Bristol had speeded up; the Rolls-Royce kept the gap and held on. Miss Gorringe was using the nightglasses. She said: "I don't recognize him. You can't see much because the rear window's curved."

"We'll organize a close-up."

The red car raised the pace, skinning a traffic-island and slewing left into a side-street on the off-side and sending up a thin tire-howl that echoed from the buildings while the gray car held it, lost it and then came up, nearly ramming as the Bristol swerved under brakes and turned right, off-siding a Keep Left sign and building up a lot of speed on the straight.

Bishop's car was heavier, but the power was there to keep it close. A constable shouted and waved a lamp as the first car went past him in the fifties along a narrow street. An Austin came nosing from the side, and clipped the Bristol's wing as the Rolls-Royce swerved, avoiding it. There was another shout.

The smaller car was snaking badly, trying to shape for a T-section too fast. Bishop held back, positioning. They both took the lights at red and straightened, swerving left again within seconds. The Bristol rocked as one front wheel hit a corner-stone and as the tire burst it went sliding from the left pavement to the middle before it got right out of control and cocked over, smashing into railings.

Bishop was out of the car before it stopped and was sprinting well. The other man was making for a wall, limping a little but keeping on, clambering over the wall. Bishop was quicker, with two good legs. As he dropped, he saw the other man halfway across a yard. There was another wall. He didn't get to it. Bishop tripped him and brought him down. The man lay on his back, hands up, one leg drawn back to kick. The breath was coming out of his body in painful grunts.

Bishop said:

"Don't get up. I want your name."

The man swore thinly. Bishop got him by one arm and dragged him to his feet and said: "I want your name, very quick."

Between breaths the man said: "Miller."

"Where's Joanna Gregg?"

"Joanna—?"

"Quick or I'll crack your skull wide open—"

"I dunno anyone call' Joanna—"

"Christine Johns then—where is she?"

"I dunno what you're talkin'—"

Bishop sent him down and dragged him up again.

"Christine Johns—quick—"

"I dunno—for Chris' sake I dunno what you—"

"The owner of that car you were driving is Christine Johns. Where is she?"

"I dunno—it's a hot one—I dunno anything—"

"A hot car?"

"Yes, I—"

"Where was it when you picked it up?"

"I don' remember—"

Bishop doubled him up and waited until Miller could get words out again. He'd gone sick-looking.

Bishop said: "Where did you find the car?"

"Dawson Mews." It came out on a gust of agony.

"How long ago?"

"Ten minutes—"

"That car was standing in Dawson Mews ten minutes ago? If you lie I'm going to smash you up. I want to know this badly. Well?"

"Ye'." The man pulled at his stomach, bending over. "Ye'. Ten minutes 'go—"

Bishop sent him a clean rising one that rocked him back head-first and threw him flat. Then he climbed back over the wall. Miss Gorringe was on the other side. There was a crowd of people round the smashed Bristol.

"Gorry, there's a bloke on the other side of this wall. He's out cold. He'll keep till you send someone over to bring him in. Get the police to sort him out. He says he stole the car but it could be a lie. I'm going to check up on something. Take our car home and I'll be ringing you—check?"

"Check."

He turned away and crossed the road quickly without looking back at the Bristol.

One of the constables who had come on the scene walked up to Miss Gorringe and said: "That's your gray car, isn't it, Madam?"

"Yes."

He nodded. "That's right. I saw you in it when you went past. Where's the driver?"

"He's—er—gone for a little walk. The crash made him very nervous. He hates loud noises."

The constable looked at her calmly. He said:

"I think we ought to go along and make a statement, don't you?"

He turned his head as a police-car came up and stopped. "Leave the Rolls-Royce where it is, please. We'll put a guard on it until they've taken measurements."

"All right," she said helpfully.

He looked back at her. He asked:

"What happened to the driver of the other car?"

She pointed to the wall. "You'll find him over there. Over the wall. He's—resting."

He gave her an old-fashioned look, and beckoned to the police-car. While the observer was coming across to them he said to Miss Gorringe:

"Odd sort of accident, this. Both drivers missing. A lady looking after everything. That's Mr. Bishop's Rolls-Royce, isn't it?"

"Yes, constable."

He nodded. "That's right. Quite a well-known motorcar, in this district. And all this little lark smacks of our Mr. Bishop."

"I—er—suppose it does, yes."

They saw her politely into the police-car.

The sergeant made sure she had a pen. A green-shaded light shone down on to the sheet of paper.

"The whole story, Miss Gorringe, please. Where you first saw the Bristol car, how far you followed it, and so on. Take your time—you won't be disturbed."

The swing-doors into the main room parted and Inspector Frisnay came through. He stopped as he caught sight of Miss Gorringe.

He looked right on his toes. Practically jerking about on invisible wires. "Hello, Gorry. Where's Hugo?"

"Gone off somewhere, Freddie."

Frisnay grunted.

"Now where's this man, Sergeant?"

"Through here, sir."

As Frisnay crossed to the other door he said: "Wait for me will you Gorry?"

"I will."

He went through the doorway and along the passage. They had Miller in a cell. Frisnay looked at him for a moment and then said:

"So it's you. When did you get out?"

Miller had been given a cigarette. They'd cleaned him up. His face still looked slightly shapeless. He said thickly:

" 'S'mornin'."

Frisnay said: "Brixton's too comfortable is it—can't wait to get back t'your mates?"

"I been a fool," Miller said.

"Course you have, and you'll go on being a fool, Miller, all your sweet life. Your type never learns—"

"I had to get money—just out an' flat-broke—"

"Don't, you're breaking my heart. You steal this car?"

"Ye'."

"Where from?"

"Dawson Mews—"

"Chelsea?"

"Ye'—"

"When?"

"Twenty minutes back—"

"Know the owner?"

"No."

"You know a woman named Christine Johns?"

"No. That other bastard talked about a woman—"

"Did you see a woman anywhere near the car when you took it?"

"No."

"Anyone call out or run after you?"

"No. It was clover, mate."

Frisnay turned round and poked his head into the passage outside.

"Sergeant, get a signal out. Christine Johns' Bristol car stolen from Dawson Mews, Chelsea, twenty minutes ago. Car recovered but no sign of Johns. Might be lying up in Dawson Mews."

"Right sir. You want a search made?"

"Leave it to Operations, there's a general search on now."

Frisnay turned back to face Miller. He was pulling on his cigarette to save his life. It was making him choke because of his stomach. In his mind, which was an ex-con's mind and full of day-dreams to sweeten life, he was doing all those things to the other bastard that the other bastard had done to him, over the wall.

Frisnay interrupted him. He said:

"Listen, Miller. You'll be going back, in any case. You know that. But if you want to be helpful, now's the time."

Miller held his stomach, dragging on the cigarette.

"If you know this woman," said Frisnay, "Christine Johns, or know anything about her, or know anything about a woman named Joanna Gregg, or anything about what's happened to her, just open up. For your own sake. Well?"

Miller's eyes were screwed up against the cigarette-smoke.

He said: "I dunno." All he wanted was to be sick and go to sleep, out of this damned bright bloody light. "I dunno anything. I on'y got out 's'mornin' di'n I?"

"Or these names—listen, Miller—Professor Scobie, Dr. Taplow, Professor Parish, Charles Moss, Sir Bernard Gregg—"

"I dunno anythin' blast you, *blast* you!"

"Clifford Jackson, Arthur Bell, Max Corbyn—"

"I dunno, I tell you!"

Frisnay watched him.

Miller said with a dry pain in his throat, softly, "I dunno . . . "

Frisnay drew in his breath.

"All right, Miller."

He turned and went out.

Miss Gorringe was waiting, talking to the sergeant.

Frisnay came in and said: "Made your statement, Gorry?"

"Yes. It looked complicated, on paper."

"From what they tell me, it was fairly complicated anyway. We shan't get much help from that chap in there."

"He just stole the car, innocently?"

"Yes, if you can steal a car, innocently. He was only out of prison this morning, so he can't have had much to do with this business."

He leaned a shoulder against the doorpost, hands in his jacket-pockets. "Though I'd hoped for a lead, of some sort. No one knows more of what's going on in London than the men behind bars. They get news in a dozen ways, and it's not often duff—"

"But would he have opened his mouth?"

"To me, just now? Certainly, if he'd known anything even remotely useful. Six words can lighten a stretch by six months if they're the right words, and every man-jack of 'em knows it. He would have talked, it's just that he'd nothing to say."

He straightened up and said: "The car was taken from Dawson Mews. That's where Hugo's gone. I'll bet my pension."

"Freddie, I must get back home, in case he wants to phone me."

"All right, Gorry. If he does, and you want to contact me, ring Ops and they'll find me on the radio. May see you again tonight." He gave a quiet smile.

"Tonight," she said, "nothing seems impossible."

11th

MOVE

THE LAMP was burning at the corner of Cheyne Mews. Dark had come down, but not totally; the moon was in a clear sky.

She left the gray car facing towards King's Road, in case it had to go away in a hurry, tonight, tomorrow, any time. It often did, and this was the quickest exit.

A man was coming towards her, from the front door of Number Ten. She gave a slight start. He raised his hat.

"Good evening again, Miss Gorringe."

"Hello, Sir Bernard—"

"I called round for a word with Mr. Bishop, but there was no answer to the bell."

"Is it something urgent?"

"No, nothing urgent. I—just wanted someone to talk to, for an hour, before I go home at twelve for this . . . final telephone-call."

She felt a prick of pity for him. He had an hour left before he tore himself apart, one way or the other, to reach the decision they'd demand.

"Yes, of course, Sir Bernard." She opened the door with her key. "Come along in, and we'll wait for Mr. Bishop."

He hovered uncertainly. "But you're a very busy woman, Miss Gorringe—"

"Only when my chief's at home." She smiled warmly, holding the door for him.

"Well, it's kind of you. Most kind."

The resilience had gone out of him. He was a man lost.

In the long room upstairs, the one lamp was still on. Gregg sank into a chair, and laid his hands along the arms, resting his fine head back.

"A brandy, sir. Napoleon."

"Hard to resist, my dear, but I must. I've lost my sense of luxury, for a time."

"Then just sit quietly, and try to relax."

He attempted to assert himself, and almost managed—

"I'm perfectly all right, Miss Gorringe, thank you. It's just that I'm—" one hand moved.

"Worried, naturally."

"Yes. You see . . . " He decided against going on. "No, it's very difficult, this."

She sat on the Regency foot-stool, drawing her legs under her. The soft light sheened across her hair. Vaguely he thought that she looked a charming woman. Her voice was quiet, modulated.

"I should like to say, Sir Bernard, that as Mr. Bishop's personal secretary I always have the privilege of sharing any confidences that might be made to him, directly, in cases such as this. I am even, sometimes, helpful."

She watched him steadily. Perhaps she could help, if only by persuading him to get it off his mind. It was to do with more than Joanna. It was pressure. He was like the others, now, at last. Like Scobie, and the others.

"I'm sure you are, my dear, and if the matter were simple, I wouldn't hesitate to confide in you. But the truth is that I called here for no particular reason, other than to pass a trying time with someone who knows a great deal of this terrible situation, with someone I feel I can trust, beyond any doubt."

He looked at the room, his eyes noting nothing. "Mr. Bishop, although I've met him only a few times, appears to be a most sterling man, especially when one needs moral confidence."

"He can sometimes help," she said quietly, "and

he's often very practical. I know he's determined to find your daughter, tonight if it's humanly possible. He's looking for her now, in a particular area where the search has focused, and I may get a phone-call any time—"

"There's a new hope?"

He said it dully. He didn't invite disappointment.

"A hope, yes. Unfair to call it more than that."

"We haven't long, now."

"They all realize that, and there's not one minute going to waste, believe me. Soon after Mr. Bishop and I left you, on the Embankment, we were involved in a car-chase that ended with a smash. It's given us a clue—"

"Was anyone hurt?"

She half-smiled. "No. Not seriously."

"I feel . . . so idle."

"You're not, in your mind."

"No, that's busy enough. Three of my friends gone, in a few weeks, and gone tragically. Now my own daughter, in danger of her life . . . "

She got up, and went over to the sideboard.

"We're going to have a brandy, Sir Bernard. It's not a luxury, it's a godsend."

She turned to look at him. She asked: "Soda, or—?"

"As it is, thank you."

She gave him a bubble-glass. In a moment he

said slowly, "Wouldn't it be useful, if the Oracle still dwelt at Delphi? I'd know what to say, at midnight. In the Comet aeroplane, one could reach Delphi in a matter of hours . . . "

"You'd find a long queue. Questions are coming faster, in this bewildered brave new world."

He cupped his white hands round the glass, breathing the bouquet. "I must make up my own mind," he said quietly. "A man must do that."

"Can't you do it now?" There was an appeal in her tone. "Quietly, in this room, while there's time left. Instead of having to drive yourself to do it, later, on the telephone. I'll leave you, if you like, quite alone."

"No, don't leave me alone." He got up suddenly, and walked to the window, looking down into the street.

She was a little startled. He had almost beseeched her.

His voice was odd. "It's not good for me to be alone."

She saw in her mind the bright fast train, the striking snake, the broken glass.

She stood up, and moved halfway across to him.

"If there's anything we can do to help, Sir Bernard, that we're not doing, or that we've not thought of, let me know."

His big shoulders were hunched. He didn't turn his head.

"You're doing all you can," he said.

"And feeling rather useless."

He said nothing for half a minute. When he spoke, his voice had changed.

"That man down there . . . "

She came to the window. He said: "At the corner, where the mews . . . I seem to recognize him, the way he stands."

She saw the man. He was standing not far from the lamp, in the shadow of a wall. Sir Bernard said: "Yes. It's Bell."

She glanced at his face.

"The porter at the Hospital?"

He nodded slowly. "Yes."

She touched his arm.

"Please come away from the window."

"Why?"

"It's just a precaution." She was firm.

When he had moved into the middle of the room she crossed over to Bishop's desk and picked up the telephone, dialling three nines. Gregg watched her in surprise.

"What are you doing?"

"Having Bell collected. He's a suspect." Into the phone she said, "Police, please."

"But I know the man well—he was with us when—"

"Hello—Carlton 2330. Miss Gorringe, from Mr. Bishop's number. Yes. There's a man in King's

Road, corner of Cheyne Mews, watching these windows. Already under suspicion in the case Inspector Frisnay is handling. Yes. Arthur Bell. Thank you."

She lowered the phone.

Gregg said: "Bell . . . under suspicion? Of what?"

"I don't know, Sir Bernard." She moved slowly to the window, but kept to one side of it. "The police have questioned him already—he was seen watching your house the night before last—"

"But there's nothing wrong with *Bell*. He's an excellent man, I assure you."

"Are you quite certain?"

"Well, he was one of the crew of our ship, in '52, and I met him again a few months ago. Remembered him very well—he was a good seaman. He said he'd given up sailing and was looking for a post, and would like to serve me in any way he could."

She could just see Bell's head, against the wall. He hadn't moved.

"Yes?" she asked quietly.

"I'd nothing for him, but I managed to get him the porter's job at my own hospital, and he seemed very satisfied. I don't believe for one moment that he's anything but an honest, reliable—"

"I'd still rather you didn't come anywhere near the window, Sir Bernard."

He stopped. "Very well, if you feel there's danger for me, but—"

"I do. We all do. For you, and Charles Moss. You must realize—" she broke off.

A black car had pulled up, quietly.

Gregg said: "Have the police arrived?"

Gently she said: "Yes."

He wanted to move to the window, but remembered her warning.

"Please tell me what's happening, Miss Gorringe."

Her voice was slow. "An incident . . . a routine incident. They're often a joy to watch, if you're English and like the way we do things, the English way. Police have just arrived, but there weren't any sirens screaming . . . just a couple of quiet men in a sober black saloon, no guns, no hustling."

She rested one hand against the curtains. He watched her.

She said: "They're speaking to Bell. Nobody's moving, just hands idly in pockets. Now he's getting into their car. The doors are closed."

Faintly Sir Bernard heard the click of them, and the hum of the engine.

"Now they're going," Miss Gorringe said. "They might be off to a theater, or their club, or a pub for a friendly drink." She came away from the window. "And the odd thing is that if Bell had pulled out a gun or thrown a grenade, they'd have taken him away, just the same. There would have been more noise, but they'd have taken him away."

She smiled suddenly, and picked up her brandy.

Gregg looked worried.

"But have they arrested him?"

"Yes. For further questioning. One man was touching his elbow, lightly, as they ushered him into the car. That kind of physical violence always means an arrest."

"But on what charge?"

"Oh, suspicion. Loitering. Acting in a manner likely to occasion a breach of the Queen's peace. Something like that. But there must be a witness, if possible, and in a few minutes I shall get a—"

The telephone was ringing. She smiled again.

"—I shall get a phone-call. Excuse me."

She lifted the receiver.

"Yes, speaking. No, he was standing at the end of the mews, looking up at the windows of this flat. I can't say, but I rang you the moment I saw him there. Right, I'll do that for you. Good-bye."

Gregg was still not satisfied.

"They can arrest a man, just for standing on a corner?"

She was glad of his interest. It had stopped him thinking about Joanna, for a few minutes, and about the thing he might do if she left the room, leaving him alone.

"Sir Bernard, in less than three weeks, three men have died. It could be murder. Tonight you're in danger. So is Charles Moss. When the police cast their net for the big ones, they're bound to pick up minnows, too. You can always throw minnows back, and less harm done than if the whole lot were allowed to slip away."

She finished her brandy and said: "They've asked me to drive you home, at once. May I?"

He drew a deep breath. He said: "I'm in your hands, and theirs. That's a comfort, but it's bewildering."

She got a coat from the hall. He said as they went down the stairs: "What about your call? If Mr. Bishop telephones?"

"It's taken care of. We leave a tape-recorder switched on."

In the car she said: "We shall have a police-escort, on the way. But you won't see it, and there'll be no sirens."

"Operations Room?"

"Speaking."

"Miss Gorringe here. Cheyne Mews. I've just

got back from taking Sir Bernard Gregg home, and there's a telephone message from Mr. Bishop on the tape. I'll play it to you direct, in case I miss details."

"Right, Miss Gorringe, go ahead."

She put the switch over, and listened again to Bishop's voice in the room.

Faintly the spools whirred as the tape went through.

"Gorry, this is Hugo. Time is ten-five. Please contact Freddie. I advise a cordon round Dawson Mews, if there's not one there already. Quietly, no fuss. If Freddie or one of his men can meet me, I think we can do some business."

Miss Gorringe lit a cigarette, walking up and down.

"I'll wait halfway down the mews, outside the garage door numbered 15. Green door, broken top hinge. I may not want to show myself till they come. No special hurry, but before ten-thirty. Come along yourself if you like. Signing off."

She turned to the desk, moving the switch. Into the phone she said:

"All right?"

"Yes, we've got that. Will you be going yourself?"

"I think so. It looks like something not to be missed."

She put the receiver down and set the recorder for any further calls coming in.

It was just after ten-twenty by her watch as she went down to the car and started up.

The Humber turned down Walton Street, cruising. The driver and observer were silent. In the back, Frisnay sat with Sergeant Flack. They had not spoken for minutes.

Hello JK-5. Hello 5.

The observer pulled the receiver out of its clip.

"Hello JK. Go ahead. 5 Over."

Hello JK-5. Message for Inspector Frisnay. Mr. Bishop is waiting in Dawson Mews outside garage Number 15, which has green door with broken top hinge. Requests to be met there by Inspector or one of his men before ten-thirty, advises cordon round mews with least possible noise. Message urgently begs approval of action. That is all. JK Over.

Frisnay said from the back of the car:

"Say plan going ahead."

"Right, sir." Martin pressed the lever. "Hello JK. Message received. Plan going ahead. JK-5 Over."

Hello 5. Location please.

"Going East along Fulham Road, nearing Church Street."

Thank you JK-5. JK Out.

The Humber swung left on hard Telecontrol and dived directly South. The synchronized clock on the facia-board was at ten-twenty-five precisely.

A shoe touched a pebble. The sound gave a tiny echo from the nearer wall. The mews was half-shadowed, half moonlit.

Very softly . . . "Bishop."

"Here."

The shoes sounded again. The shadow against the door became a man. Bishop said: "Is there a cordon, Freddie?"

"Yes. Been one here for an hour. We'd have moved in, if I hadn't known you were nosing about—"

"Glad you didn't. This place is a warren. You could have wasted your time."

"What've you got, Hugo?"

"A door."

Frisnay grunted. "A real wooden door with a handle and everything?"

Bishop said: "It's this way. Up the stairs. Careful they're timber."

They moved off the cobbles, and climbed.

At the top, Frisnay murmured: "How d'you know it's the door we want?"

"Because I've seen 'em all, the lot, every damn'

door in Dawson Mews, in the last hour."

He led the way along a half-lit passage. "I've been up fire-escapes and down drain-pipes, in and out of keyholes and round the maypole. Even that didn't get me anywhere, until I followed my nose. Along here, now."

They turned, and came to a narrow hallway. At the end were stairs. Above was a skylight. There were six or seven doors along one side.

Frisnay said: "Your nose?"

"Yes. Christine Johns wears a particularly enchanting scent. It's called Music of Roses, by Tabarin."

"So she smells like a flower-stall. So?"

Bishop stopped, outside the end door.

"No, like the music that roses would make, if you plucked their petals in the silence of the moon." His lips scarcely moved. "I couldn't break in, because there's another way out of this room, on to a flat roof at the back. If she's in here she'll make a break the moment we hit the door."

Frisnay said: "All right, you cover the roof-exit while I open up here."

Bishop nodded. Before he turned away he said: "Freddie, I think this is it."

The lightness had gone out of his voice. He was suddenly hoping like hell that this was it.

Frisnay said bluntly: "Don't hang about. Cross fingers."

He waited until Bishop had climbed through the tilting window. Then he counted ten. Then he tried the handle. The door was locked. No one made any sound, in the room. He drew back and hit the door. It wasn't much of a lock. It didn't even make much noise. He snapped the light on and blinked in the sudden glare. He heard Bishop coming down the passage, coming in.

The girl on the bed was Joanna. She was lashed on to the bed with cord. The bed was pulled halfway across from the wall. On top of it, near her shoulder, was a small cabinet and a pile of books. On top of the pile there had been a little white bottle. When Frisnay had broken the door in, the bottle had come down. It had spilled something over Joanna, over her face. Her face was white. She wasn't gagged. She was out, cold.

Bishop didn't say anything. He picked up the bottle, and looked at it.

"Freddie—" his voice cracked but Frisnay caught his arm and said:

"No, it's water. It's all right. Not acid."

He drew a finger across the girl's forehead, and put his finger to his tongue. He said: "Yes. Water."

Bishop was sweating. Color came back to his face. He looked at Frisnay and didn't say anything. Frisnay was undoing the cords. He said curtly:

251

"Lend a hand."

Bishop put down the bottle and started on the knots. His hands were shaking.

"My God," he said, to no one.

"It looked nasty, yes. But a neat job. A woman's job. She couldn't leave Joanna here while she went out. You can gag your victim but she'll moan for help, and get it, if anyone's walking past."

He ripped a loose cord free. "You can tie her up but she'll make a shindy, kicking. You can dope her but you can't rely on timing. So you rig up this kind of thing, and leave her staring up at a bottle that says Sulphuric Acid. And knowing that when she calls for help, the first person to open the door brings the bottle down. A woman's job. A yellow-gutted bitch. Like Johns."

He straightened up, wiping his face with the back of his hand. In a moment Bishop said dully: "She was lying here hoping to God nobody would open this door."

"Yes," Frisnay said. "That's what she was doing. And when I opened it, she watched the bottle come down."

"And fainted."

"Wouldn't you?" He turned away. "I'm going down to get signals out. Look after things."

Bishop called: "Don't be long, Freddie. We've got to get this kid home. Send Gorry up, if she's there."

Frisnay shouted that he would, and went along the passage, hurrying.

Bishop looked down at the girl. She didn't move. Her face was white. Cord-marks were across the bare flesh of her arms. Her lips were parted. He could hear her breathing.

He sat on the edge of the narrow bed, and began stroking her hair, just above the brow, very gently. She was going to feel awful when she came round.

He went on running his fingers through her hair, and with his other hand rubbed her arms where the cords had cut into the flesh. The line of her limbs as she lay here was glorious, but he could watch her without thinking about anything, because he hating Johns at white-heat. It had only been water, but that didn't make any difference. This kid had thought it was vitriol.

A yellow-gutted bitch, Freddie had said. Yes. Joanna began moaning softly, suddenly.

He said: "It's all right. You're all right now."

She didn't open her eyes yet. She said thickly, "Don't open the door." He could just make out the words. "Don't open the door—"

"It's all right, Joanna—"

"My face," she said and opened her eyes and looked at him. Her pupils were large, not focusing yet. She was breathing very hard. Her voice tried to get stronger and cracked with the effort—"Don't look at my face, it's—"

"All right, darling, your face is all right. It wasn't really acid—"

She was panicking now and tried to sit up. She put one hand up to her face and held it there and began crying with an ugly harsh sound—"Oh God, don't look at—"

"It was only water, in the bottle." He said it firmly, almost viciously. "Water, nothing else."

She began shaking, with her hand pressed against her face.

He got off the bed and looked round the room and saw the mirror on the wall. He jerked it off the hook and came back.

"Joanna, look—"

"No leave me alone—"

"Joanna." He gripped her wrist and pulled her hand down and she tried to hit him, twisting over on the bed. He forced her back and held the mirror steady. Her breath was scraping out of her throat. "Look," he said sharply.

Her eyes were terrified. She stared at the mirror, and it was a long time before she believed it, and closed her eyes, and went limp against him. He threw the thing on to the floor and got her to sit up, before she passed out again, this time with relief.

"Darling, everything's fine now. Take it slowly, you've all the time in the world—"

"That woman—"

"Won't come back. She's gone."

He rubbed her arms, up and down, his fingers feeling the flesh-grooves still. She sat half-upright for minutes, then opened her eyes and looked at him. She was normal. She'd switched back, suddenly.

"Sorry, Hugo." She gave a lop-sided smile that hurt him. "Dear Hugo."

He relaxed at last. He was aware that he was breathing again, that blood was coming back to his face.

"It said acid, on the bottle, Hugo."

He nodded. "I know." He held her against him and she let her head rest on his shoulder. "But it was only water." He could feel the beat of her heart. She stayed like that for minutes, then he said: "We're taking you home now. When you feel like it."

Softly she said: "Home." She played with the word. "Yes."

She lifted her head and looked at him, the faint smile still there. "Dearest Hugo."

Gently he straightened up. He said:

"See if you can put your feet on the floor, Jo-anna."

Her shoes were lying in a corner of the room. He went and fetched them, easing them on to her stockinged feet. She said:

255

"Pins and needles. Delicious."

He laughed briefly. "You don't take long to get over shock."

Her smile faded. Her eyes watched his face. "You were holding me," she said softly. "I took as long as I could."

He said quietly: "It's wonderful. But the wrong time. Can you stand up?"

She gripped his hands, and managed it. She stood there wobbling, looking at him with comic solemnity. He let go one hand, and said: "Try walking."

She was halfway across the room, still holding his one hand, when Miss Gorringe said in a monotonous mincing tone from the doorway:

"Forward—sideways . . . Sideways—back . . . One, two, three—"

Joanna giggled. Miss Gorringe said:

"Everything ship-shape, Hugo?"

"And Bristol-fashion. Got the car down below?"

"Yes. One gray Rolls-Royce and a couple of dozen smart black saloons with radio-antennae littering the whole area. Do we go, or is this a rather complicated step?"

Joanna was walking alone now, awkwardly.

"I feel like an unemptied ashtray, Miss Gorringe, but never mind. We'll go." She glanced at Bishop. "Thank you," she said, "for everything."

He was feeling for his pipe. He wanted badly to smoke.

He smiled gently. "Any time . . . "

They went out to the passage, and helped Joanna down the stairs. Bishop said to Miss Gorringe: "Take Joanna home, will you? I'll follow on, probably with Freddie."

"Right."

Joanna said: "Freddie is the Inspector? Frisnay Minor, of the Remove?"

"That's the one. He'll want to question you, as soon as you've had a rest."

"Of course."

Frisnay came up suddenly.

"All right, Miss Gregg?"

"Yes. Thank you."

"I'm not going to worry you now, but you've no idea where the woman's gone?"

"No. She said to telephone my father."

"That was some time before nine o'clock tonight?"

"I don't know. My watch had stopped. But it was twilight."

Frisnay nodded. "What was she wearing?"

She leaned for a moment against the grey car. Bishop steadied her with a hand on her arm, holding the door open.

She said: "She had a loose grey coat, dark-red gloves and shoes, no hat. Red handbag."

Frisnay said: "Good enough. Thank you, Miss Gregg. Have a good rest, and I'll be along later."

She got into Bishop's car. Miss Gorringe took the wheel and started up. Bishop said: "I'll phone Sir Bernard."

They drove away. Frisnay was standing with his hands in his mac pockets. He murmured: "Same description. She's not even changed."

"Christine Johns?"

"Yep. She won't get far. I'm going to find her, and then break her."

Bishop said: "It's not often you chaps get emotional about your job."

Frisnay turned away to his car. "No, not often, is it."

Bishop walked to the end of the mews, turned right, and stopped at the telephone-box across the road. He dialled Gregg's number and Gregg answered personally.

"This is Bishop, sir."

The edge came off Sir Bernard's tone. He said: "It's not midnight yet, but I thought it was . . . "

"Yes, I see. But you can forget that now. Joanna's on her way home, safe and sound."

There was a long pause. Gregg couldn't quite get his tone steady.

"Joanna's—coming home?"

"Yes, she'll be there in a few minutes. I'd like

to be the first to congratulate you, sir."

"Bishop, this is—" he broke off.

Bishop said cheerfully: "Yes, good news. We're all very happy about it. Inspector Frisnay's coming to see you a little later—he'll want to ask Joanna about what happened."

"I hope you'll be along, too, Mr. Bishop. I have an idea that you were responsible for—for this."

"No sir, we were in luck, tonight."

"So were Joanna and I . . . We shall look forward to seeing you, soon."

Bishop said good-bye and came out of the telephone-box, looking along the street. A few cars were going by, a few taxis. He thought of stopping one, then decided to walk. It was a clear moonlit night, and the streets were cool, and it had only been water in the bottle. A walk would be nice.

The black Humber pulled up behind the grey saloon. Frisnay said to the driver:

"Wait here. After what's happened, I doubt if there'll be any phone-call at midnight. Even so, we'll be ready to switch to Dawson Plan at a second's notice, just the same."

"Right, sir."

Frisnay got out and crossed the pavement, climbing the steps. When he rang the bell, it was one of his own men who opened the door.

"Well, Blake?"

"Nothing to report, sir. Mr. Bishop called. I let him go through."

"That's all right. There's no change of plan."

He found Sir Bernard in the drawing-room. Bishop was talking to Joanna. Miss Gorringe was talking to Gregg.

He came forward. "You're very welcome, Inspector."

"Thank you Sir Bernard. Miss Gregg's feeling better now?"

"Indeed yes." He lowered his voice. "She's not told me any details, of what actually happened—"

"She didn't come to any real harm, sir, don't worry. Mainly shock."

Gregg nodded, reassured.

"It remains for me to try to thank you," he said.

"Only doing my job, sir, and Mr. Bishop did most of it for me, this time."

Gregg smiled slowly. "You should have him in the Force."

Frisnay grunted. "He'd never stand the discipline."

Gregg took him over to the others. "You'll join us in a drink, I hope?"

"Not even to celebrate, thank you, sir." He looked at Joanna. "But I'll say 'welcome home'."

She smiled. Her face was still pale. "I haven't got used to it, yet."

Bishop looked at Frisnay, trying to catch his eye. When he managed it he said briefly: "Any luck?"

"Not yet."

Gregg asked: "Are we still to expect the telephone-call?"

"Yes, sir, but it may not come." He looked at his watch. "There's fifteen minutes. The line's rigged. We'll just wait, if we may."

"Of course."

"And if I could ask Miss Gregg a few things—I'll make it as brief as I can."

She sat down near the windows; he drew up another chair.

"Now you left Mr. Bishop's place, soon after eleven o'clock last night, to walk here alone."

"Yes. I heard the quarter strike, before I turned into King's Road."

"Please go on from there, Miss Gregg."

"I was nearly to Sloane Square when a car stopped. It was Christine Johns. She said someone wanted to see me, urgently, at Trent's Hotel—"

"Mr. Max Corbyn, would that be?"

"How did you know?"

"Did she actually say it was Mr. Corbyn who wanted to see you?"

"Not until I asked her. She just said someone at Trent's Hotel. I knew he was staying there—we were friends, once—"

"Yes, I see. You had to ask her, and she said he was the person who wanted to see you."

"Yes, Inspector."

Frisnay studied his shoes.

"You got into the car—?"

"Yes, and she drove me to the hotel. Mr. Corbyn wasn't there when we arrived, so we sat in one of the lounges and had a drink while we were waiting. After ten minutes or so, this woman went to telephone him at a place where she thought he might have been held up—"

"She gave that as her reason for going to the telephone?"

"Yes."

"Did you actually see her using a telephone?"

"No, the phones are in the main lobby."

"She just left you, saying she was going to phone."

"Yes. She came back in a few minutes and said that Mr. Corbyn was held up, and couldn't manage it—"

"Couldn't manage to come to the hotel?"

She nodded. He said:

"Didn't you think that was odd, after he'd asked to see you urgently?"

"Of course. I thought it was so odd that when

the woman offered to drive me home, I agreed. It was well out of my way, and I hoped to get her to talk to me, and find out where she fitted into this frightening business."

"You couldn't have felt very frightened, Miss Gregg. You'd heard something about this woman, I believe, and probably mistrusted her in any case—"

"I was under the illusion that I could take care of myself. I realized it was an illusion when I woke up. I wasn't in her car. I was strapped on that bed with the bottle balanced over my face—"

"You'd passed out, in her car?"

"Yes. I suppose I was drugged, somehow—"

"With the drink you'd taken in the hotel lounge."

She said: "That could have been her only chance."

"What time did you wake up, from this drug?"

"I don't know, but it was this morning. I think I must have passed into natural sleep, because I didn't feel very much ill-effect."

"When did the woman leave you, Miss Gregg?"

"Before ten, by my watch, but I hadn't been able to wind it up last night, and it might have slowed—"

"When did she come back?"

"During the afternoon. She took the bottle

away and let me move about for half an hour, but she watched carefully and had the bottle within a few inches of her hand—"

"She said she'd throw it if you cried out or tried to get out of the room?"

"Yes. I—suppose I should have risked it, but—"

"I wouldn't have, Miss Gregg. I'd rather have risked a gun. Vitriol's unpleasant stuff. When did she leave again?"

"This evening. I was tied up again, on the bed—"

"She say where she was going?"

"Yes—to phone my father."

He said: "Did she at any time ask you to give her this vital information?"

"Oh yes, persistently. I told her that even if I knew it, she could do what she liked, and not get it."

"Did she threaten actual torture—hold the bottle over you and tilt it—that kind of thing?"

"No. I think she believed me when I said I didn't know what she wanted."

Frisnay got up and moved about near her chair.

"Did you see anyone else, in Dawson Mews?"

"Nobody."

"There's a telephone in that room. Did she use it, to your knowledge?"

"No."

"What time did she leave you, this evening? You said it was twilight. You can't be more accurate than that, after a little time to think?"

"I'd no means of telling. My watch had stopped, and I couldn't hear a church-clock or anything."

"There's nothing else you can think of that might help, Miss Gregg?"

"I don't think so. I'm sorry—"

"One remembers little details, much later, after an experience of this kind. If any occur to you, even as late as tomorrow, please let us know. However slight."

"I'll try to think."

"Thank you. Did she mention Mr. Corbyn's name again?"

"No."

"Did you?"

"No."

He stood still, fascinated by his polished shoes. He said in a moment: "Well, thank you. I'm sorry to have worried you, so soon after—"

"I just wish to God I could really help."

He smiled. She was a nice kid. Bishop had told him she wasn't slinky, but nice.

"I'd say you'd done your share, Miss Gregg, if only by accident. We'll find this woman, now— she's blazed too much of a trail to get away."

He looked up as Sir Bernard approached.

"I suggest beauty-sleep," Frisnay said, "don't you, sir?"

"If I could only tell this young lady to get off to bed, Inspector, I could do a lot of other things in my own household. But we don't stand a chance."

As she left them, Gregg said to Frisnay: "I've been waiting to tell you something rather curious. I don't know if I'm right, because the last few days have been harassing and my judgment's not all it was. But when I came back here after the—er—nine-o'clock appointment in Carter Street, I went into my study for a while, to think."

Frisnay waited. Bishop came up, and stood quietly, a glass in his hand.

Gregg said: "Everything seemed to be as usual, in the study, but soon after I'd sat down at my desk I noticed one or two little things out of place—a drawer not quite closed, the paper-weight on the left instead of on the right—a book out of place on the shelf behind—"

"You think your study might have been searched while you were away in Carter Street?"

Bishop was watching Frisnay. He liked seeing a theory become solid.

Gregg said: "That could have been the only opportunity."

"Anything missing, Sir Bernard?"

"Nothing. I made a rough tour of inspection, and frankly when I'd finished I doubted if I was right. And yet—you know how one gets used to one's own patterns, especially in a room where one works—"

"Yes, quite, sir. You were in the study just before you left to go to Carter Street?"

"I was in there about an hour before, yes. After dinner."

"And noticed nothing unusual. The 'pattern' was right?"

"Oh yes. I'm still not certain, now, but I think if I had to give evidence, I'd say that someone had been in the study, and possibly made a search there."

"Not one of your staff?"

"Oh no—we've only the one woman here, Mrs. Cobb, and she's most careful. Poor soul, I give her a bad time of it if she does anything more than dust, in that particular room."

Frisnay was looking at Bishop. Bishop said:

"It had actually occurred to me, Freddie. That the nine-o'clock appointment might have been made for this reason. It wouldn't be the first time."

Frisnay said: "If there's been a search made, it was a woman's work. Some attempt to restore order. A man usually tears the place apart and leaves it in a shambles, and gets out quick. Can we look at the room, sir?"

Gregg led the way. The study was small, crescent-shaped, high-ceilinged. Beside the desk were french windows. Frisnay opened them and looked out. A lawn, a path, a cedar-tree. He bent down, using a pocket-torch, then straightened up and shut the doors.

He wandered round the room and said at last:

"It would have been too easy, sir. Wouldn't it? If these doors weren't locked?"

Gregg nodded. He looked at his desk. He hated people in his laboratory, in his study, when he was absent; even friends of his.

Frisnay said: "You see, sir, we know this woman Johns abducted Miss Gregg. But she may not have been involved in any foul play there might have been when Professor Scobie, Dr. Taplow and Professor Parish died. She may not have sent those threatening notes to you, to Professor Parish and to Mr. Moss. She may not have searched this room, or even telephoned you on those two occasions—at your laboratory, and at the rendezvous tonight: in fact it's likely that two people were concerned in the second phone-call, because this room seems to have been entered while you were answering it—"

Bishop said: "But it *could* have been one person, couldn't it Freddie? If they used a phone-box very near this house?"

"It could, Hugo, but it's unlikely, because of the risky timing required. Sir Bernard might have left here at five minutes to nine, by car, and been back by five past, leaving only two short periods of about four minutes each in which to search this room, before and after making the phone-call. Although in fact, Sir Bernard was absent for some thirty or forty minutes, so we can't overlook the possibility that one operator did both jobs, I agree. But it's unlikely."

Gregg straightened his shoulders, putting his hands behind his back. Joanna was home now; it would take time to shift the burden he'd carried before. He said in a moment:

"Perhaps we should be getting back to the drawing-room." He was looking at the clock on his desk. It was five minutes to midnight.

They followed him, closing the study door.

Frisnay said: "I'd like to get some men in, if I may. We'll cover your study for prints and so on."

Gregg hesitated. Frisnay said: "We shan't disturb anything, sir. This time, you won't know there's a soul been in there."

Sir Bernard smiled briefly.

"I'm quite sure. Please make what plans you must, Inspector."

Frisnay stopped in the hall, to give orders to Blake. The man went out to the waiting police-car.

"If Johns hasn't been back to Dawson Mews," Frisnay said as he joined Gregg and Bishop, "she'll phone, any time now. If she's the one who phoned before. But if she's been back there, we'll get a call from my chaps. Dawson Mews is a super-trap, now."

Sir Bernard asked: "What are my instructions, if there's a call?"

"Please suppose that Miss Gregg is still held in some unknown place, sir, and that she knows the vital information they want, and that you've decided to give it up, through her, in order to save her life."

Gregg nodded. "I understand, yes. So that if she hasn't been back to Dawson Mews, she'll go there now, to ask my daughter. Do I have it right?"

Frisnay nodded.

"That's it, sir. The caller might be surprised—they're often surprised when things are made easy for them. They might think fast and ask you for some kind of pass-word that'll convince Miss Gregg that the message comes from you, and isn't just a trick to make her talk—"

"Yes, I see—"

"Be ready with something. Any little thing that Christine Johns or anyone else couldn't possibly know about your daughter. Something that only you could know, and could pass on to a stranger."

"I shall think of something, very well."

Frisnay looked wooden-faced across at Bishop.

"What's the odds?" he asked.

Bishop said: "Fifty-fifty."

Frisnay shrugged. He looked once at his watch. Just before twelve he wandered into the hall. He said to Blake:

"Go outside and tell them to start up and warm the engine."

When the man came back, Frisnay said: "If we leave in a hurry, you stay. You're personally responsible for the safety of Miss Gregg and Sir Bernard, Blake."

"Yes, sir. They'll be all right."

Blake had a good tough chipped-looking face with straight eyes and a wariness that didn't often go. He had been picked for this duty. He was the best they had.

There was another man at the back. He was good, too. There was a man in Collingwood Lane, standing where Arthur Bell had stood, the night before last.

Frisnay came back into the drawing-room and stopped dead and looked at Sir Bernard as the telephone began ringing. Sir Bernard came slowly past him into the hall. Frisnay picked up the special extension that had been rigged up near the main phone.

Two miles away, a plain-clothes man was standing next to the emergency-call operator in the nearest section exchange. There was a murmur in the long high room. Forty people were talking, repeating numbers, asking for service. Above them the sound-baffle boards kept down the volume.

As the telephone rang in Gregg's house, the red light began flashing in the exchange. The operator looked at a man who stood near the detective-constable. He said:

"Ringing now. Trace."

The man of the house in Collingwood Lane, Sir Bernard said briefly:

"Hello?"

"Sir Bernard Gregg?"

He glanced once at Frisnay.

"Speaking."

"You've had time, now. Have you decided?"

"It—hasn't been very long."

Frisnay had told Sir Bernard: Hang it out as long as you can, Sir. It'll give us time to trace.

"This is the final chance. I'm sorry to say your daughter seems a little weaker tonight. That's mainly fright, of course. She's been warned that you might not move a finger to save her, and she's—"

"*You damned fiend . . .*"

He had tried his best to sound convincing; but

Joanna was just through the doorway there, in the drawing-room. He wanted to tell them they could go to hell, she was safe.

"Then I'll say good-bye to her for you, Sir Bernard."

He paused.

In the section exchange the man scribbled some words on his pad and flicked it across to the detective. The detective picked up his receiver. "Kettering. Dawson Plan. Right? Box on corner Duke Street—Reading Hill. Duke Street—Reading Hill. Still talking." In a moment he put down the receiver.

Within a rough square, area Victoria-Fulham, Thames-Bayswater, black cars stood in shadows. Signals came.

Hello JK-1—JK-2—JK-3—JK-4. C-Charlie Action. Action. Box on corner Duke Street— Reading Hill. Duke Street—Reading Hill. Surveillance only. Proceed. JK Over.

Calls went back, words sounding between the snick of gears, the rush of cylinders, the wink of lights. There was very little noise. There was as little noise as possible. But there was speed.

On the distant line, Sir Bernard said:

"Very well. You win." With an effort he said: "Tell my daughter I want her to give you the information."

The odd, familiar, toneless voice said:

"She doesn't know it. Only you know it."

"She has known it for some time. She'll tell you."

"She's refused, so far. She might think I'm tricking her into telling. Give me something that will prove to her that you want her to talk. Quickly."

Sir Bernard hesitated, trying to think of something.

Frisnay had said: hang it out, as long as you can.

Less than a mile away, a call was going in, from prowler to Base. *Hello JK. Woman under surveillance. Walking-pace twenty yards from box. She is still talking. JK-3 Over.*

The woman in the box listened. Sir Bernard said:

"My daughter's birthday is on January the Second. This year I gave her a gold compact, initialled." He kept gentleness out of his tone. "She was almost angry with me, for my extravagance."

In a moment the voice said:

"All right."

"You give me your word that—"

"I can't promise anything, until I have the information. If she refuses again, or tries to make up something, there'll be no more chances."

The line went dead.

Gregg glanced across at Frisnay. Frisnay

waited a few moments, then put his receiver down.

Bishop was standing in the doorway. He asked: "Yes-no?"

Frisnay said: "Yes. It's a cop."

He went to the front door. Bishop half-turned and said:

"Coming, Gorry?"

The gray Rolls-Royce pulled away from the front of the house in the wake of the black Humber.

In the Humber, Frisnay was receiving a signal.

Hello JK-5. Hello 5. Dawson Plan in action. JK Out.

The room was empty. The passage was dimly lighted, calm as still water. Somewhere, in a bathroom or a tucked-away closet, a tap dripped, monotonously, musically.

It had been like this for ten minutes, perhaps fifteen.

Bishop shaped his lips round words almost inaudible.

"Something slipped up, Freddie?"

Frisnay said on his breath: "No."

Nothing had slipped up. He knew what the situation was. The situation was that Christine Johns was walking back to Dawson Mews, walking through a network of men who at any given signal could pick her up, wherever she was. They could take her just as she turned a corner, or crossed a road, or put up a hand to move her hair, or move one foot past the other as she walked. They could take her at any second, come down like a camera-shutter, click.

She wasn't here yet, but she'd be here. To get her here would be to save a lot of time later, collecting evidence.

Frisnay was a human man, and had some kind of a heart; but it was nice, standing here in the dark room, thinking of the slim bright fly who was trembling in his web.

He said: "Listen."

They stopped breathing. A door had opened, a long way off, a long way below them. Seconds passed, ticked off by the drip of the tap.

High heels climbed stairs, quietly, nearer.

Bishop said: "Yes."

They waited, until their muscles ached.

The high heels came along level floor, from the top of the stairs, nearing.

They came on, steadily, until it was hard to tell where she was, because of the echoes, and the steadiness of her pace. Then she slowed, towards the open door.

Bishop had said they should close the door, and let her come in. If she saw it was open, she'd know people had been here, and Joanna had gone. And she'd panic, and try to make a run.

Frisnay had said, that's right. He wanted that. Panic. He wanted to pin a series of charges on this little bitch that would sew her up in a cocoon. Then perhaps she'd talk. He wanted her to do everything incriminating that she had time to do. And she'd been given time, and this chance now. From the moment she'd left the telephone-box, they had held back from dropping on her. They'd been paying out the rope.

She had stopped, now. She was right outside the door. Bishop, a little to the left of Frisnay, could make out the slender line of her arm, against the softly lighted wall outside. Her fingers were loose. A ring glistened. The room, the passage, the building was grave quiet.

Frisnay said loudly: "Miss Johns."

She ran with a cry stifled in her throat and her hands flying out. They saw her go past the open door, like that, like something winged in the light, the physical form of an abstract thing: panic.

Frisnay said: "Come on."

They reached the passage. She had turned right. They saw one of her shoes, lying on the carpet. It had been flung off as she had darted round the corner.

"Going up," Bishop said.

"Yes."

They walked steadily to the corner and turned right, passing the neat little suede I. Miller shoe. It looked, Bishop thought, pathetic, lying there.

They climbed the narrow steps that led up to the roof door. It had been flung open. Her other shoe lay on the top step. She would be able to run better, more softly, in her stockinged feet. Run more quickly, into their hands.

Frisnay stood in the doorway and looked across the flat moonlit roof and called softly:

"Smith—Scott."

A man called: "Right, sir."

There were chimneys, spread across this roof and the roofs beyond. They stood black and angular like man-made stalagmites against the quiet sky.

Frisnay stood with his hands in his pockets. Bishop was trying to see where she had gone. Suddenly one of the men said:

"All right—don't—"

She cried out something vicious and they saw her dart across a gap between two of the chimney-stacks. Bishop felt sorry for her. Sometimes a man feels sorry even for a rat, when it hasn't a chance.

She called out again, her voice pitching up to a hoarse reedy shrill of a cat's.

A stamp of feet came as one of the men ran

forward, crossing a pool of moonlight.

Frisnay called: "Take her now!"

Bishop heard something in his voice. Frisnay savoured this. It was unlike him; but three men had died, and he'd been prodded hard from above, and he still didn't know how they died. Two suicides and an accident, and no one knew how they'd died. But here was something, at last, a girl in the net. With her they could open everything up, if they were lucky. She might not know everything, but she knew a lot. More than he did.

Bishop said suddenly, "Freddie, she's—"

"*Take her!*"

They were running now, all of them, the two men and Frisnay and Bishop, towards the girl and the parapet. She was calling something that the tramp of their own feet drowned.

Bishop was the first to stop. He was still yards from the parapet. Her scream was coming now, a long dry scream that diminished down the empty air until it was cut off by the crash of glass.

Bishop held his breath. The scream had gone searing down his spine, and was still there, echoing along his nerves.

Frisnay was dodging past him and the two men were following. Their feet hammered down the steps and along the passage.

Windows were being thrown open. A voice called, fright in it.

Bishop went down, and into the mews. A lot of men were there now, out of sheer shadow. They had heard the scream and the glass, and had moved in.

Frisnay had gone in through a doorway, along a narrow courtyard, three or four men with him. Bishop passed a black saloon and heard a call going out for an ambulance. Miss Gorringe was beside him suddenly—

"Hugo—"

"We don't know," he said, and followed Frisnay.

Frisnay was standing over the girl, with torch-light glaring across the mass of shattered glass. The skylight above their heads was torn with a hole like a hole in thin ice.

She lay in her blood. The glare of the torches painted bright crimson across her body.

12th

MOVE

THE YOUNG man was tall, thin, quiet-looking. The Sister put him down as doctor-type. She said:

"Good morning."

He smiled. He said:

"Good morning, Sister. My name is Bishop—"

"Oh yes, Mr. Bishop. You've come to see Miss Johns."

"If I may."

He followed her to a small private room. Outside the door she said:

"Only for ten minutes, please."

"All right. What's her condition?"

"She's in no real danger, and she passed the

rest of the night fairly well. Chiefly shock and superficial cuts and abrasions—"

"She was lucky."

"Yes." The Sister was tall, clear-eyed, with a nose made for humor, a firm mouth. She seemed reluctant to open the door. "The skylight broke the fall."

He nodded. "And saved her life?"

"Yes, probably. Are you a friend of hers, Mr. Bishop?"

He smiled again, faintly.

"Not even now, Sister."

She hesitated, but he didn't say anything more.

She opened the door. Before she left him, she said quietly:

"Please see me on the way out."

He said he would.

Christine Johns had a wax-white face without make-up and without blood. She was lying down in the bed. Bishop looked at the other woman in the room, a short, neat-looking woman with good features and a quick smile. He said:

"Hello, constable."

She said: "Good morning, sir," and took her chair over to the door, sitting down, folding her arms.

He sat on the edge of the bed.

"How are you, Christine?"

She spoke strongly enough, moving her head

to look at him. Her head was bandaged. She said:

"How do I look?"

"As gorgeous as ever, even in the pudding-cloth. How do you feel?"

Her mouth curved down.

"A bit cut-up."

"That'll heal. You were lucky. You don't mind my sitting on your bed?"

"We've got a chaperone, haven't we?"

He said: "I'm not allowed to talk for very long, but there are some things I'd like to know."

"Some things Frisnay would like to know, so he sent you along to pump me. His hands too sensitive for dirty work?"

"For one thing," said Bishop, "it was I who found you, so he lets me keep up my unflagging interest in your gay affairs. For another thing, he's busy, looking for Corbyn."

In a moment she said in a dull tone, "He won't find him. Corbyn's out of town."

"Not really? When did you last see him?"

"Couple of days ago, at Trent's Hotel."

"Yes?"

"We had lunch together, and he skipped when I was putting cream in my coffee."

"You don't lie very neatly, even when you're feeling well. This is worse than ever. When you saw him last, wherever and whenever it was, did he say where he was going?"

"Like hell. I spoiled his sense of privacy."

He looked across at the window for a time and without glancing back asked her:

"The night before last, when you left Joanna Gregg for a minute in the lounge of that hotel, you said you were going to telephone Corbyn. But that was just part of your plan to abduct her?"

He looked back to her face.

She said:

"Work it out for yourself, Hugo darling."

"Did Corbyn take any part in your plan?"

"Of course. It was his job to be available on the phone, when I didn't phone him."

"Did he have any part in your plan, Christine?"

She said nothing for minutes. He thought she had dried up, for good. She closed her eyes, and then opened them and looked straight at him and said with a bitterness:

"He hadn't got the guts. Or he was too sweetly sentimental about crossing-up his ex-girl-friend. You know what men are. They've a low melting-point."

He said: "Are you still in love with Corbyn?"

"See my private diary, if you can find it."

"Is he in love with you?"

She said softly and with a forced smile: "Darling, the whole world is."

She jerked in her breath, on a spasm of pain. She didn't act it.

He said: "Anything wrong?"

Relaxing, she said: "They didn't get all the glass out. Underneath, I'm transparent, like all simple girls."

"I'll leave you, if you say."

"Would you, sweetheart? You'd stay here and give me the third-degree if I was yelling out for a priest."

"I should think that'd be the last thing you'd do."

"It's always the last thing. But go on, golden-voice, you do me good."

In a little while he said:

"When you called at my flat, out of the blue, it was to warn me off. Why?"

She said: "You tell me."

"All right. You'd heard I was digging up odd theories about Scobie's death, and Taplow's. You had the unpleasant feeling I might strike gold— the secret of the 1952 expedition. You were going after that secret yourself, and you didn't want any keen competition. Yes?"

"Not bad," she said. She closed her eyes. "Go on, Hugo. I'm not going to sleep. I'm just framing your fascinating face in my imagination, and feeling for a dream-razorblade."

He said gently: "Once those two men had died, you decided to move in, and get the secret before anyone else did. Before the killer did. You began digging, yourself, as I was. But you did it through Moss, and through Corbyn—"

"Max doesn't know the secret."

He paused, and thought that one over. It clicked into place.

He said: "No. But he went as far as the land supplybase on the expedition. It was he who first told you there was a secret. Before then, you didn't know a thing." More gently still he said: "That would have been about the time when he and Joanna broke off their engagement . . . would it?"

She took a breath and held it, then said: "They were washed-up anyway. They'd been together on that ship for a long time, hadn't they? While the party went out. They got it all out of their systems, hadn't they? Sometimes there's not much left, for—"

"I believe they broke it up because Joanna had the sudden feeling he wasn't quite straight."

Christine opened her eyes. They were very tired, but there was all the expression in the world there.

She said: "That might be. I don't blame her for taking so long about finding out. Max can look you right in the eyes . . . and your guard's liable to go down . . . when you're a woman."

"So you—"

"Let's change the subject."

He shuffled a thought into the pattern and shrugged.

"All right. Have you ever been down to Dr. Taplow's place, in Amberly, Surrey?"

"No. Did I miss good parties?"

"Did you send threatening notes to Sir Bernard Gregg, Parish, and Moss?"

"Threatening what, for God-sake?"

He watched her with needle-focus. She still wasn't lying.

"Never mind," he said. "But you telephoned Sir Bernard, three times. At his laboratory in St. Mark's Hospital, at the kiosk outside the stamp-shop in Carter Street, and at his house last night, at midnight."

"That would cost all of ninepence, so I'm a rich girl?"

She was just pulling it out of the air, meaning nothing, just tough-minded about giving him a straight yes, too weak to act.

"And you disguised your voice," he said.

"Successfully, though I says it as shouldn't."

"And you searched his study, last night, about midnight."

"His place was searched?"

He watched her.

"If not by you," he said, "by Max, while you were busy spending ninepence."

"Max is out of town—he couldn't have—"

"All right. He couldn't have. He's out of town. We think he'll be coming back."

He thought: if it wasn't her, and wasn't Corbyn, who the blazes? He believed her. When she lied, big bells rang all over her face. She wasn't lying now.

He said quietly: "We think he'll be coming back, because you're news, this morning. Pretty girl in would-be death-leap from rooftop, lies injured in hospital."

She was watching him, alert-eyed.

He said: "If you still mean anything to Max, and I think you do, he'll try to see you, here."

She looked down.

"Do I care?"

"Perhaps. But he'll care a great deal, if he comes within a mile of this hospital—"

"You can see right through me, can't you?" It came out through her teeth.

He smiled pleasantly.

"As you say, Christine, they haven't got all the glass out, yet."

Suddenly he got up, and stood looking down at her.

"Now I must go. I don't want to sap your strength when you need it so badly."

He was halfway to the door before she said in a thin dry tone—

"You've less sympathy for me than a snake's got for a rabbit."

He turned his head.

"Not very much more, I admit. Every time I smell Music of Roses I think of sulphuric acid. Odd association."

"It was plain water wasn't it?"

He nodded.

"Yes. But did she know?"

He smiled briefly to the constable. As he opened the door, Christine said with the last of her present strength—

"Officer, the gentleman is leaving. Would you please open the windows, when he's gone?"

He called at the Sister's desk, on his way out. It was pleasant to do. She was a nicer type of girl.

Frisnay was sitting on the davenport when Bishop came in. The Siamese was on his lap. He dropped her off it for the third time. He said:

"I don't like cats. Even yours. I don't like anything with more than two legs, or no legs at all. It's unnatural."

Bishop looked at Miss Gorringe. She was at her desk.

"My dear Freddie. Have a drink?"

"No thanks."

Bishop closed the door and came across the long room to his desk. Miss Gorringe said:

"I've been telling Freddie about Sir Bernard's visit here, last night."

Bishop sat down gently.

"Ah, yes," he said. "You thought he was quietly suicidal. And not altogether because Joanna was still missing."

She said: "He—was worried about her. Terribly. But I had the impression it was something else, slowly breaking him down. He said his mind was burdened . . . "

Frisnay said: "Like Scobie's, Taplow's, Parish's."

"I think we ought to take care of Sir Bernard," Miss Corringe said precisely. "When the others died, there was no warning."

Bishop said in a few seconds: "And if Gregg were to go next, you wouldn't feel very surprised, after his attitude last night."

She shook her head. "I'd have to tell the coroner that the last time I saw the deceased, he seemed depressed in his manner, and even in some of his remarks. Suicidally depressed. I'd hate to think we had the chance of saving him, and didn't take it."

Bishop looked at Freddie, who sat wooden-faced.

"He's still under police-observation, Freddie?"

"Yes. But we can't protect him sixty seconds a minute, you know. Protect him from outside attempts on his life, surely, but not from *inside* attempts."

He looked vaguely at the cat, waiting for it to jump on to him again. It did not. He said: "We've lost people before now, even when we've had them in protective custody. If they want to take their own life, you've got to turn your back for two seconds, no more. It's too easy. Death's a damn' sight easier than birth."

He got up, and moved nearer Bishop. Bishop sat back in his chair and stared at the chess-pieces on the board. He said soon:

"I wonder if we could possibly find out, more certainly, whether he means to go the same way as the others? Either by a deliberate act of his own, or by deliberately submitting to the hand of a murderer?"

Frisnay said: "He'd talk to you more freely than to us. We're official. Always a sort of barrier."

"Well, I'll try. I'd try very hard, to save a man like Gregg."

Miss Gorringe was staring at her telephone. She said:

"Hugo, last night he said he wanted to talk to you, and although I assured him he could say anything to me—was that right—?"

"That was right—"

"—He decided against it. I really believe he'd got something to say to you, and to nobody else."

Bishop said after a little time: "Yes." He looked at the clock. "It's nearly twelve noon. I'll phone Joanna, and ask her if she'll lend me a hand. Freddie, I phoned your office, spoke to Sergeant Flack—"

"Yes, I got your message. But if Christine Johns doesn't actually know where Corbyn's hiding-up, he's on the wanted list, and there's a watch at airports, docks, so on. What's your guess?"

Bishop said with conviction: "I think he'll try to reach her at the hospital. I think the darlings are in love."

Frisnay said: "Well, he's quite at liberty to go there. We'll just save him the cab-fare home when he leaves her."

"What about the others?" Miss Gorringe said. "Bell, and—"

"We've questioned Bell. Odd type. He says he's been shadowing Sir Bernard in order to protect him from anything that might come along."

Bishop looked up at him.

"Implausible enough to be the truth."

Frisnay nodded.

"Yes. He's independent, not to say aggressive. He seems to be nothing more or less than an honest, loyal admirer of a good man and a brilliant scientist: Gregg."

He looked at Miss Gorringe. "His story checks with what Sir Bernard told you last night, Gorry. Bell was on the *Snow Goose*. Back in London, out of a decent job, he thought he'd ask Gregg if he had a place for him. Sir Bernard seemed to be involved in bad trouble, Bell put it. He wanted to help him, if he needed help."

He lit a cigarette and watched the chess-pieces for a few moments. "But we're watching him. We're watching him, and Jackson, and Charles Moss—we're watching *everyone*. When the next move comes, we'll be there, on the spot."

The telephone began ringing.

Bishop reached out a hand. He said:

"Yes?"

"Hugo, this is Joanna."

"Talk of angels. I was just going to ring you, Joanna."

"Yes?" She sounded glad.

"How d'you feel?"

"Very good, thank you."

"Better than little Christine. She has windows to see cushions through. Joanna, would your grand old man be interested in lunch, the three of us? I know it's short notice, but—"

"Today?"

"Yes." He looked at the clock again.

She said: "I expect he'd like it. You're very

popular with my grand old man, after saving his erring daughter."

"I hope you agree with him—"

"Unreservedly." Her voice had run into crushed velvet. He said briskly:

"Then I'll collect you both, may I?"

"There's only me here, just now. He's gone to the Runway Club, to talk to Charles Moss."

He did a mental double-take and then said:

"How was it arranged, Joanna?"

Miss Gorringe was watching him. Frisnay was too. His voice was edgy.

Joanna said: "I don't understand—"

"I mean did he want to see Charles, or did Charles invite him over?"

"Oh. It was an invitation, I think. Is it important?"

"No. I just wondered. Look, I'll pick you up in the car, and we'll go on to the Runway Club, and give your father another invitation to be going on with. All right?"

"Yes, all right, Hugo. Everything's fine?"

"Everything," he said, "is dandy."

They said good-bye and he rang off and looked at Frisnay and said: "Gregg's with Moss at the Runway Club. Moss wanted to see him. You heard what I'm doing. Want me to change anything?"

Frisnay said: "No." He looked down, thinking.

He dropped ash off his cigarette. "We're watching Gregg, we're watching Moss. We'll be watching you two. If you happen to look round, don't blow a kiss. It makes people nervous when they know there's an imp on their shoulder."

Bishop left in five minutes, and drove to Sloane Square.

Joanna came down the steps looking fresh in a gray suit and with a wonderful diminutive white hat on the back of her head.

She got in. Bishop said:

"You appear dream-like."

She said gravely: "Hello, darling."

They looked at each other and didn't say anything else until he just put the gears in. She looked away, through the windscreen, clasping her small gloved hands round her knees. He said: "Before I'm pulled-in for being in charge of a horseless-carriage whilst under the influence of dreams or drugs . . . we'll go."

They met traffic up Sloane Street, the beginning of the lunch-hour rush.

"I've got the day off, Hugo."

"To recuperate after dire adventures."

"M'm." She hadn't smiled since she'd come down the steps. As they neared the traffic-lights by Knightsbridge Tube she said: "I like you so much that I can't stick it."

The lights went red-amber to green and he

changed into third and said:

"I've been trying to find the right words all morning. Those are them."

"You mean those are they."

He said: "I mean they'll do."

When they reached the Runway Club he said:

"Will you go and find him, or shall I?"

"Both."

They went up the steps. She said:

"It all looks very plushy."

"Yes, doesn't it." The steward was looking attentive. Bishop told him: "I think Sir Bernard Gregg is here—"

"That's right, sir—with Mr. Moss."

"Would you please tell him that we're here? His daughter, and—"

"Mr. Bishop. Certainly."

He busied himself at the tiny switchboard and said in a moment:

"Did you get your message to Miss Johns all right, sir?"

"Message . . . ? Oh. Yes, I did."

Joanna was looking at him. He smiled non-committally. The steward said suddenly—"Here's Mr. Moss ringing through, same time." He clicked in a lead. He said into the phone: "Desk, sir?"

Bishop heard the faint voice coming over the line.

"Please come up quickly to Mr. Moss's room—"

"Something wrong, Sir Bernard?"

Bishop was watching the man's face. It was soft with surprise.

"Yes—please hurry, there's—"

Gregg broke off. Bishop stood hard down on his feet, wanting to run up the stairs, making himself stay here to listen—

"No—Charles, don't!"

Gregg's voice. Desperate.

Bishop snapped at the steward: "Keep that line open and listen!"

He was going up the stairs three at a time. Joanna was calling something, he didn't hear what. He was in the corridor and hitting the corner-wall to right himself when he heard the shot. It unnerved him and broke his run but he kept on.

The door wasn't locked. He wrenched at the handle and it opened. He reeled in, on momentum.

Sir Bernard was leaning heavily against the table where the telephone was. The phone was still in his hand. He was looking down at Moss. Moss was on the floor. A gun was on the floor a few feet away from him.

Bishop looked at Moss's head, and turned back as he heard Joanna coming. He met her in the doorway and guided her back. She began struggling. He said fiercely:

"He's all right—your father's all right. It was Moss."

"I must see, I must—"

She stared past him with her eyes trying to focus. She saw her father, and screwed up her eyes in the pain of relief. Bishop said: "Go and call an ambulance, quickly."

She left him. Bishop came back into the room. An ambulance wouldn't do anything for Moss, but it had been something to make her go away for.

He looked at Gregg, and Gregg, with his head lifting slowly, looked back at him. His eyes were bright. There were tears in them. He looked an old, broken man.

His voice was old, and broken, and rough with pain.

"Bishop, you were too late."

"Yes. I'm sorry."

He heard the steward in the passage. He turned and met him. "Get the police."

The man said: "Yes, sir," mechanically, and looked at Moss, and went out, shaken.

Gregg was murmuring like a man in a dream. He was trying to say clearly:

"My fault. It was really my fault."

Bishop bent down and looked more closely at Moss, then straightened up. In a moment he said:

"What happened, sir?"

Gregg was staring at nothing. The telephone was still in his hand. He wasn't aware of it, of anything in the room.

"Dear God," he said, his voice stronger, angry. "You'd no right—"

He broke off, and looked suddenly at Bishop.

"All my friends, Bishop. All my friends."

There were people coming along the passage. Bishop turned to the door. A man came in. Bishop recognized him. One of Frisnay's men. He didn't say anything.

Bishop closed the door quietly. The man was noting everything, everything with his eyes, standing perfectly still in the middle of the room, just by the dead man's feet.

In a moment Bishop said:

"Others on their way?"

"Yes, sir."

Sir Bernard was aware at last of the telephone he was holding. He looked down at it, and then put it back on to the contact.

Frisnay came within two minutes. He had been near the Club, before Bishop had come. Moss had asked Gregg here. That was all right, but it might be all wrong.

He looked at Moss. Yes, it was all wrong.

Sir Bernard had turned and was looking out of the window, his hands behind him. He was trying to get the set of his shoulders straight, and he couldn't, yet. It was like an actual, physical weight on him.

Frisnay looked at Bishop. Bishop said:

"I was too late, Freddie." He said it in his teeth, as if every word were an oath.

Frisnay said gently: "Never mind." He looked at Gregg. "Can you tell me what happened, Sir Bernard?"

His voice was perfectly strong now.

"Yes, Inspector." He turned away from the window. Other men came in, one of them with a medical bag. Frisnay looked at the second door, crossed the room, and opened it, and said:

"Let's go in here."

Gregg and Bishop followed him. It was a small bedroom.

As Bishop was closing the door he saw the steward coming back. He said quietly to the steward: "Please get me a neat brandy."

In the bedroom, Sir Bernard said:

"Mr. Moss asked me to see him. I came." He managed to get a brevity in his tone that steadied him. "While we were talking, I asked him if he'd lend me a revolver. He keeps more than one in his luggage. He uses them abroad, when—" he broke off, moving a hand, dismissing detail.

"I thought it might appear cowardly, to ask the police for such a thing. They're doing their best, to protect me. I know that. Moss . . . understood. He brought out that—the gun that's on the floor there, and said he'd clean it for me."

Bishop stood by the door. Frisnay was looking down at his shoes. Gregg stumbled over the rest.

"While he was cleaning it . . . it went off." He looked up slowly at Bishop. "So you see, it was really my fault."

The silence drew out, along their nerves.

Frisnay said:

"It was you who asked him for the use of the gun, sir? Mr. Moss didn't suggest it, first?"

"No. I asked him."

"I wish you'd asked us, sir."

"You've detailed men to guard my life, Inspector. It would have seemed that I couldn't rely on them, or on—"

"We're not so sensitive," Frisnay said drily.

There was a hesitant knock on the door. Bishop opened it. The steward was there. Bishop took the tray and thanked him.

"Brandy, Sir Bernard."

Automatically Gregg's hand was raised to take the glass, but he stopped himself.

"No. But thank you. A kind thought."

Frisnay was making notes.

"What time did you arrive here, sir?"

"I should say about half an hour ago."

"Was Mr. Moss alone?"

"Yes."

"How was his manner? Normal?"

Gregg was having to think. Bishop was watching him think.

He said: "Yes, quite normal."

Bishop knew his answers must tie-up with the accident story.

"Did you see him fetch the gun," Frisnay asked, "from his luggage?"

"Yes. It was in this room." He moved a hand. "In that case."

Frisnay nodded. Gregg said: "He loaded it for me, and as he was cleaning it—"

"It went off?" asked Frisnay.

Gregg nodded. "Yes."

Bishop was looking at Frisnay. He said:

"Sir Bernard, before you say any more . . . "

Gregg looked at him.

"What?" He looked confused.

"I ought to give my evidence, now. And it's going to conflict with yours. Isn't it?"

"I—don't follow."

Frisnay said in a matter-of-fact tone: "Well, sir, you've just told me that Mr. Moss loaded the gun and then began cleaning it." He looked steadily at Gregg. "A man like Mr. Moss wouldn't do that. And you can't really clean a gun when it's loaded. Not all of it, or even properly. So Mr.

Bishop feels we might all help each other out, and . . ." He snapped a sharp look at Bishop and said: "Well?"

Bishop said, "I know I wasn't in the room, so that I can't give any visual evidence. But I arrived here with Miss Gregg, about ten minutes ago, and I asked the steward to phone this room, telling Sir Bernard we were here. Before he could deliver the message, he found himself connected with this room. Someone had just put a call through to the desk. It was apparently Sir Bernard."

Gregg watched him, a little wearily.

"It was 'apparently'?" murmured Frisnay.

"I mean it was Sir Bernard's voice I heard on the phone. I assume—I can't do more—that he had picked up the phone to make the call."

"Go on, Hugo."

"His voice was faint but quite clear. It's a very short line. He asked the steward to come up quickly to this room. The man asked if there were any trouble. I heard Sir Bernard say, yes, there was. He sounded desperate. Then he called out to someone in here. He called: 'No—Charles, don't!' I told the steward to keep on the line, and ran up here. As I got to the top of the stairs, at the other end of the passage, I heard a single gun-shot. I ran along to this suite and came in. The door wasn't locked."

Frisnay was making notes again. Gregg was sitting quietly on the bed, holding his knees, staring at the floor. He looked ill.

Bishop said: "When I got here, Sir Bernard was leaning against the table, with the receiver in his hand. Moss was on the floor, and the gun was where you saw it. I didn't see anything of anyone else."

Gregg began speaking. "Inspector Frisnay, I—"

"Just one moment, sir."

Frisnay went into the larger room and told one of his men to fetch the steward. The steward came in a few seconds; he had been hovering in the passage. Frisnay got him into the bedroom and shut the door and said:

"Will you please tell me what happened when Mr. Bishop asked you to phone this suite?"

The steward was still shaken. He was a youngish man with a thin English face. He said:

"There was a call came through, sir, from up here, just when I was on the switchboard. It was Sir Bernard. He told me to come up quick, as there was trouble. Then Mr. Bishop run up the stairs, and—"

"Hold on. What were the actual words Sir Bernard used, as far as you can remember them?"

"Oh." He looked quickly to Gregg, then back to Frisnay. "He said something like—'No, Charles, no'. Then, after Mr. Bishop had gone, he shouted out—'put it down, you fool'. Then I heard the shot. I come up right away, after Mr. Bishop and Miss Gregg."

He stopped, and tried not to look at Gregg, and had to look at him. More quietly he said: "I'm sorry I wasn't quicker, Sir Bernard."

Distantly: "I'm sure you did your best."

Frisnay sent the steward out, and when the door was shut he said to Gregg:

"Well, sir?"

"I—think that should give you the truth, Inspector."

"You don't want to contest any of this other evidence you've heard?"

"No. It's quite so."

"Did Mr. Moss shoot himself, deliberately?"

Quietly: "Yes."

"You tried to stop him, sir?"

"Yes."

"Did you realize that the steward downstairs— and Mr. Bishop too, as it happened—might have heard what went on, over the telephone?"

"No. But I suppose I'm glad, to be able to keep to the truth, although I'd hoped to keep the stigma of suicide from my friend's name. An old, out-worn consideration, perhaps."

Frisnay sat down on the bedside-chair and said in a resigned tone:

"What actually happened, Sir Bernard?"

On a long breath Gregg said: "When I called here, at the invitation of Mr. Moss, I found him depressed. I thought it was the inaction he was going through—his leg still in plaster—an active man. He—had been drinking. Not a great deal, perhaps, but in a short time."

The silence went on. Frisnay didn't break it.

"He told me he had decided to end it. This—burden we've all been carrying. There was an argument. He suggested we should hand over the vital secret to the authorities—as indeed we had suggested before, between ourselves, the night Parish was found dead."

Bishop leaned against the door. Behind its thin panel he could hear men moving about in the sitting-room, with their equipment. Prints, photographs, measurements were being made.

Gregg's voice came heavily.

"I agreed with him—I gave in, seeing the mood he was in. Then I realized, when he fetched the gun, that I'd said the wrong thing. He told me I was soothing him, placating him, treating him as a child, or a coward. I didn't think he had the guts—and those were his words—to bear the secret any longer. I argued with him again—difficult to know which point to argue, in that frame of mind—and he became defiant."

In a moment Frisnay said: "Defiant, sir?"

Gregg nodded.

"He said he was damned if they'd get it out of him, as late as this. He said . . . he'd make certain they didn't. He had the gun in his hand. I decided I couldn't talk him out of it. I got hold of the telephone to call for help, and he moved the safety-catch of the revolver. I—cried out for help, as you have heard from other witnesses. Moss . . . put the gun to his head. I tried to jerk his arm down, but he—fired."

Second followed second. Bishop was watching the clock on the book-shelf. The hand swept silently round, drawing the minutes away. It was electric. It didn't tick. It seemed the more relentless, for that.

"I'm afraid I sound rather garbled, Inspector. I'll be more able, later, to—"

"No, sir, it's quite clear, in the main. When Mr. Moss said 'they' wouldn't get the secret from him, who did he mean?"

"We don't know, do we? But it seems that someone is trying to get at it, very desperately."

Frisnay took a brief turn round the room.

"When you got hold of the telephone, sir, was it to save Mr. Moss? Or only partly?"

Gregg gave a slow smile that hurt.

"You see the situation clearly, even though you weren't in the room. It was to save myself, as well. For a moment, as he took up the gun, and released the safety-catch, I admit I thought he was going to kill both of us, and safeguard the secret completely."

Frisnay nodded.

"He might have had it in mind, sir. And might have changed his mind. You weren't in a very good position."

He closed his note-book. Bishop looked at him and said:

"Miss Gregg's downstairs, in my car. Can Sir Bernard come with us now?"

"Yes."

Bishop looked at Gregg. "We were going to have lunch, the three of us, Sir Bernard. But now I'll drive you home."

Gregg was brooding, looking at neither of them. He was thinking of his friends. He didn't want to go back through the room where the last of them lay dead. He didn't want to do anything. Everything was cold, numb, over.

Bishop touched his arm gently.

"Sooner the better," he said.

They went down to the car. Frisnay stayed behind, looking round the main room.

He thought: suicide, in front of four witnesses. And we're looking for something else.

One of his men dropped a cushion, as he worked over the furniture.

Frisnay snapped: "For Pete's sake, you'll smother any prints in dust."

The man was nearing the wide stone steps. He had a top-coat on, though the day was warm. He was walking very steadily, and not turning his head to look at anyone. Above the wide steps there was the name of the hospital, in huge carved letters. He did not look up at it.

He reached the first step, and a man who was standing at the top looked down at him, and did not look away.

They met, at the top. The first one turned and ran, suddenly, and the other went after him. The first one was flinging open the door of a small car. He got in and banged the starter home. The door swung shut as he jerked into gear. The other man stopped, and raised one hand. A large black saloon pulled out from across the street. Its tires left soft gray marks on the surface of the road.

A bus hooted and slewed to a halt. The black car swerved once, righted, then drove down the crown of the road and turned, heeling against the springs as a man jumped out and lurched on his feet to match the speed. The small grey car had hit the pavement. People were trying to get out of the way, along the pavement. A woman cried out. The bus was waiting, with the driver craning round from his cab to see what was happening.

The man was trying to get out of the grey car, which had cocked half-across the pavement on impact. The man from the black car helped him out, and opened the door of the black car and pushed him inside. It drove off quietly. Some other men stayed by the grey car, and began straightening the wheels, pushing it neatly back into the kerb, as if it had just been parked there.

The bus started off again. Everyone asked questions. Nobody really knew.

In the little room above the great stone letters that said the name of the hospital, the woman was crying, and calling out vicious things, calling out that she loved him. She loved the man they'd taken, down there.

She had heard the shrill of the tyres, the voices, the running footsteps, heard them through her high window.

She cried out a lot, that she hated everyone, and loved the man.

Frisnay said into the telephone:

"They picked up Max Corbyn, five minutes ago."

Bishop stroked his cat. She sat on his desk.

"Good," He said into the telephone.

"He was trying to see Johns. They stopped him as he was going up the steps of the hospital. Tried to get clear in a car."

"Fool, not using his feet."

Frisnay said: "They always think a car's quicker."

"When d'you grill him, Freddie?"

"Any time. I'll let you know what we find."

"Anything on the Runway Club shooting?"

"Only physical evidence supporting Sir Bernard's, and yours, and the steward's, and Miss Gregg's. His own prints are on the phone-receiver. Moss's prints are on the gun. The gun was fired at almost zero-range. Powder-marks."

The Siamese stared at Bishop with huge eyes. She was listening to the tiny man shouting in the black shape of the telephone. It always interested her.

Bishop said to the tiny trapped man:

"So this time it's really suicide."

"In front of four witnesses, more or less."

Bishop looked at the chess-board. He said in a moment:

"Freddie, I've been getting odd ideas, since this morning. With Scobie, Taplow, Parish there was the possibility of murder. You admit that much. A possibility. But now we've got four witnesses to a suicide, and physical evidence supporting

311

those witnesses. All we haven't got is the negative evidence."

Frisnay asked: "What?"

"The negative evidence that nobody else was
there. The shadow-man wasn't there. The one
on the train, the one at Taplow's house, on Parish's fire-escape—"

"All right," Frisnay grunted. "He wasn't there.
We don't expect him to be. This is suicide."

"But let's make dead certain, shall we Freddie?"

"What the hell are you talking about?"

"Listen." His tone had gone very crisp and
clean. "We can't be quite certain the shadow-
man wasn't there at the Runway Club this morning, just because nobody saw him this time. Do
something for me. Only a little thing."

"Well?"

"Has the *outside* door-handle of Moss's room
been checked for prints?"

"No. There's no purpose."

"But have it done, would you, just for me?"

"Look here," said Frisnay irritably, "we've got
enough to do, without—"

"Freddie, do I ever waste your time for my own
amusement?"

Frisnay sighed. He said: "We'll do it."

"I appreciate that. Will you let me know what
you find?"

"You think we'll find anything interesting?"

"Yes. I think he was there, again, this morning, in broad daylight, at the Runway Club, killing Moss. And that's the one we really want to find. The shadow of death."

"Oh, for God's sake, Hugo, why can't you go and buy a Yankee Comic and get your fun that way?"

He rang off. He wasn't furious with Bishop. He was furious with Frisnay, for doing almost anything Bishop wanted, sensible or silly. It was a hell of a spot for a big grown man to be in.

Bishop put down the telephone. Miss Gorringe said from across the room:

"What's broken, Hugo?"

"They've picked up Max Corbyn."

"That's very nice," said Miss Gorringe.

After thinking about it for a minute or two he said:

"Yes."

She watched him. She said: "You don't sound very happy about it."

"About Corbyn's arrest? Oh, it'll help us to see things a bit straighter, once he's been grilled. But he doesn't close the case."

"Then who does? Christine's in. Corbyn's in. The police are watching Jackson and Bell—"

"That was the situation a few hours ago when Charles Moss died. He still died."

"Corbyn wasn't in, then."

"Corbyn was too busy keeping out of our way."

"He was free, at large, in London. You've told Freddie you believe the shadow-man was there at the Runway Club. Couldn't it have been Corbyn?"

"It could." He filled his *meerschaum,* with quick-moving restless fingers, prodding the tobacco in too tightly. "But it wasn't. If those four men were murdered, even directly, by Corbyn, what would his motive have been?"

"To get at the secret. We know he was after it."

He nodded and got up, striking a match. He said:

"Exactly, Gorry. That would have been his motive. We know he wants the secret: he even asked Joanna for it. I don't think Corbyn is the shadow, because I don't think the shadow wants the secret."

Miss Gorringe blinked. She said:

"That's quite a switch of thought."

"Yes, and it's turned on the light, for me." He came over and perched on the corner of her desk. She moved her pot of ink. He said: "I've gone over this whole thing a lot of times in my mind, and every time I hit a brick wall. Now I've twisted the situation right round to the reverse. Look at it from the angle that whatever motive there was for those men's deaths, it wasn't to get at the secret. Assuming those deaths were murder—indirect murder, because Moss was directly a suicide—I believe they were made by the shadow-man. And I believe he's known the big secret from the start."

"But how in God's name—"

He said: "Listen." He put his hand down flat on her desk and looked at her steadily. "There were five men who found it. Two years ago. How many people do five men talk to, in two years? Hundreds? Thousands? I think that one of those people learned the secret, or in some way came by chance to learn it, perhaps not even realising what it was, how vitally important it was—until a few weeks ago."

He slid off the desk and walked about. Miss Gorringe stared at the smoke he had left in the air.

She said: "And as soon as he realized what he'd got in his hands, he began taking steps to make it his exclusive property?"

He came back to her. He said:

"Exclusive of Scobie, Taplow, Parish, Moss, Sir Bernard Gregg." His voice went low, and he brought out each word very clearly. "If Gregg dies now, the secret is the shadow-man's, alone, for good."

Miss Gorringe said: "I can't switch my mind

round, yet. Doesn't anything stick out from the original pattern? Surely if the—"

"Nothing sticks out, Gorry. I've thought about it, for hours now. Nothing sticks out of the original pattern. All that's happened is that the brick wall's come down. I'm not hitting it any more. With this theory, everything fits."

Frowning she said: "Sir Bernard told me that this secret's of vital concern to the whole world—"

"So that one man, with this thing in his hands alone, could become the most important man in the world . . . Wouldn't that be his motive for murder?"

She sat there trying not to be impressed, but she was impressed. Things began fitting, now. It was absurd, melodramatic, unthinkable, but it looked so right.

She said: "There have been lesser ones, Hugo. And a motive like that could still fit Max Corbyn."

Bishop shook his head slowly, this time with real conviction.

"No, not Corbyn. He's too small. The man we want is big, as big as the secret, a man with a brain, with vision, with the ability to see himself standing astride the globe like a Colossus—"

"Oh, for—"

"All right—it's comic-strip stuff, it's a great big gaudy balloon to play with. But get me a pin, and pop it. I don't think you can. Gorry darling, we're upsides with an unusual person. A person who murders four men is unusual. He is a megalomaniac. We're up against a megalomaniac. Try to wind the mind round the character. It'll help you to see the rest."

She got up and crossed the room, walking slowly with her arms folded. She didn't like this new idea. It was too big, and too bright. It smelled of speciousness. Yes, it was a big balloon. But she couldn't find a pin. There was nothing she could think of, in the whole pattern of these deaths, that could bring down the new theory, and pop it.

She swung around and looked at Bishop.

"All right, our man's as big as the whole world. And still too small for us to see him. Let's bring a paradox into it and really bite the carpet."

Gently he pressed his tobacco down and took another match.

"No, I've seen him, once. He's quite ornery-sized. About as big as a man. He was on the fire-escape, at Park Mansions. Other people have seen him, talking to Scobie on the train. He was described as a man. Jackson heard Dr. Taplow talk to him when he was on the telephone. So he's a man with ears. And he's a man with gloves. Imitation pigskin gloves that left prints at Grey Gates, prints in Park Mansions—"

He shrugged as the telephone rang.

"He's an ordinary man, Gorry. So we can get him. He's not got up in zip-fastened ectoplasm or anything ga-ga."

He took the receiver. "Yes?"

Frisnay said: "There's another bit of information that's come in, Hugo."

Bishop said: "Yes, Freddie?"

"We covered Sir Bernard's study for prints, after it was searched in his absence last night. I've just asked for any results. They found prints. The usual. Gloves."

Slowly Bishop said: "The imitation pigskin gloves?"

Miss Gorringe watched him. She sat down again at her desk. She was worried. She still couldn't get her mind round to the new angle. It fitted too beautifully, and was therefore suspect.

"Yes," Frisnay said. "There's no mistake."

Bishop stared at nothing, holding the phone drawing on smoke, exhaling it, thinking. Frisnay said:

"Hello?"

Bishop stared vaguely: "Hello, sweetheart." His tone sharpened. "Listen, Gorry and I are working on something new. A new angle. It fits so well it worries us. But if we're right it means there'll be another death—another killing—Sir Bernard

Gregg's—unless we do everything in our power to stop it."

"But—"

"His life's been in danger ever since Scobie pitched out of that train, but he's never been nearer death than he is now."

Bored-voiced Frisnay said, "We're working on those lines, Hugo. We have been for a long time. There are men watching Gregg's house, and men inside it, men watching the hospital where he works, men trailing him whenever he makes a move. Sir Bernard Gregg has got more body-guards than a visiting president."

Bishop said: "Fine. But Charles Moss was under surveillance this morning. And there were powder-marks."

"We're doing all we can," Frisnay said sharply.

"Don't let me get your hackles up, Freddie. I'm just thinking aloud."

"Then fit a baffle. That's my information—the gloves. Be seeing you."

Bishop didn't have time to say good-bye. Frisnay had rung off.

"As I was saying, Gorry." He sat down at his desk, and fumbled for a match. "Our man wears pigskin gloves. He was wearing them when he searched Gregg's study at nine o'clock last night."

Miss Gorringe drew a breath.

She said, "I'm beginning not to catch up. Things go too fast. What was the study searched for? The secret. But it was the shadow-man who searched the study, because of the glove-prints. And we say the shadow-man *knows* that secret, already. So I feel slightly dizzy."

"Was he *searching* the study? Try that one."

"I can't." She stared at her telephone, wishing it would ring, or explode, or something. Anything would do. Her mind was circling, unscrewing her head at the base.

Bishop said gently, "I'll try it for you. He might simply have been waiting, in the study, for Gregg to come in. While he waited, he picked things up, put things down, looked at some books—a nervous man, right on the brink of his nerves because he was going to make another killing."

In a minute Miss Gorringe said: "He wasn't searching for anything. He was waiting for Sir Bernard to come in. Waiting to kill him." She said it all slowly, getting it right in her mind.

"Why not? Moss was the fourth to die, but it could have been Gregg—does the order make any difference? These deaths have been planned in the order of opportunity.... And last night, the shadow-man missed it, because it was Miss Gorringe who brought Sir Bernard home by car. Very well, he turned his attention to Moss. And Moss is dead."

"Suicide," she said helplessly. "Witnesses."

"Murder," he said, obstinately. "Foul, subtle, remote-controlled murder. Let's not make any mistake about that."

He got up, restlessly. She watched him. He was odd, on edge. She said quietly:

"Hugo, you're running a high mental temperature. Why?"

He said tightly: "Listen. I've got nerves. It's getting on them, this thing. Personally. I telephoned Taplow, fifteen minutes before he was bitten to death. I rang Parish's doorbell, and heard the poison-glass fall from his hand and smash on the floor. I called at the Runway Club and heard the sound of the bullet that ploughed into Moss's brain."

He stood quite still in the middle of the room. "Even the first of them, Scobie, had a place here at our table, the night after he was mangled on the lines at Henford Tunnel. Every time, Gorry, I've been in at the death. And this time I can smell it coming. It's coming for the last of them. Gregg—"

"Better keep away from him then."

Her nerves had gone into her voice. "Better not ring his bell. Had you?"

He said: "And that's the frightening thing. Because I've got to see him, talk to him, get him to help me work this out and find the shadow-man, before the shadow-man finds him, at home this time, and wide open to the kill."

His voice seemed to leave ugly echoes in the room.

Miss Gorringe said: "Then I don't know. I can't think it out straight."

"If I could, I'd be very happy. As it is, I'm scared about Gregg. He wanted to tell me something— maybe the big secret—last night. He called here, perhaps for that. Today, you and Freddie and I decided that I should try talking to him. We fixed up a lunch, with Joanna, to pave the way. We got badly tripped. The fourth green bottle came down off the wall."

He moved across to her desk, and picked up the telephone.

She said: "Are you going to ring him now?"

"No." He dialled Gregg's number. "I'm ringing Joanna. She's still in danger, too."

He waited, listening to the soft burr-burr.

Miss Gorringe said: "Well, Hugo, it's your move. I don't envy you."

"I don't envy anyone, tonight."

The ringing-tone went on. It pulsed in his stomach. He said: "I want you to look after Jo-anna, just until we've got the man we want, dead or alive."

"She'll be coming here?"

He nodded, looking down at her.

"Yes. Can you do it?"

"Of course. If anyone can."

The ringing-tone stopped. The line opened. He took a breath. Voice said: "Hello?"

He said: "Joanna? Hugo. How are you?"

"All right, I think."

"Why only 'think'?"

She laughed softly, forcing it. "I get butterflies in my stomach, when the phone rings."

He said: "Don't we all. Would you like to come over here, and stay for a meal this evening?"

"Love to. But it doesn't sound a casual invitation. Is anything wrong again, so soon?"

"No. Nothing. But things are getting a fraction tricky. Can you get here without anyone knowing where you've gone?"

She tried to sound easy-voiced. She didn't.

"Yes, I should think so. My father's at his laboratory. Mrs. Cobb's here, but I won't tell her where I'm going."

"Don't tell a soul. The police will be on your tail, in any case, but make sure no one else is. Take a couple of taxis, dodge about a bit—you know?"

"All right."

"I'd pick you up myself, but it'll make things more conspicuous."

"Yes, of course." She had steadied. He admired her clear steady voice. "Shall I come now?"

"If you can. And don't worry about this. We're merely taking rather absurd precautions, because we all love you."

For a moment the line was silent, then she said:

"I'll—be there soon. Good-bye, darling."

When he had put down the receiver he looked at Miss Gorringe and said:

"That's all right. She's on her way. Just make her feel at home."

He went to the door.

"Where are you going, Hugo?"

"See Freddie. Back in thirty minutes, unless I phone. Check?"

"Check."

She stared at the closed door.

There was a late sparrow on Frisnay's window-sill. He was watching it. He could think very well, looking at sparrows. They were always on the move. He got his thoughts geared to small movement. Some people watched tropical fish, but he watched sparrows. He didn't like anything without any legs, like fish or black mambas, and they wouldn't have let him move in a tank full of fish, to his office. Sparrows had two legs, and were natural.

Bishop was striking a match again. He had

struck three, so far, in here. He had been here three minutes.

"So you couldn't trip Corbyn," he said.

"No."

The sparrow flew off. Frisnay thought about Corbyn.

He added: "I think he was telling most of the truth."

"And he's not our man."

Bishop got his tobacco alight at last.

"If you mean our theoretical killer, no. Corbyn's got two unquestionable alibis at the times when Scobie and Taplow died. We've checked up. They're cast-iron. I think he's like the Johns woman."

Bishop watched him.

"You mean they realized someone was after the big secret in a big way—"

"And tried to beat him to it."

Frisnay span his chair round and put his hands on the desk, watching them. He moved his fingers all the time, turning the nails to catch the light. Soon it would be dusk. The window was a flush of pink, catching reflected sunset.

He said in a moment: "Same goes for Jackson, possibly for Bell. A lot of people suddenly got interested in the 1952 expedition, because the names of the five men became linked after Taplow—the second of them—was found dead."

Bishop began to interrupt, then stopped. Frisnay was only halfway through.

"Different people might have been responsible for different things, Hugo. The murderer, if one exists, might not have sent those threatening notes to Gregg, Parish and Moss. We know he didn't abduct Joanna."

"But we know he searched Gregg's study, or waited in that room for Gregg to come in, waited there to kill him. Because he left the glove-prints."

After a time Frisnay glanced up and said:

"Waited to kill Gregg? I see."

"It fits in with our new idea, Freddie. If the man has already learned the secret, he could be killing off the rest. To keep it for himself. It's a bigger motive. It's even more plausible."

"It's damned plausible. But so are a lot of other theories. We've checked on all of them, with what facts we've been able to screw out of people like Johns and Corbyn. So far, we seem to have cleared up a whole gang of suspects, big and small. Johns and Corbyn were heavily involved. The woman was working through Moss, and through Corbyn, trying to get at the secret. Corbyn was working alone—or trying to. The only suspect we haven't roped in is your shadow, the man who's been seen or heard near the scene of every death—except the one at the Runway Club this morning."

Bishop tilted his head.

He said: "You told me you'd check on that for me. The door-handle on the outside of the suite."

Frisnay nodded.

"We are. We'll get a report any time."

"Any time. You don't think it's important, worth hurrying?"

"It'll come under routine findings. There's no rush-tag. I'll phone through, before you leave here. We should get it by then. Don't rattle me."

Bishop said gently: "My object is to be of some slight help."

Frisnay gazed at him wooden-faced.

"And don't mistake my tone. I've just been sitting down on a long murderous job and I've been kicked so hard behind by those above me and chiefly by myself that I'm smarting."

"Some jobs are like that." Bishop spoke very evenly. He was a free-lance. He didn't have pressure put on him. Frisnay did. "I left Gorry swinging on the chandelier, out of her mind. Gorry is a very straight thinker, but she's foxed now. So am I. So are you."

"All right, I'm a really good boy after all and we all forgive each other like—"

"Let's shut up," said Bishop.

There was silence. They finally gave each other a slow twisted smile.

"The trouble with you," Frisnay said, "is that

you're worried to death about what's going to happen to Gregg."

"Because he's the last of them—"

"Because he's that. But look, if we took more precautions than we have, we'd need to put a couple of boys in his coat-pockets. Just try to relax, about Gregg."

"All right."

"And stop worrying about Joanna, too. I know she's a sweet little example of all that's—"

"Yes," Bishop said amiably.

"And you've got her nicely cooped-up in your fortress, with Miss Gorringe feeding her sedatives—"

"You've been quick—"

"So has she. She was at your place within five minutes of your leaving it. When people move about, we've practically got red lights floating across our wall-map. Relax, if you'll be so kind."

Bishop said: "All right. Everyone's as safe as houses. Why not just find out if we can get the report?"

"What report?"

"The door-handle. That worries me more than—"

Frisnay picked up an inter-phone and asked for Prints.

They told him the report was on its way up.

He put down the phone and said:

"It's coming. You have some other place for that bee to go, now your bonnet's becoming vacant?"

Bishop got up and sprinkled a lot of ash from his pipe into the ash-tray on Frisnay's desk, and felt for his tobacco-pouch.

Frisnay looked at his ash-tray reflectively. He said:

"I haven't any pipe-cleaners."

"I don't want any." He filled his pipe. "What time are you going home tonight, Freddie?"

"I don't know. I haven't thought about it."

"You don't want to go. Do you? You're just about as nervy as I am, until something fails to happen to Gregg."

Frisnay swore lightly and added: "Leave Gregg out of it."

Someone knocked at the outer door and he said: "Come in," with a tone of voice that he would have used for "Get out."

Flack came in.

"My God," said Frisnay, "I thought you'd gone home."

"No, sir."

He put a narrow typed report on the desk. Frisnay looked at it without moving in his chair, without touching the slip of paper.

Bishop said to the sergeant: "How's Mrs. Flack?"

"Lovely, sir."

Frisnay looked up at Bishop as if he hadn't realized he was in the room at all, or as if he didn't know who he was. He said:

"The report says that your finger-prints were found on the outside door-handle of Moss's suite at the Runway Club. That would be when you opened the door, after you heard the shot."

He looked down again at the slip of paper.

"It also says that there's another trace, about a square millimeter of which is hard-clear. After patching up with other positives, the result is conclusive. It's the pigskin glove."

Flack was looking stonily at his chief. Bishop struck another match, and said:

"Yes, that's right."

Frisnay was staring at him. He said: "How the hell did you know?"

"I didn't. If I'd known, I shouldn't have troubled you with making the test. I only suspected. Freddie, I can tell you now where you'll find some more of those prints. Good ones, recent ones. They should be on the inside door-handle of my car, down below in the yard. Nearside rear door. Shall we try it?"

Frisnay got up and looked at Flack and said: "Bring a kit."

He went out. Frisnay said to Bishop: "What have you been keeping back? Real evidence?"

Their voices had gone very serious.

"No. This is the only real evidence. If we get confirmation with this test, we can crack the rest of it cold."

They went down to the yard. The gray Rolls-Royce was facing towards Whitehall. Flack came down soon after they reached there. He had a kit.

Bishop opened the nearside rear door of the car, and Flack put his kit down on to the running-board.

Frisnay stood with his hands behind him. He said:

"Need a lamp."

"Got one, sir."

Bishop got down on his haunches, watching. Flack handed positives to Frisnay for comparison, then dusted the door-handle neatly. Smudges came up. He gave Frisnay the glass. Frisnay used it, for two or three minutes. He didn't say anything.

"All right?" said Bishop.

Frisnay straightened up. They waited while Flack took four or five flash-shots from different angles. Finally Frisnay said to Bishop:

"Try it yourself, with the glass."

Bishop spent only a few seconds. He wasn't an expert. He relied on their word. He said:

"It looks like the glove, doesn't it Freddie?"

"Yes. It wouldn't convict, but it convinces. Flack—get that stuff rushed through."

As Bishop straightened up, Frisnay said to him: "Well?"

Bishop said, "I'd like to phone." He was looking pale.

Inside the building they gave him a direct line. When the ringing stopped, it was Miss Gorringe's voice.

She scarcely recognised his.

He said:

"This is Hugo. Is Joanna there?"

"Yes. You want to—"

"No. Gorry, when you feel like it, start dinner without waiting for me. I'll be a little delayed."

"All right, Hugo." The tone of her voice was trying to ask what had happened. She thought something bad had happened. It was in his voice. But Joanna must have been in the room. It would worry her, if she overheard anything like that.

Bishop said: "And Gorry, open a good bottle. Take the edge off her mind, just a little. Just a slight anesthetic."

Tightly Miss Gorringe said: "Yes, Hugo. Fine."

"There'll be bad news, I think. I'll leave her to you. She's perfectly safe. No one will come."

They said good-bye and he rang off. Frisnay was standing near him. Bishop dialled through to the house in Sloane Square.

Mrs. Cobb answered.

Bishop said: "Is Sir Bernard there, Mrs. Cobb?"

"No, sir, he's still down at the hospital, as far as I know."

"I see. Thank you."

"Is there any—"

"No," he said, "no message. Good night."

He said to Frisnay: "Gregg is still at the hospital. Let's go there."

Outside, Frisnay said: "Use your car?"

"Yes. There's no special hurry, as far as I can see." He got in and started the engine, turning on side-lights. "But we won't waste any time."

The grey car pulled up outside the hospital. Frisnay got out. Bishop switched off the engine and left the side-lights on. He didn't lock the doors.

They walked up the steps.

There was a new porter, starting the night-shift.

Frisnay said to him: "Sir Bernard Gregg is still here?"

The porter glanced across at a man who was standing near the swing-doors. The man nodded. The porter looked back to Frisnay and said:

"Yes, sir."

"We'd like to see him." He showed his card. As the porter took them down the passage, Bishop murmured:

"Is that the only man you've got? By the doors?"

"No. Another one down here. Why?"

"Doesn't matter. We don't need this chap."

Frisnay caught up with the porter and said:

"That's all right, we know our way now."

The porter hesitated, then went back along the passage. Down at the bottom of the steps was another man. He was the one who had been in the Greggs' house, last night.

They stopped. Frisnay said quietly:

"All right, Blake?"

"Yes, sir."

Frisnay looked at Bishop and said very softly:

"What kind of a wrong tree are you barking up?"

Bishop said: "Let's go into the lab."

Frisnay knocked. There was no answer, so he pushed open one of the double-doors and went inside. Bishop followed him. The door swung shut behind them.

The laboratory was bright. Every lamp was burning. It looked clean and gleaming, and quiet, and empty. There was no one down here except for Sir Bernard. He was sitting on one of the high stools along the end of the nearer bench, where there was a desk, and filing-cabinets.

As Frisnay and Bishop walked down alongside the bench their footsteps echoed drily across the big room. Gregg heard them. He looked up.

He wasn't doing anything. He was sitting on the stool, with a small note-book in his hand. He dropped the notebook on to the sloping desk and said:

"Good evening, gentlemen."

Frisnay stopped.

"I'm sorry to disturb you, Sir Bernard."

He thought Gregg looked ill. He looked as he had looked this morning, in the Runway Club.

He said: "You're not disturbing me, Inspector." He waved a vague hand, "If you'd like to sit down—only the stools I'm afraid." His voice trailed off.

Bishop was watching him through a mental microscope. Gregg's fine eyes were blank. Dull, dead, blank.

"I've finished my work," he said. His voice was like that, too. A slow record.

Bishop looked at the bench, the equipment, the charts, instruments, graphs, specimens, slides. He looked back at Gregg.

"You've—finished your work, sir?"

"Yes. The major part of it." His voice rambled over the words as if he'd been reading them over and again for a long time, until they meant nothing, but had to be said. "Someone else can tidy up the loose ends. I'm too tired."

Bishop said quietly: "It's been a long time."

"M'm? Ten years, yes. Fifteen. I don't know when I started, really. Cancer's a big problem. I've not found the cure, but I think I've found a clue."

Frisnay was perching on one of the stools, looking down at his shoes. Bishop stood where he was, just by the bench.

He said: "That's going to help a lot of people."

"Yes, it'll help. I'm tired, but happy."

He lifted his white hands and pressed the fingers together, looking at them. It was impossible to imagine what he was thinking about, even what he was really looking at. Not his brilliant white hands.

"And the other problem," Bishop said steadily.

Frisnay was looking up at Gregg now. He wasn't sure why they had come here to see Gregg, but Bishop had some idea. Better to wait. Gregg was all right, looked sick, but not in danger.

Bishop said: "The other problem, about how to keep the big secret. That's finished, too?"

Gregg looked up from his hands. In a moment he nodded.

"Yes. That one's left me just as tired, but not happy. I'm satisfied, but I'm sad."

"And you're dying."

Frisnay flicked a glance at Bishop. The few words went on echoing in the big bright room.

Sir Bernard said: "Yes, Bishop, I'm dying. And you want to ask me a lot of questions. I'm sorry, there isn't time, now. I was going to see you, later this evening, but you've come to see me, instead, and I'm caught on the wrong foot."

He gave an odd dry laugh, a drunken man's laugh, but he was sober, and dying.

Bishop was trying not to think about Joanna.

He said: "We want to ask things, sir. We have to—"

"There's no time—"

"Otherwise people might be blamed, or suspected. You'll cause a lot of needless trouble, and pain—"

"Very well."

The old man tried to take a grip on himself, on his voice. "Be quick, Bishop. Please be—"

Bishop said: "You killed Scobie, Taplow, Parish, Moss."

Frisnay's hand froze and then pulled out a note-book.

Bishop said: "To make sure they'd never give up the information."

Gregg's lips moved feebly. The word scarcely left his throat.

"Yes."

But he was still trying to rally, to help them.

As quickly as he could, Bishop said: "Three years ago, in the Antarctic, the five of you swore to tell no one, ever. You came back, time passed, you began to think, rightly or wrongly, that the secret wasn't safe anymore."

He stopped as Gregg moved, putting one arm along the bench to steady himself. His face was bloodless.

Bishop said: "Scobie was running into financial difficulties and was desperately worried—you must tell me if I go wrong, sir—and he could have sold the secret for a million, to the first bidder. Big temptation for any man, so you caught the same train as he did, that night, instead of coming down here as you said. And you pushed him through the door of the train. He died bewildered, with your check in his pocket to prove how you'd tried to save him—get it all down, Freddie, time's short—"

"Don't worry—"

"Sir Bernard, you saw that Taplow was suffering under the strain of keeping silent. He was heading for a nervous break-down, during which he might have revealed the secret, even in delirium."

Gregg had closed his eyes. His head was still erect. There was still strength left but Bishop watched him hard.

"You looked round his snake-house on the night he died—got him to show you round, as he'd done often before. You slipped the catch of the mamba's den, when Taplow's back was turned. He died later that night—"

"Yes, yes, that's what happened—quickly Bishop—"

Frisnay's pencil grated in the second's silence.

"You sent those notes to yourself, Parish, Moss, partly to divert suspicion, partly to get their reaction. You invited them to a conference—and found Parish scared, and Moss indifferent. Parish had already put in the advertisement—*who wants the secret of the snows?*—that appeared the next day. You didn't know he'd done that but you knew how scared he was. So you called on him, soon after he'd left your house and gone home, and you had a drink together. His was poisoned."

Gregg had not opened his eyes. There was a pulse-beat throbbing in his blue-veined temple. Bishop thought that if the man slumped, he'd hit the bench, and not the floor. He also thought that it wouldn't make any difference where he fell.

"Please hurry." The words came out of a ghost.

"When I broke into that room, you were in the big cupboard. When I left the room to phone the police, you came out to the passage and made for the fire-escape through an emergency door. You left behind you the scene of a suicide, in a room locked from the inside, with no one there but Parish, at the time when I broke in."

He moved slowly closer to the man on the stool. It wouldn't make any difference if he fell, but he didn't want to see him fall, without anyone to help.

"Moss had to die because he'd become indifferent, and because Christine Johns was trying to get the secret out of him—and Moss was an adventurer, as weak as only a strong man can be, with women. You went there for a gun, to protect yourself with, and when it was in your hand you picked up the telephone and told the steward to come quickly—then you began shouting to Moss, telling him not to do it—he didn't know what you meant, thought you'd gone mad for a minute—and as he got out of his chair you shot him at close range and wiped the gun and clamped his fingers round it before you let it fall on to the floor beside him. You took the phone again and were holding it when I came in. You looked grief-stricken, dazed. You were. He was your friend, but you'd had to do it, and you bore witness, with three others, to a suicide so obvious that you could safely pretend, for a few minutes, that it had been an accident—for the sake of your friend's good name. The secret was safe, at last. But the problem remained. Didn't it?"

Gregg opened his eyes. Frisnay was watching him.

Bishop was pale. There were a lot of things he'd rather do, than this.

"It followed naturally," he said as gently and as quickly as he could, "once I realized you'd been driving yourself so relentlessly with this cancer-research that your mind became prey to fantasy—to the obsession that one man could save the world, and that the man was you—"

"But I was right—I was right—"

His voice, his eyes, were feverish.

"That depends, sir. It depends how dangerous the secret is. And I don't know it. Only you know it, now—and last night you were struck by a sudden doubt . . . that if you killed the last of them—Charles Moss—the secret would last very long. Because your own days are numbered, and your work has been killing you. You realized suddenly that you couldn't take the secret with you—that *someone* must know it, and keep watch on the big danger when you'd gone—the danger of another expedition going out there to find what you found. And you chose me, and came to tell me, last night. But I was out. Could you trust Moss, and leave the world in his hands—?"

"No—he was indifferent, and there was the woman—he had to go, before I could. And Joanna's a young girl—too young for a burden as big as—"

"And you hadn't time, you were distracted, because after killing four men and then a fifth—yourself—you were going to leave the secret without a guard—"

"Bishop." Gregg's eyes were bright. He had the strength of fever in him. "You'll guard it. I can trust you—"

"You can't know and you can't trust me. But you've got to, because time's short and there's no one else to turn to as late as this."

Gregg was breathing heavily. Bishop said:

"Trust our Government."

"No! A government's not human—it's a big machine—it's got to be. And governments make war, and that's a single step that no one man would take, alone. Bishop, I'm going to tell you, alone."

Bishop said briefly: "I'll take over the secret, but not your obsession. I can't make a single promise."

"You'll do what's right." He looked pleadingly at Frisnay. "Inspector, please give us a moment alone—"

"I'm sorry, sir. I can't leave this room."

"Then if you will, stand over by the door, where you can see us. Mr. Bishop will come to no harm."

Frisnay looked at Bishop.

Bishop said: "Up to you." He said it very softly.

Frisnay got off the stool and walked down the length of the bench. When he got to the doors, he turned round and stood facing them.

Bishop waited.

Gregg said quietly and with a steadiness that was surprising:

"Bishop, listen. I have to be very quick, now. You can find out where our party went—that's common knowledge. There's no exact spot, it's a large area. In the Antarctic land-mass there's a uranium-field, too immense to measure—"

"Uranium?"

"In vast quantity. If the world finds it, there'll be a gold-rush on a global scale, with only two protectors . . . East and West. There'd be world-war, overnight, if they knew there was the limitless means of winning that war within a few weeks' holocaust."

Bishop waited again. Gregg's voice had trailed off.

"I'm tired, now. Bishop, you understand?"

"Yes, I understand."

"And—and . . . "

"And I'll keep your secret, for as long as I think it's right."

Gregg began saying something. His face had changed. He had something of a smile there; it was relief. Bishop said:

"Now let me get a doctor, sir—"

343

"No . . . no, don't leave me, Bishop." His voice began letting the words down again; he struggled for coherency.

"When I—saw you come in, I knew—would happen. Carried it with me, days . . . small pill, tripentacyn . . . painless and doesn't take long, put an old body like this out of—misery."

Bishop held his arm. Gregg's eyes were still open. He tried clearly to say: "Done, now. Fifteen years—help a lot of people . . . poor Gordon . . . I hated doing . . . "

Bishop didn't turn his head. He called clearly:

"Freddie."

Frisnay's footsteps echoed along the room. Gregg was trying to get breath.

"In—Inspector, it was good of you to—give us that little time . . . between us we've saved the world . . . no, that's an obsession, isn't it . . . yes—"

Frisnay spoke very quietly, very clearly.

"Sir Bernard, I must formally charge you with the murder of Charles Edward Moss, on the morning of—"

"Yes—yes, I was responsible for . . . "

Bishop grabbed his shoulder as he slumped against the edge of the bench and between them they saved his head from hitting against the heavy microscope, but it didn't matter. It was just to keep decency here, grossness away.

Bishop said: "Sir Bernard."

Gregg did not hear.

Frisnay's face was wooden. His voice was gentle.

"And may God have mercy upon your soul."

Bishop stood away.

He said: "Amen."

Adam Hall is the pseudonym of Elleston Trevor, the author of over 20 novels. Mr. Trevor resides in Cave Creek, Arizona.